The Duke's Bridle Path

GRACE BURROWES

THERESA ROMAIN

D1260492

Cover design by Wax Creative, Inc.

ISBN: 1-941419-57-7
ISBN-13: 978-1-941419-57-1

TABLE OF CONTENTS

HIS GRACE FOR THE WIN

GRACE BURROWES

CHAPTER ONE

"Will I see you at the race meets, Your Grace?"

Lowered lashes and an arch smile suggested Lady Ambrosia Warminster wanted to see every naked inch of Philippe Albinus Bartholomew Coape Dodge Ellis, twelfth Duke of Lavelle.

Many women sought the same objective—those inches were handsome, titled, and wealthy, after all. Alas for Lady Ambrosia, an equestrian gathering was the last place she'd find Philippe.

He took her proffered hand and fired off a melting smile.

"I've neglected my acres, my dear, and must forgo the pleasure of even your company to make amends with my dear sister at Theale Hall. Might I ask where you'll spend the Yuletide holidays?"

He kept hold of her hand and looked hopeful, that being the protocol when declining an assignation, or when dodging the forcible trip to the altar such an encounter would likely engender.

"Papa hasn't decided, or Mama hasn't," she said, retrieving her hand.

Philippe let her hand go, slowly. "I will live in hope of a waltz next season. Please give my felicitations to your family."

Add a touch of eyebrow, a slight flaring of the nostrils—Philippe's older brother, Jonas, had taught him that bit—allow the lady to be the first to turn away, and... With a curtsey and a smile, she was off, pretending to see a dear, dear friend on the other side of Lady Pembroke's music room.

"How do you do that?" Seton Avery, Earl of Ramsdale, had been born with an inability to whisper. He growled quietly or not so quietly. On rare occasions, he roared.

"How do I avoid capture?" Philippe asked. "I give the ladies a little of what they want—my attention—and they give me what I want."

"Their hearts?" Ramsdale wore the expression Philippe usually saw when he and the earl were sharing an interesting game of chess.

"My freedom. You are coming out to Theale Hall with me next week?"

Ramsdale lifted two glasses of champagne from a passing footman's tray and handed one to Philippe.

"If I allow you to abandon me in Town, the disconsolate widows and hopeful debutantes will swivel their gunsights in my direction. One shudders to contemplate the fate of a mere belted earl under such circumstances."

Ramsdale grew restless as autumn came on, while Philippe felt the pull of his family seat, despite the memories. Ada bided at Theale Hall, doing more than her share to manage the estate, and Philippe owed his sister companionship at this time of year above all others.

"Then have your belted self ready to depart no later than Wednesday," Philippe said. "The nights grow brisk, and harvest will soon begin in Berkshire."

Ramsdale lifted his glass a few inches. "Of course, Your Grace. My pleasure, Your Most Sublime Dukeship. We'll take that rolling pleasure dome you call a traveling coach?"

When did Philippe travel a significant distance by any other means? "If it's raining, you're welcome to make the journey in the saddle."

"And deprive you of my company? Don't be daft. Let's leave on Tuesday. I've grown bored with Town, and the debutantes circle ever closer."

"Monday," Philippe said. "We'll leave Monday at the crack of dawn."

* * *

"Such a beauty," Lord Dudley cooed. "Such lovely quarters and elegant lines, such a kind eye. Makes a fellow itch to get her under saddle."

Titled men seldom rode mares, and thus his lordship's innuendo was about as subtle as the scent of a full muck cart. Harriet Talbot stroked the mare's shoulder, silently apologizing to the horse.

Utopia deserved better than a strutting clodpate.

"Shall I return her to her stall?" Harriet raised her voice to aim the question at her father, who was leaning heavily on his cane near the paddock gate.

"Your lordship?" Papa asked. "Have you seen enough? She's a superior lady's mount and enjoys working over fences. At the fashionable hour, she'll make an elegant impression, and she'll be eager to hack out of a fine morning."

Please don't buy her. Please, please do not buy this mare.

"She's very pretty," Dudley said, "very well put together. I like her eye."

Harriet did not like the covetous look in Dudley's eye. "While I commend your judgment, my lord, I hope you realize that she's not up to your weight. I was under the impression—we were, rather—that you sought a guest mount for a lady."

For one of his mistresses, in fact. Dudley's stable master had made that clear. "Utopia has some growing yet to do," Harriet went on, "some muscling up. With another year or two of work, she'll have more strength and stamina, but I'd advise against buying her for yourself."

His lordship stroked the mare's glossy backside. "Oh, but she's a chestnut. I cut quite a dash on a chestnut."

Besides, what lordling worth his port would make a decision based on a woman's opinion?

Utopia switched her tail, barely missing his lordship's face. This would not end well for the viscount or the mare.

"We can find you another handsome chestnut," Harriet said, before Papa could cut in with more praise for his lordship's discernment. "Utopia needs a chance to finish growing before she's competent to carry a man of your stature."

The mare had the misfortune to be beautiful. Four white socks evenly matched, excellent conformation, a white blaze down the center of her face, and great bloodlines. She was doomed to become some nobleman's plaything, though she truly wasn't large enough to handle Dudley.

Utopia was also not patient or forgiving enough. His lordship was tall and portly, and while many a large or stout rider sat lightly in the saddle, Dudley's horsemanship had all the grace of a beer wagon with a loose axle and a broken wheel.

"I do believe I shall take her," Dudley said. "I'll get her into condition and show her what's what."

The mare would be lame by the end of the year, possibly ruined beyond repair. Why had Papa agreed to show her to Lord Dunderhead?

"Papa," Harriet called, raising her voice. "His lordship has declared himself smitten with Utopia. I'll leave the bargaining to you." And yet, Harriet had to give herself one glimmer of hope that the mare could yet enjoy a happy life. "Regardless of the terms you strike with my father, please recall that we stand behind every horse we sell. You may return her at any point in the next ninety days for a full refund, regardless of her condition."

That term was Harriet's invention, quietly tacked on to sales when she lacked confidence in the purchaser's ability to keep the horse sound and happy. Several times, Harriet's guarantee had spared an unhappy horse a sorry fate.

Papa took a different approach: Buying a horse was like speaking vows to a bride. The purchaser became responsible for the creature for life, to have and to hold, and to provide fodder, pasture, shelter, farriery, veterinary care, gear, grooming, and treats until such time as a subsequent sale, old age, or a merciful bullet terminated the obligation.

Papa was a romantic. Harriet hadn't had that luxury since her mama had died five years ago.

"Take the filly back to her stall," Papa said. "His lordship and I will enjoy a brandy in my study."

"Brilliant!" Dudley replied, slapping Papa on the back and falling in step beside him. "She'll be a prime goer in no time."

The mare would be back-sore before the first flight had pulled up to check for loose girths. Harriet was no great supporter of the hunt field, for it lamed many a fine horse while subjecting Reynard to needless suffering.

"Come along," Harriet said to the mare. "I can still spoil you for a short while, and you'd best enjoy the time you have left here." Dudley's stablemen would take as good care of Utopia as they could and argue for her to be bred when she became unsound under saddle. The situation could be worse.

And yet, Harriet's heart was heavy as she slipped off the mare's bridle and buckled on the headstall. Five years ago, Papa would have listened to her when she'd warned against the likes of his lordship as a buyer for the mare.

Five years ago, Mama would have been alive to make him listen.

"There's a gent waiting for you in the saddle room, miss," Baxter, the new lad said. "Doesn't look like the patient sort either."

Gentlemen in search of horseflesh were seldom patient. "Did he give you a name?" Harriet asked, unbuckling Utopia's girths.

"No, but he knew where he was going and knew not to intrude on your dealings with Milord Deadly."

"Dudley," Harriet muttered, though stable lads would assign barn names however they pleased.

A buyer who knew his way around the premises wasn't to be kept waiting. Harriet handed the mare over to Baxter with instructions to get her out to the mares' pasture for a few hours of grass before sunset.

Harriet peeled off her gloves, stuffed them into a pocket of her habit, and hoped whoever awaited her in the saddle room was a better rider than Lord Dead—Lord Dudley.

She tapped on the door, because wealthy gentlemen expected such courtesies even when on another's premises, then swept inside with the confident stride of a woman who'd been horse-trading with her betters for years.

"Good day," she said to the tall, broad-shouldered specimen standing by the window. "I'm Harriet Talbot. My father can join us shortly, but in his absence…"

The specimen turned, and Harriet's brain registered what her body had been trying to tell her. She'd come to a halt halfway into the room, assailed by an odd sensation in the pit of her belly—happiness and anxiety, both trying to occupy the same space.

"Philippe. You've come home."

He held out his arms, and Harriet rushed across the room, hugging him tightly. "Oh, you've come home, and you gave us no warning, and Papa will be so happy to see you."

Harriet was ecstatic to see him, though her joy was bounded with heartache old and new. Old, because this was a courtesy call on Papa, a gesture of affection toward the late Duke of Lavelle's retired horse master. New, because every time Harriet saw His Grace—His Current Grace, she must not think of him as Philippe—the gulf between them was a little wider, a little more impossible.

She was the first to step back, though he kept hold of her hand.

"Do you ever wear anything other than riding habits?" he asked.

"Yes. I often wear breeches, but you mustn't tell anybody."

He smiled, Harriet smiled back, and her heart broke. She hadn't seen the duke for nearly a year, and yet, this was how it was with them. Always easy, always as if they'd parted the day before with a smile and a wave.

Philippe slipped an arm across her shoulders. "I will keep your secrets, Harriet, because you have so graciously kept mine over the years.

You won't tell anybody I'm hiding in here, for example. If that strutting excuse for bad tailoring, Lord Dimwit, should see me, I'll be required to invite him over to the Hall for a meal. He'll make a guest of himself—guest rhymes with pest—and my reunion with Lady Ada will be ruined."

"His lordship and Papa are secreted in the study bargaining over a mare. You're safe with me."

Philippe had always been safe with her, and she'd always been safe with him—damn and drat the luck. He folded himself onto the worn sofa Harriet had donated last year from her mother's parlor. When occupied by a duke, the sofa looked comfortable rather than at its last prayers.

When embraced by a duke—by this duke—Harriet felt special rather than eccentric.

He did that, made everyone and everything around him somehow *more*. Philippe was tall, dark, and athletic. In riding attire, he'd set hearts fluttering, though alas for Harriet, His Grace of Lavelle had no use for horses or anything approaching an equestrian pursuit.

For Harriet, by contrast, the horse was a passion and a livelihood—her only passion, besides a doomed attachment to a man to whom she'd never be more than an old, mostly overlooked friend.

* * *

On some stone tablet Moses had probably left up on Mount Sinai—stone tablets were deuced heavy—the hand of God had written, "Thou shalt not hug a duke, nor shall dukes indulge in any spontaneous hugging either."

The consequence for this trespass was so well understood that nobody—not Ada, not Ramsdale in his cups, not Philippe's mistresses, back when he'd bothered to keep mistresses—dared transgress on Philippe's person after the title had befallen him.

Harriet Talbot dared. She alone had failed to heed that stone tablet, ever, and thus with her, Philippe was free to pretend the rules didn't apply.

She was a fierce hugger, wrapping him in a long, tight embrace that embodied welcome, reproach for his absence, protectiveness, and—as a postscript noted by Philippe's unruly male nature—a disconcerting abundance of curves. Harriet was unselfconscious about those curves, which was to be expected when she and Philippe had known each other for more than twenty years.

"You do not approve of Lord Dudley," Philippe said. "Did he insult one of your horses?"

"He'll ruin one of my horses," Harriet replied, coming down beside him on the sofa. "One of Papa's horses, rather."

Philippe didn't have to ask permission to sit in her company, she didn't ring for tea in a frantic rush to offer hospitality—there being no bell-pulls in horse barns, thank the heavenly intercessors—nor tug her décolletage down with all the discretion of a fishmonger hawking a load of haddock.

"Then why sell Dudley the beast?" Philippe did not particularly care about the horse, but Harriet did.

"Because his lordship has coin and needs a mount for a lady, and Papa has horses to sell and needs that coin. Papa has explained this to me at regular intervals in recent months."

Never had the Creator fashioned a more average female than Harriet Talbot. She was medium height, brown-haired, blue-eyed, a touch on the sturdy side, and without significant airs or graces. She did not, to Philippe's knowledge, sing beautifully, excel at the pianoforte, paint lovely watercolors, or embroider wonderfully.

She smelled of horses, told the truth, and hugged him on sight, and to perdition with beautiful, excellent, lovely, and wonderful.

"Do you have reason to believe the lady who will ride the horse is incompetent in the saddle?" Philippe asked.

"I have no idea, but his lordship is a terrible rider. All force and power, no thought for the horse, no sense of how to manage his own weight. He rides by shouting orders at the horse and demanding blind obedience."

Women criticized faithless lovers with less bitterness than Harriet expressed toward Dudley's riding.

"He might return the mare," Philippe said. "He might also pass her on to a lady after all."

"I live in hope," Harriet said, sounding anything but hopeful. "How are you?"

To anybody else, Philippe could have offered platitudes about the joys of the Berkshire countryside at harvest, the pleasure of rural quiet after London's madness.

This was Harriet. "Coming home at this time of year is both sad and difficult, but here is where I must be. At least I get to see you."

She fiddled with a loose thread along a seam of her habit. "Papa will invite you to dinner."

This was a warning of some sort. "And I will accept."

"You need not. Papa will understand."

Philippe hated that Harriet would understand. "I'll even bring along Lord Ramsdale, because you are one of few people who can coax him to smile."

"The earl is a very agreeable gentleman." Harriet affected a pious tone at odds with the laughter in her gaze.

"The earl is a trial to anybody with refined sensibilities. What is the news from the village?"

They chatted comfortably, until the wheels of Dudley's phaeton crunched on the gravel drive beyond the saddle room's windows and the snap of his whip punctuated the early afternoon quiet.

The sound caused Harriet to close her eyes and bunch her habit in her fists. "If his lordship isn't careful, some obliging horse will send him into a ditch headfirst."

"He's also prone to dueling and drinking," Philippe said. "Put him from your thoughts for the nonce and take me to see your papa."

"Of course," Harriet replied, popping to her feet. She never minced, swanned, or sashayed. She marched about, intent on goals and tasks, and had no time for a man's assistance.

And yet, somebody's assistance was apparently needed. The roses growing next to the porch were long overdue for pruning, the mirror above the sideboard in the manor's foyer was dusty, the carpets showed wear. Harriet's habit was at least four years out of fashion, but then, Harriet had never paid fashion any heed.

Philippe was shocked to see how much Jackson Talbot had aged in little over a year. Talbot still had the lean height of a steeplechase jockey. His grip was strong, and his voice boomed. Not until Harriet had withdrawn to see about the evening meal did Philippe notice the cane Talbot had hooked over the arm of his chair.

"You're good to look in on us," Talbot said. "Good to look in on me."

"I'm paying a call on a pair of people whose company I honestly enjoy," Philippe said. "Harriet looks to be thriving."

She looked... she looked like Harriet. Busy, healthy, indifferent to fashion, pretty if a man took the time to notice, and *dear*. That dearness was more precious than Philippe wanted to admit. He'd come home because duty required it, but seeing Harriet made the trial endurable.

"Harriet," Talbot sniffed. "She thinks because my eyesight is fading that I don't notice what's going on in my own stable. I notice, damn the girl, but she doesn't listen any better than her mother did."

That was another difference. Talbot's eyes, always startlingly blue against his weathered features, had faded, the left more than the right. He held his head at a slight angle, and his desk had been moved closer to the window.

And never before had Philippe heard Talbot disparage his daughter. Criticize her form over fences, of course, but not cast aspersion on her character.

"How much vision have you lost?"

Talbot shifted in his chair. "I can't read the racing forms. Harriet reads them to me. I still get around well enough."

With a cane, and instead of inviting Philippe to stroll the barn aisle and admire all the pretty horses, Talbot had barely stood to shake hands.

"Women are prone to worrying," Philippe said.

"Now that is the damned truth, sir. Harriet will fret over that mare, for example, though Lord Dudley's no more heavy-handed than many of his ilk. Will you have time to join us for dinner before you must away back to London?"

"Of course. I've brought Ramsdale along, lest he fall foul of the matchmakers while my back is turned."

"Man knows how to sit a horse, meaning no disrespect."

This birching to Philippe's conscience was as predictable as Harriet's outdated fashions, though far less endearing. "Talbot, don't start."

"Hah. You may play the duke on any other stage, but I know what it costs you to eschew the saddle. You are a natural, just like your brother. You'd pick it back up in no time."

"All my brother's natural talent didn't keep him from breaking his neck, did it?" The silence became awkward, then bitter, then guilty. "I'm sorry, Talbot. I know you mean well. I'll be going, and if you send an invitation over to the Hall, expect me to be on better behavior when I accept it. I can't vouch for Ramsdale's deportment, but Harriet seems to enjoy twitting him."

Perhaps Harriet was sweet on Ramsdale. She liked big, dumb beasts. Ramsdale might have agreed to this frolic in the countryside because he was interested in Talbot's daughter.

The earl was devious like that, very good at keeping his own counsel— and he rode like a demon.

"No need to get all in a lather," Talbot said. "Young people are idiots. My Dora always said so. Let's plan on having you and his lordship to dine on Tuesday."

Talbot braced his hands on the blotter as if to push to his feet, and that too was a change.

Not for the better. "Please don't get up," Philippe said. "Bargaining with Dudley was doubtless tiring. I'll see myself out."

"Until Tuesday." Talbot settled back into his chair. "Do bring the earl along with you. He's the only man I know who can make Harriet blush."

Talbot shuffled a stack of papers as if putting them in date order, while Philippe took himself to the front door. A sense of betrayal followed him, of having found a childhood haven collapsing in on itself. He'd always been happy in the Talbot household, had always felt like *himself*, not like the spare and then—heaven help him—the heir.

Harriet emerged from the corridor that led to the kitchen, a riding crop in her hand. "You're leaving already?"

Was she relieved, disappointed, or neither? "I have orders to return on Tuesday evening with Ramsdale in tow. Where are you off to?"

"I have another pair of two-year-olds to work in hand. I'll walk you out."

Philippe retrieved his hat from the sideboard and held the door for her. "You train them yourself?" When had this started?

"The lads have enough to do, and Lord Dudley's visit put us behind schedule. The horses like routine, and I like the horses."

She loved the horses. "So you're routinely doing the work of three men." The afternoon sunshine was lovely, and over in the stable yard, a leggy bay youngster stood in bridle and surcingle. Still, Philippe did not like the idea that Harriet had taken on so much of the actual training.

Perhaps all of the training?

"The work of three men is a light load for a woman," Harriet said. "I'll look forward to seeing you and his lordship on Tuesday."

She pulled gloves out of her pocket and eyed the horse as she and Philippe walked down the drive. Already, she was assessing the beast's mood, taking in details of his grooming.

She paused with him by the gate to the arena. "You walked over?"

"Of course. Most of the distance is along the duke's bridle path, and Berkshire has no prettier walk."

"Well, then, have a pleasant ramble home. I'll look forward to seeing you on Tuesday."

She was eager to get back to work, clearly. Eager to spend the next hour marching around in the sand, her side pressed to the sweaty flank of a pea-brained, flatulent horse.

Of whom Philippe was unreasonably jealous.

The least Philippe could do was give Harriet something to think about between now and Tuesday besides horses. He leaned close, pressed a kiss to her cheek, and lingered long enough to whisper.

"Until next we meet, don't work too hard." Up close, she smelled not of horse, but of roses and surprise.

Her gloved hand went to her cheek. "Until Tuesday, Your Grace."

Now here was a cheering bit of news: Ramsdale was not the only fellow who could make Harriet Talbot blush. Philippe offered her a bow and a tip of his hat and went jaunting on his way.

CHAPTER TWO

Dinner with the duke was a special kind of purgatory for Harriet.

Cook had outdone herself—two peers at the table, and one of them their own Lord Philippe!—and Papa tried to recapture the jovial spirit he'd exuded before Mama's death. Harriet attempted to play hostess, which was harder than it looked for a woman who got out the good china only at Christmas and on the king's birthday.

Philippe regaled them with tales of polite society's follies, while Ramsdale was mostly quiet. His lordship's dark eyes held a lurking pity that made Harriet want to upend the wine carafe into the earl's lap.

Sorely missing a friend was *not* the same as being infatuated with a man far above her touch. "If Ramsdale is insistent on being trounced at the chessboard," His Grace said when the clock struck ten, "then I'll see myself home. There's a lovely moon tonight, and I certainly know the way."

Thank heavens, or thank Philippe's faultless manners. He was a considerate man, and Harriet would ever regard it as a pity that he eschewed equestrian activities. A little consideration went a long way toward success with most horses.

"Be off with you," Ramsdale said, waving a hand. "Lord knows, you need your beauty sleep, Lavelle, while I relish a challenge."

"And you shall have it," Papa rejoined, rising more energetically than he had in weeks. "It's your turn to be white, my lord, and if memory serves, you are down five games and very much in need of the opening advantage."

As Ramsdale politely bickered about the tally of victories, and Papa hobbled off with him to the study, Harriet's difficult night took a turn for the worse.

"He's lonely," she said.

Philippe paused by her chair. "Ramsdale? You are doubtless correct."

"Papa. He misses this. Misses the company of men, the jokes over the port, the slightly ungentlemanly talk that doubtless flows when he's at chess with Ramsdale. With the lads and grooms, Papa has to be the employer. With the buyers, he's the deferential horse master. With you and Ramsdale… he's happy."

Philippe bent closer, as he had when last they'd parted. "What of you, my dear? If your papa is lonesome for the company of men, whose company are you missing?"

Yours. "My mother, I suppose." And the father she'd once known, who'd been gruff but kindly, a hard worker, and a tireless advocate for the equine.

Philippe sighed, his breath fanning across Harriet's neck before he straightened to hold her chair. "Ada says you hardly ever call at the Hall."

Harriet *never* called at the Hall unless Papa insisted. "I am the daughter of a retired horse master, while your sister is a lady and always will be. I'll see you out."

"A horse master is a gentleman," Philippe said, "every bit as much of a gentleman as a steward or a vicar, and this might come as a revelation, but Ada is, like you, a woman living without benefit of female relations and in need of company."

Lady Ada was also a lovely person who adored her brother and took management of the ducal estate very much to heart. Harriet would endure Ramsdale's silent pity because she must. Pity from the duke's sister was unthinkable.

"If her ladyship needs company," Harriet said, "perhaps her brother should spend less time larking about London and more time where he belongs. It's a wonder women don't end every meal cursing," she muttered, disentangling the hem from beneath a chair leg. "These infernal skirts—"

"Are very becoming," Philippe said, offering his arm.

"I don't need an escort to my own front door, and I'll see you out on my way to the mares' barn."

Harriet wanted to elbow His Grace in the ribs, but he and she were no longer children; moreover, her elbow would get the worst of the encounter. Philippe was the duke. Over the past ten years, he'd transitioned from spare, to heir, to title holder. Generations of wealth, consequence, and yes—arrogance—regarded her patiently, until she took his arm simply to move the evening toward its conclusion.

I hate you. That pathetic taunt might have salvaged her pride in childhood, but now it was a sad echo of truer sentiments: *I miss you when you're gone for months. I worry about you. More often than you know, I wish I could talk to you or even write to you.*

I read the London papers for news of you. I dread the day I hear of your nuptials. For dukes married as surely as horses collected burrs in their tails.

"You're worried," Philippe said when they reached the foyer.

A single candle burned in a sconce on the wall, and when Harriet retired, she'd blow that one out.

"Papa will pay for this night's pleasures," Harriet said. "He forgets sore hips when he's in company or showing a horse to a prospective buyer, and I can't get him to touch the poppy or even white willow bark tea. I mentioned keeping a Bath chair on hand for the days when he's too stiff to walk out to the training paddock, and he nearly disowned me."

"I'm sorry. He's proud, and that makes it difficult to look after him." Philippe took Harriet's cloak from a hook near the sideboard, settled the garment around her shoulders, and fastened the frogs.

He knew exactly what he was doing, and not because he had a sister. Countless nights escorting ladies—titled ladies—to the opera, the theater, or this or that London entertainment had doubtless given him competence to go with his consideration.

Harriet treasured the consideration and resented the competence. "I can do up my own cloak, Your Grace."

Philippe shrugged into a shooting jacket and donned his top hat. "She's Your-Gracing me," he informed the night shadows. "I have transgressed. Perhaps my sin was complimenting my hostess's lovely attire. Maybe I misstepped when I commiserated about her father's waning health. Perhaps I've presumed unforgivably by performing small courtesies."

"You are being ridiculous." Harriet said. "So am I. I'm sorry." For so much, she was sorry.

"You are tired," Philippe replied, holding the door for her. "You work, you don't sit about stitching sanctimonious samplers while plotting adultery. You supervise men, instead of scheming how to get your hands on their coin or their titles. You want for respite, not a new diversion to go with the endless list you've already become bored with."

The moon was full, which meant Harriet had enough light to see Philippe's features.

The evening had apparently been trying for him too. All those stories about lordlings swimming in fountains, or young ladies whose arrows went astray, that was so much stable-yard talk. The reality was cold mornings and hard falls. Aching limbs and colic vigils. London had left Philippe tired and dispirited. He was bearing up and hiding it well.

"I'm glad you've come home," Harriet said, twining her arm through his. "I'll walk you to the bridle path."

"Unlike some people, I won't grouse at an offer of good company. As a youth, I spent many a moonlit night wishing my true love would accost me under the oaks."

He referred to a ridiculous local legend: *The first person to kiss you under a full moon on the duke's bridle path is your true love.*

"The legend is very forgiving," Harriet said as they made their way between paddocks. "It doesn't specify that we're to have only one true love. I suspect many a stable lad has been relieved that subsequent interests aren't precluded by that first kiss."

And maybe many a duke? Tears threatened, and for no reason. What did it matter which squire's daughter, daring tavern maid, or merry widow had first kissed a young Lord Philippe on the bridle path?

"So who was your first true love?" Philippe asked.

Not a hint of jealousy colored his question. He was merely passing the time while tramping on Harriet's heart.

"He was tall," she said. "Quite muscular, a fellow in his prime. Splendid nose, moved like a dream, all grace and power."

"You noticed his nose?"

Was that disgruntlement in the duke's voice? "One does, when kissing."

"Not if one goes about it properly."

He spoke from blasted experience, while Harriet was spinning fancies. "I noticed his dark, dark hair, his beautiful eyes, his scent."

"You found a lad here in Berkshire who could afford French shaving soap?"

"He wasn't a lad, Your Grace. He was quite the young man, and all the ladies adored him." Which was why he'd been sold as a stud colt and was still standing at a farm in Surrey. "I kissed him good-bye under a full moon on the bridle path, and I will never, ever forget him."

Philippe slowed as they neared the trees. "You kissed him good-bye?"

"Years ago."

This part of the bridle path ran between two rows of stately oaks. Nobody knew when the path had come into use, but the oaks were ancient. In places, the path wound beside a stream. At other points, it left the trees to cut along the edge of a pasture. Every square yard of the footing was safe. Every inch of the way was beautiful.

Especially by moonlight.

Philippe stopped at the gap in the oaks. The night was peaceful enough to carry the sound of horses munching grass in their paddocks. Harriet's slippers were damp—her only good pair. She'd neglected to change into boots, because shooing away His Grace had been the more pressing priority.

Shooing away His Grace, whom she missed desperately even when she was standing beside him.

"May I trust you with one more secret, Harriet?"

In the shadows of the trees, she couldn't make out his expression. "Of course. We are friends, and friends…"

He took off his hat and set it on a thick tree limb. "I waited in vain on this path. Nobody fell prey to my youthful charms, not on Beltane, not at harvest. Nobody would kiss the duke's younger son, though I witnessed several young ladies bestowing favors on Jonas."

That must have hurt. "Lord Chaddleworth was a rascal." A lovable rascal.

A foal whinnied, and the mama answered. A sense of expectation sprang up from nowhere, and two instants later, Harriet realized His Grace was through waiting for somebody to kiss him.

He touched his mouth to hers. Harriet stepped closer, and then his arms came around her.

The kiss resumed, and while Harriet noticed many things—how her body matched the duke's differently in the darkness, how the breeze blew her hair against her neck, how warm he was, and how his shaving soap smelled of sweet lavender—she did not notice his nose at all.

* * *

Philippe had gone to university, and thanks to the Oxford tavern maids, he'd learned how to kiss. Those women instructed a fellow without regard to his title or wealth, demanding that he give pleasure where pleasure was offered. Thus Philippe had been introduced to the democracy of the bedroom where all—rich, poor, handsome, plain, young, and not so young—were reduced to common humanity in pursuit of common pleasures.

Then he'd kept discreet company with a young widow who ran a boarding house in Oxford. After university, he'd graduated to the wonders—and horrors—of London. Jonas had lectured Philippe at length about the French gout, fire ships, and other dangers, and a tour of Covent Garden after the theaters let out had underscored the need for caution.

Caution was expensive and tiresome, in the form of mistresses who expected regular visits and even more regular bank drafts. When Philippe realized that he'd not paid a call on his mistress for the duration of three bank drafts, he'd bid her a fond farewell—she pronounced him hopeless at debauchery—and resigned himself to the occasional frolic at a house party.

Two years later, he'd stopped accepting invitations to house parties. As Ada had pointed out, if he wanted to while away a few weeks in rural splendor, the peaceful, debutante-free luxury of his own Hall would suffice.

And all along, from university, to London, to the shires, and back, Philippe had wondered if something wasn't amiss with him. Intimate congress was pleasurable, but so was a ramble along the bridle path—and a good deal less complicated. Kissing had inspired sonnets and panegyrics in many languages, and yet, Philippe had regarded it as so much folderol to be got through while the lady made up her mind.

With Harriet, he never wanted the intimacies to end. Her kiss was everything—soft night sounds, breezes teasing the leaves that would soon fall to the lush grass, homecoming, joy, warmth of the heart and warmth—blazing warmth—where desire dwelled.

She wrapped her arms around him and shifted, so her breasts rubbed against his chest. He suspected she had no intention other than to be closer, which was a fine, fine idea. He explored the contours of her back with one hand, not stopping until he cupped her derriere and pressed her closer.

She was luscious, eager, artless, and—some vestigial artifact of his gentlemanly scruples shouted—she was *Harriet*. Harriet, the pest who'd spied on him and Jonas; Harriet, who'd beat Jonas racing on her pony because she'd jump anything without checking her mount's speed;

Harriet, who'd forget Philippe for another year because he hadn't a mane, tail, or hooves.

Philippe was a duke, a creature of discipline and duty.

His almighty discipline was barely sufficient to inspire a pause in the kissing.

"The full moon always makes the horses restless," Harriet panted.

What had horses—? Philippe eased his embrace and rested his cheek against Harriet's hair. The scent of roses was partly her, partly the night breeze.

"A mere kiss is not lunacy, Harriet. Not when we're on the bridle path. Kissing on the bridle path is what one does in this corner of Berkshire."

He felt the change in her, felt his attempt at levity fall flat and knock the wonder from the moment. Harriet doubtless had some equestrian analogy handy to better describe the unwelcome return of sanity.

"I thought bridle paths were for riding along," she said, pressing her cheek to his chest. "I can feel your heart."

Philippe's attention was on another part of his anatomy, and yet, his heart was involved as well. He'd kissed Harriet Talbot, *his friend*, under a full moon on the bridle path. The kiss had been spectacular, but then, he was out of practice, and Harriet brought focus and energy to all she did.

He should turn loose of her.

He really should.

He stroked her hair, which was marvelously soft. "Are we still friends, Harriet?"

She stepped back and handed him his hat. "Of course, Your Grace. We will always be friends, and now when you are asked about our local legend, you can take your place among the village boys and stable lads who've at least kissed *somebody* on the duke's bridle path."

Her gaze wasn't on him, but rather, on the horses at grass under the full moon.

"You came out with me to check on a horse."

"A mare who has the audacity to be presenting us with an autumn foal. Such a thing shouldn't be possible, and if winter is early, it's surely not wise. She got loose, though, and was found the next morning disporting with Mr. Angelsey's stud. Heaven help the foal if it breeds true to the sire line, for that stud is cow-hocked and... I'm babbling."

Harriet wanted to see to her mare. Philippe wanted the last five minutes to never have happened, and he wanted to resume kissing her.

"Away with you," Philippe said, bowing over her hand. "I'll wait here until you're at the mares' barn. Thank you for a lovely meal and a lovely kiss."

He owed her that. He also probably owed her an apology, except he wasn't sorry. Confused, yes. Sorry, hell no.

"Good night, Your Grace." A quick curtsey, then Harriet stooped to remove her slippers, and off she went across the damp grass, her shoes in her hand.

Philippe remained by the oaks even after she'd disappeared into the mares' barn on the far side of the paddocks.

What had just happened? Harriet had kissed him as if she'd been longing for him to take that very liberty and needed to make up for lost time. Then she'd scampered off into the night—Cinderella taking both of her slippers with her—abandoning him yet again for the company of some smelly equine.

Philippe ducked into the shadows of the bridle path, and made his way back to the Hall, hat in hand.

* * *

"Somebody must have moved my mares' barn a mile or two down the bridle path," Jackson Talbot said.

Ramsdale's mind wasn't on the game, not on the chess game at any rate. Apparently, Talbot's wasn't either.

"Or perhaps," Ramsdale said, "like any self-respecting equestrienne, Miss Talbot saw a water bucket half empty and tarried to fill it. Or a mare who needed more hay, or a—"

Talbot waved his pipe. "The lads mope if Harriet steals all of their work. They take their responsibilities seriously."

"His Grace of Lavelle takes everything seriously." Though, because the duke also took his flirting seriously, and his gentlemanly bonhomie, and his cordial socializing, nobody seemed to notice—including the duke himself.

The front door closed, and a vague worry left Talbot's eyes. "All's well in the mares' barn. We're expecting a woods colt or filly."

The game had not yet progressed to the interesting phase. Ramsdale and his host were settling in, exchanging civilities, recalling each other's strategies.

"A maiden mare?" Ramsdale asked.

"No, but having chosen her swain for herself, I can't breed the damned horse to another until spring. Every foal counts, and this one, having a disgrace for a father, will be ewe-necked, over at the knee... It's your move, my lord."

Ramsdale moved his king's knight into position to threaten Talbot's queen. "An occasional outcross can strengthen a bloodline."

A duke's horse master had greater responsibilities in some regards than the land steward or house steward. He oversaw the coachmen and carriages, the breeding stock and farm stock, the stables and paddocks, the training and riding, the teams stabled at coaching inns all over the realm, and the money it took to keep that aspect of a dukedom functioning.

Anything associated with a ducal equine fell under the horse master's purview, and now Talbot was reduced to managing a few brood mares, some youngsters, a handful of riding stock in training...

And one smitten daughter.

"An occasional out-cross makes sense," Talbot said. "My darling mare chose the worst possible stud though. Damned colt should have been cut before he was weaned."

Talbot did not see the danger to his queen. "Lavelle is a gentleman." Which was half the problem. Somewhere along the way, His Grace had confused strawberry leaves for holy orders.

"His Grace is also a man without many close allies," Talbot said, moving his rook in a completely useless direction. "Harriet is ferociously loyal and unwise to the ways of men."

"To the ways of scoundrels, you mean." Ramsdale decided to draw the game out, for he had a delicate point to make, and he and delicacy were not well acquainted. "Lavelle hasn't a drop of scoundrel's blood in his veins."

"But every drop is male, and Harriet's future is dull enough to inspire her to rash acts. Her mother resorted to rash acts to gain my attention."

Ramsdale took a pawn with his bishop, a warning. "Her mother's strategy worked."

"I was a baronet's younger son. She was an earl's granddaughter. We knew what was expected of us, and times were different."

Talbot fell silent, and Ramsdale gave up on delicacy. "They would suit."

Talbot moved his *king*. Perhaps the horse master had begun a mental decline.

"Lavelle might make Harriet his mistress for a time," Talbot said, "and I'm sure he'd be generous and kind. Harriet was not raised to be anybody's fancy piece, not even a duke's fancy piece, not even a good duke's fancy piece."

Talbot wasn't angry, so much as he was bewildered. He'd never envisioned himself the father of a duke's fancy piece, or perhaps he worried about how to keep a stable afloat without Harriet to run it?

"I meant no insult to the lady," Ramsdale said. Then too, to be mistress to a duke was hardly the same as walking the London streets. "I meant that they're very nearly in love, and whom Lavelle falls in love with, he'll be inclined to marry."

Ramsdale wasn't sure what it meant to be in love, but whenever he accompanied Lavelle to the ancestral pile, the duke called first upon the Talbots, even before visiting the family graveyard. For a man who eschewed anything having to do with a horse, Lavelle was uncommonly fond of his papa's old horse master.

Also of the horse master's daughter.

"A duke must marry wisely," Talbot said. "Harriet is in no regard a suitable duchess. She knows that."

Ramsdale moved his queen again, though the king's shift by a single square was inconvenient to his intended strategy.

"Lavelle never wanted to be a duke, and every time somebody refers to him as such, he misses his older brother. In London, His Grace is endlessly popular, beloved by all, but known by virtually nobody. They were all too busy fawning over Lord Chaddleworth as the heir and didn't notice the younger brother. Now they notice him, and he can't be bothered."

His Grace was always polite, always charming, and always—to Ramsdale's discerning eye—bored with the life meant for his older brother. The boredom had become restlessness, and the restlessness was building toward some bad end.

Excessive drink, perhaps, or dueling, or—the worst fate imaginable—a Society match.

"My lord, your move has put us at a stalemate."

Ramsdale surveyed the board. "Bloody hell. My apologies. My mind is elsewhere."

"As is mine. Shall we call it a night, and shall I have a gig brought 'round to get you home?"

"I will enjoy a moonlit stroll and the peace and quiet of the Berkshire countryside. My thanks for a very pleasant evening, and I hope you'll join us for dinner at the Hall on Friday."

Talbot pushed to his feet. "His Grace left it to you to do the inviting, did he? Harriet would have conjured some excuse had he asked her directly—the mare, perhaps. No harm in a meal between neighbors, I suppose. Until Friday, my lord."

Talbot's grip was firm, though his gaze was troubled.

Best beat a retreat before Talbot also conjured excuses. "I'll see myself out. I promise you better play when next we meet."

Anything was better than playing to a stalemate, for God's sake. Ramsdale reserved the pleasure of reviewing the game move by move for the futile hours involved in falling asleep. As he made his way home down the legendary bridle path, a different challenge occupied him.

Harriet Talbot was from good family. Solidly gentry and entitled to a few upward pretensions. Had she been wealthy, a match with Lavelle would have been unusual, but not scandalous. Ramsdale was prepared to spread rumors of the young lady's magnificent dowry to still any wagging tongues.

A heart full of love, for those inclined to such nonsense, qualified as a magnificent dowry.

Ramsdale had no doubt that Harriet would make a fine duchess, given some time and a few pointers from Lady Ada. The problem was Lavelle.

How could a peer who detested all things equine possibly become a suitable mate to a woman who—save for her interest in the duke—loved horses, only horses, and always horses?

CHAPTER THREE

Philippe had, as usual, not slept well.

London hours were backward. A man about Town sauntered forth with the setting sun to amuse himself with the social entertainments of his choice. When he'd waltzed to his heart's content—across some lady's sheets in many cases—he joined friends at the club for late-night cards and drinking.

By dawn's early light, the typical gentleman rode or drove in the park, and then he took himself off to bed, there to rest from his exertions in preparation for more of same.

In sheer defense of his sanity, Philippe had instead taken a serious interest in both his dukedom's commercial interests and in affairs of state. This was usually the province of men years his senior, and while Philippe liked taking a hand in politics, he didn't regard Parliament as the ultimate venue for blood sport.

In truth, he was glad to be back at the Hall for many reasons.

He was not, however, glad to regard Ramsdale over the breakfast table. His lordship wore a preoccupied expression that suggested blunt truths were about to issue forth from his unsmiling mouth.

"Have some ham," Philippe said. "Country air puts an appetite on a fellow."

"Country air must have addled your wits. I don't care for pork in any of its presentations, save for when it's on the hoof and downwind."

"Unpatriotic, Ramsdale, to turn up your nose at good English ham. Did Talbot trounce you last night?"

"Did Miss Talbot trounce you?"

Ramsdale was what some referred to as a worshipper of Aurora, goddess of the dawn. He began the day early and galloped at it headlong. By evening, he was a calmer, more settled creature.

"Now isn't that just like you, being adorably direct." Philippe caught the eye of the footman at the sideboard, who like any good house servant was impersonating a marble statue. "Thomas, you'll excuse us. Lord Ramsdale is about to deliver a proper dressing-down, and a peer of the realm wants privacy for his humiliations."

"I don't intend to humiliate you," Ramsdale said when the footman had bowed and withdrawn.

"I cannot say the same where you're concerned. You are a guest in my home, and I'll thank you to act like it. Your mention of Miss Talbot trouncing me bordered on ungentlemanly."

While stealing a kiss from Harriet by moonlight leaned in the direction of roguish.

Ramsdale rose, a slice of buttered toast in his hand. "The Talbots are not thriving." He wandered to the sideboard, added a dollop of scrambled eggs to his toast, and took a bite.

"I noticed as much last year, but told myself the evidence was simply a lack of the late Mrs. Talbot's guiding hand. She always ensured the roses were pruned, the fences whitewashed, and the carpets beaten. All the beating in the world does not make a worn carpet new, though."

The Talbots' manor house had been spotless, which made the creeping shabbiness more apparent.

Another portion of the toast met its fate. "What will you do about it?"

When Philippe hadn't been reliving his kiss with Harriet, regretting his kiss with Harriet, and longing for another kiss with Harriet, he'd asked himself the same question. His working theory was that Harriet had succumbed in a weak moment to his inappropriate overtures.

Like all theories, it wanted for supporting evidence. Her succumbing had been wonderfully enthusiastic, and a kiss was hardly a declaration of undying love. Nonetheless, Philippe had noticed the neglect on the Talbot property.

Weary, overwhelmed women were more prone to succumbing. So were weary, overwhelmed dukes.

"I have a few ideas for how to address the Talbots' situation," Philippe said. "I gather you do as well?"

Ramsdale's peregrinations next took him to the window, where mellow autumn sunshine illuminated dust motes and picked out the gold threads in his lordship's waistcoat.

"Talbot has his pride," Ramsdale said. "You'll have to tread lightly, but then, you've been treading lightly since your brother died."

"A man can choke to death on a slice of toast, Ramsdale." Though the earl was correct: Philippe had taken up his brother's responsibilities with equal parts resentment and reluctance. "Jonas was reared to become the duke, and he would have made a fine job of it."

Ramsdale turned, so the sunlight pouring over his shoulder lent him the air of a stern heavenly messenger. "You make a fine job of being a duke, but what about being a neighbor, a man, a brother?"

Or a lover? A husband even?

"I'm meeting with the vicar this morning, and I'll call on every one of my tenants over the next two weeks. For a duke, that's neighborly. I will lead my sister out at the blasted harvest ball and host the autumn open house the same as I usually do." The same as Jonas and Papa had done.

"And about the Talbots?"

"I have several options," Philippe said. "One is to ask Jackson Talbot to come out of retirement. My current horse master has been offered a post at a racing stable." In Berkshire, no mere ducal estate could compete with the joy and challenge of training racehorses.

Ramsdale finished his toast and circled back to the table to resume his seat. "Talbot is half blind and half lame. The horse master's post could well be the death of him."

"Or it might be the reason he lives another ten relatively happy years. If he took over for a few months and had reliable underlings, I'd be able to compensate him enough to tide him over."

This was a workable plan and afforded Philippe many opportunities to spend time with Talbot, which could result in opportunities to spend time with Harriet.

Maybe.

"You'd be gambling with his life, in other words," Ramsdale said. "How is Miss Talbot to manage without her father's presence on their property?"

Harriet would manage, but this was the fly in the horse lineament: Harriet would have to work harder than ever if her papa took a leave of absence to resume employment on the Lavelle estate.

"Another option is to buy the Talbot property and grant Talbot a life estate."

Ramsdale poured himself a cup of coffee. "Oh, right. Then when the old man dies, the young lady has some cash—assuming it wasn't frittered away putting the property to rights—but her pride and joy is in your hands, and you have not the slightest interest in adding a stable to your assets."

"I would never deprive Harriet of her stable."

Ramsdale stirred cream into his coffee. "She would never take charity from you. Has it occurred to you that the poor woman might be in want of a dowry?"

Philippe set his plate aside, and to hell with one's patriotic duty. "Why should she need a dowry?"

"So that she could marry a suitable successor to her dear papa. A man who could learn the business without displacing the woman who loves that business. A dashing horseman, a younger son who comes around pretending to be interested in buying a nag or two. Miss Talbot is comely, and she'll inherit a fine Berkshire stable. She could aspire to a title if she was ambitious."

Which Harriet was not.

Ramsdale took a sip of his coffee. His expression was thoughtful, and he was in *riding* attire. He'd tarried at the Talbots' last night, and he'd never turned down an invitation to join Philippe in Berkshire.

The earl was attractive, if a woman could overlook unruly dark hair, a lordly nose, and the shoulders of a blacksmith. Ramsdale and Harriet got on well. His title was ancient, and he needed heirs.

As did Philippe. "I'm considering another option. Considering it seriously."

"Do tell."

"The Talbots breed first-rate riding stock, they take excellent care of their horses, and their location is perfect for starting youngsters who won't have a career at the races. All they need is for polite society to take a little notice of them."

While Philippe needed for Harriet to take *more* than a little notice of him.

"You are polite society personified. If you were any more polite, you'd have to carry a harp and halo with you on occasions of state."

"Precisely the point. I am in a position to draw notice to the Talbots and increase their custom." Which was why this option, complicated though it was, had earned the majority of Philippe's consideration.

"You'll become a horse trader? Waste your coin on spavined, underfed, racing stock that will never be up to your weight? Shall you raise malodorous hounds and wear those execrable pinks for five months of the year?"

"Of course not. If I want to call attention to the fine stock in Jackson Talbot's stables, if I want to establish before all and sundry that I approve of the Talbots' operation, I have only to make one small gesture in the right direction, and all will come right."

Provided Philippe survived that small gesture.

"You'll dower Miss Talbot. Capital notion. She's a fine woman and deserves every happiness in this life. I'm sure once Talbot recovers from the apoplexy your insult serves to his pride, he'll remember to thank you."

"Ramsdale, have a little faith in your friends. I would happily dower Harriet—Miss Talbot—should the need arise. Until such time as it does, I'll do the one thing I promised myself I would never, ever do."

Ramsdale sat back and crossed his arms. "You'll marry her?"

Philippe nearly spluttered tea all over himself. "You consider marriage a small gesture?"

"Gentlemen do not discuss size."

While schoolboys discussed little else. "My plan was to ask for Talbot's assistance in regaining my skills in the saddle. I'll be home for the foreseeable future, Talbot was my first riding instructor, and I'm sure he'll have a mount that will suit me, once I recollect the basics."

The silence in the breakfast parlor was so profound, Philippe could hear his heartbeat pounding in his ears.

"You'll *get back on a horse* merely to help a former employee find a few more customers?"

"No, Ramsdale. I'll polish some neglected skills because it suits me to do so. I live in Berkshire, where every other farm aspires to produce the next champion stud. If in spring, I'm inclined to hack out in Hyde Park during the fashionable hour, or join a lady for a morning gallop, that is entirely my business."

"Please tell me you're not trying to impress that Warminster creature. All Mayfair will sigh in relief when she decamps for the Midlands."

Ramsdale hadn't laughed at Philippe's plan, which was encouraging.

He also hadn't tried to talk Philippe into changing his mind, which was no damned help at all.

"You said it yourself, Ramsdale. Jonas has gone to his reward, and it's time I got on with being the duke." And if Philippe had to climb back onto a horse to impress his prospective duchess, then onto a horse he would climb.

* * *

Harriet handed off the second two-year-old to a groom and headed for the house, intent on finding a midday meal, or a midafternoon meal. The hours in the stable flew, until she became famished. Only when famished progressed to thirsty, light-headed, and snappish did she force herself to do something about her hunger.

Snappish and young horses was a bad combination. Some bread and cheese, a mug of ale, and Harriet would return to the barn...

She had batted aside a skein of blown roses drooping over the front steps when raised voices from inside the house came to her notice. Papa had a grand bellow, such as anybody who'd taught riding had to have. Harriet hadn't heard her father using his arena voice for some time though, and this was not a happy bellow.

The other voice was softer, but equally emphatic. Harriet let herself through the front door, and the voices became clearer.

"You can't... damned... foolishness, Your Grace."

Your Grace? She stripped off her gloves and sat to unbuckle her spur.

"Damned stubbornness... simple request, Talbot."

Philippe, and he hadn't stopped by the paddocks to greet her. Harriet had hoped the duke would return to London, and when next they saw each other, they could make light of a kiss shared for the sake of legend.

Not a legendary kiss, not a kiss that had changed Harriet's view of herself and her future, merely a gesture between old friends.

She hurried down the corridor, tapped twice on the door to Papa's study, and walked right in. The horses had taught her that: walk into the barn as if all was well, the day was beautiful, and great good fun awaited Harriet and her mounts.

Horses, unlike stable hands, customers, and fathers, *paid attention*.

"Pardon me," Harriet said. "Your Grace, good day. Papa, I was on my way to the kitchen. Would you gentlemen care to join me in a sandwich?"

"No, thank you," Papa growled.

The duke rose from the chair opposite the desk. "Miss Talbot, greetings. Sustenance would be welcome."

The two men Harriet cared about most in the world glowered at each other. Had they been a pair of yearling colts, she would have left them to their posturing and pawing.

"You're apparently having a difference of opinion," she said. "You could be heard halfway to the mares' barn."

His Grace snatched a pair of gloves from the desk. "Mr. Talbot is being unreasonable."

"The duke asks too much."

His Grace was not in the habit of asking anybody for anything. Even last night's kiss hadn't been the result of an overt request.

Harriet's gaze fell upon Philippe's mouth, which was set in a determined line. She knew the shape and taste of that mouth, knew its skill and the pleasure it could bestow.

"What has His Grace requested?"

"It's of no moment," the duke replied. "I'll just be going."

This was not good. Philippe had a temper—Harriet had seen it exactly twice. The first time, he had been thirteen and had come upon a bitch and her puppies in a shed at the back of the mayor's garden. The space had been filthy, the mama emaciated, the stench unbelievable. He'd bought the entire litter and their mama on the spot and sent Harriet for a dog cart to ferry them to the Hall.

The mayor had lost the next election.

The second time had been years later. Philippe had come down from university on holiday and stood up with the local young ladies at a tea dance at the parish hall. Harriet's mama had forced her to attend as well.

Bascomb Hardy had deliberately tromped on the vicar's daughter's hem.

Elspeth had been slow-witted, but sweet, an easy target for unkindness. Tearing the hem of her best dress should have meant that she missed out on the rest of the dance, the first that the ducal spare had attended.

Philippe had knelt at Elspeth's feet, used his cravat pin to hide the damage, and invited her to partner him for the next set. To the young lady, he'd been attentive, charming, and kind.

To Harriet, his ire had been evident from the tension in his shoulders and the determined quality of his gaze. At services the next week, Bascomb had sported a noticeably swollen nose.

Harriet had learned to see her childhood friend with new and admiring eyes. Elspeth had married the blacksmith's son, who'd also stood up with her at that tea dance, and they now had five rambunctious children.

While Harriet had an argument to settle. "What is the issue?"

His Grace paused by the door. "Stubbornness."

Papa remained seated, which was rude, also an indication of how much his hip pained him. "Unreasonable expectations."

The duke strode back to the desk, his boot heels thumping on the thin carpets. "You were the one who suggested it! You all but dared me to try. Now I'm taking you up on your offer, and you spout inanities about suitable mounts and busy schedules."

Papa used the arms of his chair to push to his feet. "Autumn is always busy at a stable. Much of the training will cease when the weather turns nasty, and we must work while we can, especially with the youngsters."

His Grace picked up Papa's cane, the handle of which was carved into a horse head. "Talbot, you confound me." The duke studied the cane for a moment, then passed it across the desk. "Miss Talbot, you mentioned food."

The mood had shifted with the passing of the cane. Harriet had no idea what had caused this argument, but the duke had decided to retreat.

"Nothing fancy, Your Grace. A sandwich, a few biscuits, a peach or two."

The pair of peach trees had been a gift to Mama from the old duke, and the trees—unlike the rest of the facility—were having a good year.

"I adore a succulent peach," the duke said. "Talbot, good day. My apologies for any untoward remarks."

Papa subsided into his chair. "Likewise. Harriet, get the man something to eat."

With the horses, Papa was the soul of civility. He never commanded when he could invite, never insisted when he could suggest.

Harriet had given up expecting the same consideration. "Yes, Papa."

The duke looked like he was about to renew the altercation with Papa—perhaps scolding him for his peremptory tone—but Harriet was hungry, and arguing with Papa solved nothing.

"Your Grace, shall I serve you in the breakfast parlor?"

"Certainly not. I've taken the majority of my meals here in the kitchen, and we need not stand on ceremony now. Or perhaps we should make a picnic of our repast. One never knows when winter will come howling down from the north two and a half months early. We must enjoy the fine weather while it lasts."

With that parting shot, he held the door for Harriet, who paused long enough to kiss her father's cheek before joining the duke in the corridor.

"You have offended my father," she said. "We will sort that out once I've had something to eat. What did you ask of him?"

"He has offended me," the duke replied, accompanying Harriet down the steps. "Though I don't think he meant to. He teased me the other night, and I took his remarks to heart."

The kitchen was empty, the cook being in the habit of joining the housekeeper for a dish of tea at midafternoon. Long ago, the boy Philippe had downed many a mug of cider in this kitchen. The top of his head nearly brushed the dark beams now.

Philippe was not a boy. He was the man who'd kissed Harriet not twenty-four hours ago.

She'd kissed other men and then wondered why anybody would seek to repeat the experience. Mouths mashed together, teeth banging, hands landing in awkward locations then not knowing what to do. A very great bother, and for no reason.

"Are we drinking our ale from tea cups?" the duke asked.

Some hen-wit had begun assembling a tea tray. "We are not." Harriet set the tray aside. "I grow scatterbrained when I go too long without eating."

"Please do get off your feet," the duke said, leading Harriet by the hand to the hearth. "I recall well enough how to slice bread and cheese. I wonder if you recall how to sit for five minutes on anything other than a horse."

The hearth stones were cool, even through the fabric of Harriet's breeches and habit. Sitting down felt too good. Watching the duke impersonate a scullery maid felt even better.

Philippe was the duke—always would be—but part of him was still Harriet's friend. One kiss hadn't changed that. "The butter's in the—"

"Window box," he said, brandishing a small crock. "Same as always."

He unwrapped the morning's loaf of bread, unwrapped the cheese wheel, and put together sandwiches. The bread was sliced unevenly, the cheese was too thick, and he applied butter as if Papa had an entire herd of fresh heifers.

Moving around the kitchen, he also showed off a pair of riding breeches to spectacular advantage.

"What did you and Papa argue about?"

"I mistook a jest for a sincere offer," the duke said. "Where are the mugs?"

"Above the dry sink."

Harriet felt as if she'd fallen half asleep and was having one of those waking dreams that arose from sheer exhaustion in broad daylight. Dozing in the barn, she sometimes imagined the barn cats and horses could speak, or that the coronation coach awaited her in the drive.

A duke was preparing food for her, the same duke who'd kissed her last night.

And yet here, in the kitchen, he was also simply her Philippe.

Whom she'd like very much to kiss again.

* * *

A skilled artist should sketch Harriet seated by the hearth. She was like a setting sun, momentarily stilled above the western horizon.

Her coiffure, which had likely started the day as a sensible braid wrapped into a tidy bun, was now a frazzled rope down the middle of her back. She sat immobile—no part of her moved, not her hands, not her booted feet, not even her gaze. She leaned back against the hearth stones and simply watched Philippe bumble about in the kitchen.

This was why a man went to university—so he'd learn to make cheese toast, brew a pot of tea, and otherwise fend off starvation in the midst of plenty.

Or perhaps, so he might tend to a woman who was clearly in need of nourishment.

"Come sit," he said, patting the back of a chair. "Tell me about your day and lie to me about my skill at sandwich making."

Harriet crossed to the table and let Philippe hold her chair. "You got the cheese between the bread, which is the important part. Papa's hip must be paining him severely today."

Philippe took the opposite chair, the better to enjoy looking at her. "I gathered as much. When I joined you for a meal yesterday, he was in high spirits."

"He'd been at the brandy, you mean." Harriet bowed her head to give thanks, and Philippe spent a pious little silence mentally undoing the rest of her braid.

He *was* thankful, not only for his pathetic attempt at sandwiches, but also for a chance to spend time with Harriet.

"As the weather cools, Papa's joints are affected," Harriet said, opening her sandwich and nibbling the buttered side. "Autumn also makes the horses frisky."

From Harriet, that was small talk—not flirtation.

"I had hoped to prevail on your father for some assistance at the Hall."

She set down her bread and butter. "Is something amiss?"

Such concern in her eyes, but nothing of longing, nothing of intimacies recalled. "I merely sought to consult with an experienced horse master. My current horse master will take a post at a racing yard at the first of the month."

"That started an argument?"

"The argument began before I could pass that news along to your dear papa. This is good ale."

"The last of the summer ale." Harriet swiped the tip of her tongue across her top lip, something she'd never have done in the dining room or breakfast parlor.

Philippe consumed better cheese and coarser bread than he was used to and rearranged chess pieces in his mind. His plan had been to have Talbot brush up his riding skills here, where nobody at the Hall would know what was afoot.

A duke could land on his arse in the dirt and usually walk away unscathed. His reputation before his employees was a more delicate article than his backside. Then too, a duke could change his mind more easily with a smaller audience.

Say, an audience of one.

He ate in silence while Harriet demolished her food. "You are a hungry woman. I should have made you more than one sandwich."

"You can slice the peaches. I'll make more sandwiches." She rose and set a bowl of ripe fruit before him, as well as a cutting board and a knife.

"Will you make peach jam?"

"Mama was the jam maker, though Cook assisted, of course. It's a messy, tedious job, and I haven't time."

The peaches were perfect—ripe and juicy but firm. By the time Philippe had pitted and cut up two of them, Harriet had another pair of sandwiches put together. Hers were tidy—evenly sliced bread, cheese a uniform thickness, not too much butter.

"Try a slice," Philippe said, holding a glistening portion of peach across the table.

Harriet reached for it, and he drew his hand back a few inches. "You'll get sticky."

She nibbled from his fingers delicately, her eyes closing as she swallowed. "That is luscious. Of all the generosity the old duke displayed toward us, Mama treasured those peach trees the most."

Philippe shared the rest of the peaches with her, until his fingers were covered with juice and sharing a peach topped his list of erotic ways to spend an autumn afternoon.

"I was hungry," Harriet said, rising. "I get so involved in what I'm doing with the horses, I forget to eat. Shall we take our ale out to the porch?"

"A fine notion." In view of the arena and the barns, Philippe had a prayer of behaving. He had not come here thinking to renew intimacies with Harriet, but in her company, little else would wedge its way into his thoughts.

He washed his hands while Harriet wrapped up the bread and cheese, then they carried their mugs to the front porch.

"I love this time of year," Harriet said, taking a seat on a wrought-iron chair. "The harvest is a happy occasion, the animals are fat and healthy, and the light is beautiful."

Harriet was beautiful, with her hair coming undone and her habit dusty to the knees.

Across the stable yard, a groom was reviewing with a bay yearling filly the etiquette of work in hand. The groom walked a half-dozen steps and stopped. Walked a half-dozen more and stopped again, until the young horse recalled that she was to match her handler's behavior, not barge about on the end of the lead rope like a half-ton kite.

"She fancies him," Harriet said. "Trusts his patience and his calm. Jeremy is like you in that regard, seldom discommoded regardless of the circumstances."

Philippe was discommoded—by the interview with Talbot, by the breeze teasing at the curls lying against Harriet's neck. He'd come here for a reason, and Talbot had stymied him. Too late, Philippe had realized that Talbot's health was more precarious than anybody grasped.

Anybody save Harriet, perhaps.

To teach regular riding lessons required hours at the arena rail, in the cold, in the damp, in the hot sun, the flies, the relentless wind. The horse master of Philippe's youth had made those lessons the high point of Philippe's day, but that man was no more.

"I had best be going," Philippe said. "Perhaps you'll walk with me to the bridle path?"

Harriet set her mug on the porch railing. "Of course. I'm looking forward to dinner on Friday."

Philippe set his mug beside hers. "Because?"

"Because dinner at the Hall is always an enjoyable occasion," she said, starting down the steps. "Lord Ramsdale passed along your invitation to Papa over the chess board."

Philippe would thank Ramsdale just as soon as he finished thrashing him for his presumption. "I'll look forward to it as well, but I've been anticipating something else more joyously than another shared meal. Something I've been meaning to ask you about."

Did you enjoy our kiss? Did you spend half the night recalling it? Have you not brought it up because you hope I'll never presume to that degree again?

They ambled along the fence, to where the young horse was being put through her paces.

"Jeremy," Harriet said, "that's enough for today. She's being a good girl, and you want to stop before she's bored."

Jeremy, who looked to be about sixteen, petted the filly's neck. "Aye, Miss Talbot. Good day, Your Grace."

"Jeremy."

The groom led the horse away, praising her fine performance.

"He's one of the miller's boys, isn't he?" The entire family had height, white-blond hair, and prominent teeth.

"One of eight sons. Jeremy works hard and loves the horses, but the first time he has to sell a favorite or put a bullet in an old friend who's stepped in a badger hole, he'll be back at his papa's side, grinding corn."

For the rest of the distance to the tree-line, Philippe pondered how anybody—even a determined duke—could bring the conversation around to stolen kisses after an observation like that.

Harriet walked past the break in the trees, right onto the bridle path itself. "Will Ramsdale join us on Friday?"

"I assume so."

"I don't think he and Papa got very far with their last chess game. Both queens and kings were still on the chess board when I brought Papa the morning mail. What did you want to ask me about, Your Grace?"

She watched the retreat of the groom and filly, her question all but idle.

"Did you know your braid is coming undone?" The ribbon had nearly slipped off the end of her plait. Philippe moved behind her, tugged the ribbon free, and held it before her. "I'll do you up. Hold still."

Harriet gave him her back while Philippe undid and then rebraided her hair. He hadn't put his gloves back on after their meal, and so he was free to torment himself with thick, silky, lavender-scented skeins of cinnamon-brown curls.

"Do you do this sort of thing often?" Harriet asked, gaze on the hedgerow before her.

"What sort of thing?" Stare at the nape of a woman's neck until his tongue ached?

"Braid a lady's hair."

Philippe completed his task and tied the hair ribbon snugly about the end of the plait. "Like that kiss we shared, this is a first for me. I doubt my work will hold for long. Your hair is too... soft."

Harriet turned, and because Philippe wasn't about to step back, they stood quite close. Nobody would see them here between the hedgerows. The moment was perfect for another kiss, if she *wanted* another kiss.

The moment was also perfect to tell a presuming duke to take his kisses and bugger off.

"You had a question for me," Harriet said, smoothing the fold of his lapel. She looked up, her gaze simply honest—no reproach, no flirtation.

He caught her hand in his. "Harriet... would you mind...?"

"Yes?"

"Would you mind...?" Her lips were parted. Philippe had touched peach slices to those lips. His dreams tonight would surely include ripe, succulent, sweet peaches.

She leaned nearer. "Your Grace?"

"Would you mind... teaching me to ride?"

CHAPTER FOUR

Harriet had been on many a horse who at the last instant refused a jump. She'd sink her weight into the stirrups—or stirrup, if she was riding aside—fix her eye on the next obstacle and anticipate the magnificent rise of more than a half ton of muscle and might beneath her—

And find herself clinging to coarse mane and scrambling to regain her balance on a beast that had barely, barely managed to remain upright.

The duke's question left her similarly disconcerted. Her momentum had all been in the direction of a kiss, not... not... *What had he asked her?*

"I beg your pardon?"

Harriet stood so close to him that she could see how agate and slate came together to put the silver glint in his eyes, so close she could feel his breath fanning across her cheek. Her fingers had gripped his sleeve, and his hand rested on her shoulder.

"Will you teach me to ride again?" he asked. "I needn't qualify for the race meets. I simply want to acquit myself competently in the saddle of a morning in Hyde Park. I'd like to ride my acres as my father did. It's time, Harriet. Your father was right about that."

He brushed her hair back from her brow, and Harriet wanted to smack his hand. "Time for you to learn to ride again? You rode competently as a boy." More than competently, he'd ridden joyously.

His lashes swept down. "That was before Jonas's accident."

Before Lord Chaddleworth had died. His horse had either refused or slipped at a stile, and his lordship had come off, straight into the wall. He'd never regained consciousness and taken less than two hours to expire.

Harriet's ire slipped from her grasp, like wet reins in the hands of a beginner. "Oh, Philippe. Of course, I'll help."

He rested his forehead against her shoulder, and Harriet wrapped her arms around him.

"Thank you, Harriet. Your father refused me, after he'd been the one to goad me into trying. I thought perhaps…"

This was a conversation to have heart-to-heart rather than face-to-face. Harriet rested her cheek against Philippe's chest and found the rhythm of his life's blood steady but pronounced.

"You thought Papa judged the task impossible," she said. "For him, it likely is. He can barely stand for ten minutes, and that's with the aid of his cane. Trudging through deep footing is hell for him, and his pride pains him as badly as his joints."

Philippe's hand cradled the back of Harriet's head, and thus they remained, embracing, for the time it took a golden leaf to twirl down through the afternoon sunshine. She willed him to understand that his request touched her—getting back on the horse was more than a metaphor for seizing one's courage after a setback.

Getting back on the horse could be the defining challenge of a lifetime.

"My pride pains me as well," Philippe said. "Might I further impose and request that our lessons take place here?"

"You will save me the time needed to hack over to the Hall," Harriet said, "and Papa will likely watch from the porch or a handy window and pass along pointers to me at supper. I'll swear the lads to secrecy, and nobody will be the wiser."

For a time. No power on earth could permanently still the tongues that wagged in a stable yard.

Philippe's embrace eased. "I should have asked you in the first place, but you have much to do already. You'll tell me if I'm imposing?"

Never. "I enjoy teaching, and you used to enjoy riding. This will be easier than you anticipate."

He brushed a kiss to her cheek. "I am in your debt. Shall we begin tomorrow afternoon?"

"Rain or shine, Your Grace. Two of the clock, and wear your oldest pair of boots."

"I have my orders." He bowed over her hand and then strode off down the path.

Harriet perched on a fallen log and sorted through her feelings as more leaves drifted to the golden carpet covering the grass.

She was proud of Philippe for taking this step.

She was proud of herself for being a good enough friend that he'd trust her to help.

She was happy that her stable would have the honor of reacquainting the Duke of Lavelle with his equestrian skills.

The next leaf smacked her in the mouth and refused to complete its descent. She brushed it aside and set it on the log.

Proud and happy weren't the entire list. Harriet was also confident that she could help Philippe—she'd coached other riders past a loss of courage and worked through the same problem herself more than once.

She was also determined. Very, very determined.

The duke would get back on his horse, and Harriet would have more kisses.

* * *

"I am a very, very bad man," Philippe informed Saturn.

The dog panted happily at his heels as they strode along the bridle path.

"There I stood, thinking *untoward thoughts*, while Harriet offered me her moral support and compassion. I am the lowest scoundrel ever to steal a kiss." Though that's all he'd stolen—a kiss, a hug, a tender embrace that for Harriet had likely been between old friends, and for Philippe had been the sweetest torment.

"I'm not nervous," he went on. "Not about sitting on a horse again."

He was, though, looking forward to time with Harriet more or less alone, but for the presence of an equine.

He reached the boundary between the ducal estate and Talbot's property. Philippe hopped a stile rather than deal with the gate. Saturn wiggled under the gate, which was a bit of a squeeze for such a grand fellow.

"I should have made it apparent that Harriet will be compensated for her time."

Saturn stuck his nose into the carpet of leaves and began snuffling intently.

"I will insist on paying her in good English coin, and she'll have nothing to say to it. I'll be quite the—"

Philippe tripped over a tree root hidden by the fallen leaves and nearly went sprawling. The dog regarded him pityingly, then went back to his investigations.

"I'll be quite the duke," Philippe finished. "Though I'm not quite the duke." He was a spare pressed into service out of necessity, plain and simple. There were worse fates—bashing headfirst into a plank wall and expiring, for example.

He increased his stride. "Riding isn't difficult. The horse goes on the bottom, as Talbot used to say. The rest of it—the hands, seat, legs, and whatnot—are details."

Important details. Philippe had been on a runaway pony once. Amazing, how an equine who'd barely moved when pointed away from the barn could cover ground in the opposite direction.

"But I stayed on. The little fiend was utterly winded by the time we trotted into the stable yard. Had to walk him for an hour."

An hour of ignominy, for all the lads had known exactly what had happened. Talbot had pretended Philippe had meant to go tearing hell-bent across field and furrow, but the stable hands, Philippe, and the demon pony—Butterball—had known differently.

"I got back on and learned to keep a firm hold of the reins. A simple enough concept."

The break in the trees that led to the Talbot paddocks came into view, and Philippe's belly did an odd leap. Saturn lifted his leg on an oak sapling, which gave Philippe an excuse to pause, reconnoiter, and say a prayer.

Let me not be put to shame.

"Watch over me, Jonas. If I follow your example and go early to my reward, the title ends up with dear cousin Oglethorpe, and the peerage will never recover from that abomination. Ada will kill us both all over again for abandoning her to his charming company."

Saturn finished watering the hedge and went trotting forth as if he well knew Philippe's destination, rotten beast. He'd been a puppy at the time of Jonas's death—Jonas's personal hound.

"I'm coming. We have plenty of time, and it's not as if Harriet has nothing else to do."

When Philippe emerged between the Talbot paddocks, Harriet was in fact striding along behind the two-year-old filly Jeremy had been working with the previous day. The filly was in long reins, Harriet marching smack up against the horse's hip.

This was a step in the direction of carrying a rider, allowing the horse to learn how to go along in a bridle without having to carry a rider's weight. Philippe had watched Talbot educate many a young horse in this manner. A surprising degree of fitness was required to manage the horse while marching about in deep footing, but Harriet managed it easily.

The horse turned, and Harriet came more fully into view.

"Gracious devils, have mercy upon me."

She was wearing breeches and tall boots, only an oversized riding jacket preserving a modicum of modesty. She spoke to the horse as they halted between two jumps, for this was also the phase of training at which voice commands could be taught.

"Walk on, Rosie, there's a girl."

The filly minced forward as daintily as a cat. Harriet steered her all about the arena, around jumps, past stable boys grinning on the rail, down the middle, and over to the mounting block, all the while guiding, chiding, and encouraging.

"And ho, Rosie. Ho."

The filly came to a smooth stop in the center of the arena, and after she'd stood quietly for half a minute, much patting and praising ensued. Jeremy left the rail to take the horse back to the stable, and Harriet waved at Philippe.

"Your Grace! Good day."

So she *had* noticed him. "Harriet. Very nicely done."

"She's a good girl. Is it two of the clock already? How time flies when the weather's fine. Come along, your mount should be ready."

Philippe joined Harriet at the arena gate. "Before you start lessons, don't you typically discuss compensation?"

Her coiffure was in good repair, which ought to have helped Philippe keep his mind on the business of the day. Instead, he wanted to take down her braid and bury his hands in her hair.

While he was kissing her.

While she was kissing him back and clutching him in that lovely firm grip of hers.

I have lost my mind.

"We can discuss remuneration once I've done something to earn it," Harriet said as they reached the barn. "This is Matador."

A mountain of gray horsehair stood in the middle of the aisle. An equine nose tipped with pink protruded from the hair—a nose about a yard long. Two big brown eyes regarded Philippe from beneath two hairy ears.

"Hello, Mastodon."

The horse's lower lip drooped, giving him an air of permanently injured dignity.

"I'll need to use the ladies' mounting block to board him," Philippe said. "He does move without hoisting sail? Stops, turns, backs up—the whole lot?"

"He'll do as you tell him," Harriet said, unfastening the crossties. "Let's see what you recall."

"*Now?*"

Harriet went about disentangling the reins from the throatlatch, then had to hop to loop the reins over the beast's great head.

"It's two of the clock, Your Grace, and I have much to do."

Whose ideas was this? "I'm a duke. I can't be seen riding a plough horse." Though dukes weren't supposed to dither, fuss, or prevaricate either.

Harriet stroked the horse's neck. "Matador is a retired drum horse. He's attended more funerals of state than you have, and you should be honored to have the use of him. He would still be in work, except his partner succumbed to colic and nobody could find another to match Matador's size and coloring."

Shamed by an orphaned mastodon. "Very well," Philippe said. "As I recall, one walks on the horse's left."

The equine cortege came along docilely, hooves the size of soup tureens clopping inches from Philippe's boots. Though the animal was apparently well trained, Philippe was abruptly aware that he was about to entrust his well-being to a creature ten times his size who had no respect for the ducal succession.

And yet, the horse was a placid beast, handsome in its way, and Philippe was no longer a small boy with only a small boy's strength.

"Let's use the rail to get you into the saddle," Harriet said. "The first thing you should know about Matador is that he'll stand until Domesday. He's stood for hours in the line of duty, put up with crowds, barking dogs, disrespectful children, and drunken fools. There isn't much you can do to unnerve him."

"His job sounds rather like being a duke," Philippe said, swallowing back some inconvenient welter of emotion. Excitement to be taking on a challenge, impatience at the indignity of being a beginner, fear of mortal harm—might as well be honest—and also hope, that this adventure ended well for all concerned.

Then he was perched on the fence railing, making an awkward job of clambering into the saddle. The horse sighed as Philippe slipped his boots into the stirrups.

"Now what?"

Harriet led Matador a few feet from the rail. "Now we adjust your stirrups. You have longer legs than most stable boys."

The next few minutes were taken up with Harriet *handling* her pupil. Philippe lifted his legs, sat tall, had his boots turned to rest nearly parallel to the horse's sides, and generally endured fussing. When Harriet stepped back, Philippe's stirrups were at the correct length, and his insides were in a muddle.

He'd made the mistake of looking down, thinking to feast his eyes on the sight of Harriet's hands on his person. He'd instead seen the ground, miles and miles below where it should have been.

"Your stirrups are on the fourth hole," Harriet said. "Remember that, because when we're finished here in the arena, we'll review saddling and unsaddling."

"Right, fourth hole." Not that Phillippe could count to four in his present state. With no warning, his heart had decided to take off at a gallop, his mouth had gone dry, and his wits were probably somewhere in the muck heap.

"Now, you follow me," Harriet said. "Horses are herd animals. This shouldn't be difficult." She drew off her jacket—probably one of Talbot's castoffs, judging from the poor fit—and slung it over the railing. "Follow the leader, Your Grace, and I'm the leader."

She strode off. Matador swung his enormous head to sniff at the toe of Philippe's boot.

Get on with it, mate.

"Keeping you from your oats, am I?" Philippe gave a scoot with his seat.

Nothing happened.

He tapped his heels ever so gently at the horse's sides, and one hoof shuffled forward.

A firm tap produced a funereal toddle, which suited Philippe splendidly. The horse moved like an equine sea, rolling, rhythmic, and relentless, but also deliberate. One-two-three-four, one-two-three-four...

"Are your eyes up?" Harriet called without looking back. "Look where you're going. Don't stare at his mane."

Well, yes. Philippe tipped his chin up, and the rolling sea became a plodding horse. This was all in aid of the Talbots' future. A secure old age for a man who'd worked long, hard years. Harriet swung left around a jump, and Philippe guided his mount in the same direction.

She didn't even glance back, which Philippe suspected was her way of allowing him some privacy at an awkward moment. Two more turns, a halt, and onward… until Philippe realized that this game of follow the leader would be the undoing of him, for the leader, striding along in her breeches, had a very fetching derriere.

* * *

Harriet got an education while teaching the duke.

By the second lesson, she realized that His Grace was an athlete. Being unwilling to ride meant that he walked far more than most of his peers. He mentioned that on holidays he'd go for a twenty-mile jaunt over the hills and consider that a pleasant day. He fenced, he rowed, he swam—the Duke of Lavelle was an intensely physical man.

He had the muscles to show for it. As Harriet moved his leg—here for the signal to move forward, there for the signal to move sideways—she grew distracted.

Ye gods, his calves. His *thighs*.

As she adjusted his hands on the reins—black leather gloves notwithstanding—she grew muddled, for those hands had coaxed terrible longings from her.

As she watched his progress from behind—lest he be sitting subtly to one side or the other—she lost her train of thought entirely. Such broad shoulders, such excellent posture. Such…

"That's enough for today," Harriet said. "Posting the trot will leave you sore, regardless of your otherwise fine physical condition."

Posting the trot—rising in the stirrups to the rhythm of the horse's footfalls—made for a smoother ride than trying to match the horse's movement with the seat in the saddle. Matador had a nicely cadenced trot, but his gaits were enormously springy.

Philippe had caught Matador's rhythm easily, though this lesson would exact a toll in aching muscles tomorrow. Sunday he'd be uncomfortable in the extreme, if the duke's tutelage followed the usual course.

"I had hoped we might canter today," Philippe said, giving Matador a whacking great pat on the neck. "Two lessons and the whole business is already coming back to me."

"We'll canter soon enough," Harriet said. "Today, you can take off his saddle and bridle and groom him yourself."

Philippe kicked his feet out of the stirrups and hopped off as nimbly as any cavalry officer. He ran the stirrups up their leathers, loosened the girth, and looped the reins over Matador's head.

"We have not discussed your compensation," he said, leading the horse to the gate. "Come with me to the barn, and we can have that argument while I get horsehair all over my clothing."

"As you wish."

"You don't fool me, Harriet Talbot. You'll be agreeable until I put the HMS Mastodon into dry dock, and then you'll turn up contrary. If we had children, you'd reserve all your ire for when the little ones were tucked up into their beds and then open fire on your unsuspecting spouse."

If they had children... "Today you pick out Matador's feet, Your Grace."

Philippe was doing quite well in the saddle. Papa had said he had a natural seat, and Papa was—once again—right. On the ground, where a horse could rear, strike, bite, or knock a man flat, the duke wasn't as confident.

Matador had confidence enough for ten students and an abiding affection for his paddock. He'd endure fumbling and bumbling under saddle for the promise of an hour at grass. The duke couldn't know that. Matador had not earned His Grace's trust, and His Grace had not earned Matador's either.

Philippe was conscientious about removing the bridle and saddle, putting on the headstall, and fastening the crossties. He also went about the grooming—curry, coarse brush, then fine brush—without skimping anywhere. The bliss of a thorough brushing had Matador's eyelids drooping and his head hanging as low as the crossties would allow.

"You've groomed the baby to sleep," Harriet said. "Or tired him out. Soon, I might assign you a different mount."

"You dare not," Philippe replied, draping an arm across Matador's withers. "Mastiff will think he's fallen out of favor with me."

"Mast—Matador is accustomed to his pupils moving on to other mounts." Harriet had never quite got the knack. When her students went to other teachers—always to men, of course—she worried. Would this one learn to sit *straight*? Would that one ever keep her eyes *up*?

"About your compensation," Philippe said, giving Matador's shoulder a scratch.

The horse groaned like a heifer flopping into spring grass.

"You haven't cleaned out his feet." Harriet took a curved pick from a nail on the wall. "I'll do the first one. You'll do the other three."

Horses were trained to lift their feet for this process. The groom had simply to scrape the mud, stones, or manure from the concave area on the bottom of the hoof. Balancing on three legs was difficult for an animal weighing a ton, though, and thus a quick, competent touch was necessary.

Harriet reviewed the basics—run a hand down the horse's leg, tug at the hair on his fetlock, give him a moment to lift his foot, then cradle it like so in one hand...

"And use the pick with the other. *You* put his foot back on the ground. He doesn't get to snatch it away."

Philippe took the pick from her. "He outweighs me by a factor of ten. He gets to do as he jolly well pleases with his feet, and my primary concern is for my toes."

"Then don't bother trying," Harriet retorted. "Don't put your hand on this horse unless you are prepared to tell him exactly what he needs to do to earn your continued goodwill."

Matador was awake now, head up, listening to the conversation. He wouldn't grasp the words, but he'd grasp tone of voice. He'd note the posture of the humans on either side of him and probably even their expressions and subtle changes in their scents.

"I'm to be the duke even in this?" Philippe said. "Hurl orders and thunderbolts, demand proper address, brook no disrespect?"

Was that how he saw the title? "You are to be a person Matador can rely upon to see to his safety and well-being. That means he learns to obey you in small matters so that large matters never become an issue. Right now, you are his groom, Your Grace, nothing more."

Philippe bent to Matador's off foreleg, hoof-pick in his hand. "*Your Grace.*" He ran his hand down the horse's front leg, tugged on the hair in the general vicinity of the fetlock, and nothing happened. "Now what?"

"You have to mean it," Harriet said. "He has to know you're not mucking about for show."

A second attempt yielded the same result. This was Matador's version of a game, getting back a bit of his own. He'd been a good boy for well over an hour, doing exactly as he'd been told. In what passed for horsey thinking, he was owed a bit of sport.

Rotten timing, though.

"I have grooms," Philippe said, stepping back. "They will deal with the distasteful business of scraping manure from horse feet when the need arises."

"So if you're out on a hack, enjoying some solitude in the saddle, and your horse begins to go uneven in front, you'll make him walk all the way back to the barn with a stone lodged against his sole rather than dismount, get out your penknife, and solve the problem on the spot? A stone bruise can lead to an abscess and worse."

Matador shook all over, sending gray hair cascading in every direction. For him, the grooming session was done.

"Now you have me killing my horse before I've even cantered him," Philippe said.

Harriet waited.

She'd been waiting for Philippe in a corner of her heart for years. She could afford to wait a moment more. If he gave up now, that would be for the best, because the challenges only increased from this point forward. Philippe had made a good try, but he had reasons for stepping back, and if that was his choice...

Harriet would be eternally disappointed.

"You," Philippe said to the horse, "are a disrespectful backbencher from the West Riding who doesn't know his place. Lift your damned foot, horse."

Matador obliged for a moment, then came within inches of putting his foot down atop the duke's boot.

Philippe passed Harriet the hoof-pick, and she nearly began to cry. *You cannot give up. Not on yourself, not so soon.*

Then he shrugged out of his jacket, slung it in the direction of a trunk, and caused Matador to shy.

"The hoof-pick, please."

Harriet passed it over.

"Now that I have the attention of yonder pleasure barge," Philippe said, "perhaps he'll condescend to allow me to scrape the manure from between his royal toes."

Matador hadn't bargained on his groom's strength or wiliness. Philippe went through the routine—bend, run a hand down the leg, tug at the feathers around the fetlock—but at the last instant, Philippe shoved his shoulder against the horse's side.

The gelding lifted his foot as if to step to the side. Philippe caught it and curled the foreleg up to put the underside of the hoof skyward. In a few brisk swipes with the pick, he'd scraped out a pile of dirt.

"Two more to go, horse. I value this shirt more than your dignity, so plan accordingly."

The first back hoof went smoothly. On the second, Matador tried to wrestle his foot away, but he was merely playing, and Philippe was in earnest. The duke finished with the foot easily.

"Well done," Harriet said. "Now you can put him up."

Philippe led the horse to his loose box, which had the generous dimensions of a foaling stall. "If you'd bring me my coat?"

Harriet obliged, though seeing His Grace without benefit of his riding jacket was the best distraction of the day so far.

"The left pocket holds a carrot," Philippe said, unfastening Matador's headstall. "We're to end on a good note, despite our wrestling match."

Harriet had reminded him of that. End every lesson on a positive note, even if that positive note was merely a smooth halt or a quiet circuit of the arena on a loose rein.

Philippe broke the carrot in half, took a bite, and put the remaining portions on his flat palm. Matador whispered his lips over Philippe's hand. The carrot disappeared amid loud mutual crunching.

"I've done the same on many occasions," Harriet said. "They also like apples."

"I like a fellow who has some backbone," Philippe said, stroking Matador's neck. "I'm not sure I like an insubordinate horse."

"Did you follow every instruction from your tutors and professors? Did you never ask them a clever question to see if they were as learned as they pretended to be?"

Philippe stepped from the stall and closed the latch on the half door. "I challenged them all the time." He leaned near. "You are a good teacher, Harriet. A very good teacher. How do I repay you for your time, your patience, and your wisdom?"

Since undertaking these riding lessons, Philippe hadn't flirted with Harriet, not once. She'd touched him in the course of instruction, and he'd listened patiently to her lectures, as if he'd never kissed her, as if she were in truth the son Jackson Talbot should have had.

She was not that son, though lately she hadn't felt much like a daughter either. She'd felt like an exhausted drudge, except for when Philippe had kissed her.

He was asking how to repay her for her time, her patience, and her wisdom. Harriet had a few ideas, and none of them involved pounds and pence.

CHAPTER FIVE

Riding lessons created a welter of conflicting emotions for Philippe.

He liked the scent and sounds of the horse barn. That hadn't changed. When he walked into the stable and caught a whiff of hay, manure, and equine, he relaxed, and his cares and worries temporarily roosted somewhere besides his too busy mind.

He did not like that horses, for all their size, could move at blinding speed. A jerk of the horse's head, a startle at a swooping barn swallow, a casual stomp of the hoof to dislodge a fly, and the nearest human could well be injured.

Though perhaps the need to remain ever alert was part of what made Harriet so vibrant.

She was a very competent instructor. Being around her was wonderful—and awful. Philippe did not enjoy his lessons, so much as he endured them. Harriet's tutelage was a barrage of admonitions worthy of Philippe's men of business:

Think ahead.

Eyes up; look where you're going.

For God's sake, the horse is ten times your size. You must plan carefully when moving that much muscle around the arena.

Riding a horse was too much like being a duke. All responsibility with very little recreation. The moments before and after the lesson were Philippe's reward for heroic sacrifice in the name of inchoate courtship.

He posed the question of compensation to Harriet and then propped a shoulder against a worn beam to await her answer. She was again in breeches and had again lost her jacket partway through the lesson.

"How do you pay me?"

"Coin of the realm, goods in kind, services rendered." Philippe draped his jacket over her shoulders. "Your time is valuable. What do I have that will compensate you for the thankless task of yelling at me for an hour?"

"Let's discuss this in the saddle room."

His spirits rose as he followed her down the barn aisle. If Harriet wanted privacy, then she was inclined to be honest with him, and honesty in private locations could lead to interesting destinations.

"Shouldn't you be returning to the Hall?" Harriet asked right outside the saddle room. "You're having guests for supper."

"Harriet, you needn't be embarrassed to discuss money with me. Contrary to popular perception, a titled man spends much of his time concerned with financial matters. If I'm not meeting with solicitors, I'm reviewing their reports, looking over ledgers, or writing bank drafts. Lady Ada is endlessly corresponding with me about this improvement or that expenditure at the Hall. I'll happily write a bank draft to your father."

Though he'd even more happily put coins directly into Harriet's hand. Talbot would use the money to paint fences, while Harriet might need the money for new fabric.

Or a bonnet. Every woman deserved the occasional new bonnet.

She let him hold the door for her. "I seek a different sort of remuneration from you, Your Grace. Coin is all well and good, but like you, I have requests I cannot make of just anybody."

Philippe stepped closer. "I fully intend to sing the praises of Talbots' stables when you've repaired my equestrian capabilities. I'll buy my personal mounts from you, credit you with restoring my skills in the saddle, and otherwise recommend your services from here to Mayfair."

Harriet took down a sidesaddle from the rack protruding from the wall. "That is very… That is decent of you, but our reputation is already excellent among the discerning."

Not excellent enough, if the carpets in the house were any indication. Still, Harriet's dismissal was understandable. She didn't circulate among her clients socially and wouldn't grasp what a duke's cachet could do for her father's prospects.

She brought the saddle over to the windows, where afternoon sun fell on a worktable. Philippe had carved his initials on one of the table legs years ago.

"I insist on compensating you," Philippe said, getting the basket of rags and tin of leather balm down from the quarter shelves in the corner. "Nonetheless, I have no idea what a fair wage would be. You must tell me."

He brought the rags and balm to the table, took up a chair, and waited for Harriet to pass him the stirrup leathers and the girths. They'd spent many a rainy day as children cleaning the saddles and bridles. Bridles were the worst, for Philippe could never figure out how to get the dratted things back together.

"Thank you," Harriet said, dipping her rag into the tin. "You mentioned services in kind. I'd like that sort of payment."

"Shouldn't you take off the stirrup before you start on the saddle, Harriet?"

"Of course." She passed Philippe the rag, then the stirrup with its leather attached.

"What sort of service might I render you, my dear?"

Harriet took inordinate care selecting another rag from the basket. "Lessons."

"My Latin is serviceable, my Greek rusty, and my French in good repair. I'm proficient at adding and subtracting numbers in my head, and I know a fair amount of history. Other than that, the only subjects I know intimately are those relating to the dukedom. How many sheep per acre on the upland tenant farms, how many heifers on the home farm, that sort of thing."

Harriet's ears had turned pink. "I need you to teach me how to gain the notice of a gentleman." She chose a second rag and dipped it into the tin.

If she'd entered Philippe to ride at Ascot, he could not have been more unhappily surprised. "What need have you of such skills? Simply kiss the poor fool and he'll be your slave for life."

She swiped a dab of conditioner onto the flap of the saddle. The scent hinted of lanolin and beeswax, and it brought back pleasant memories.

This conversation had abruptly become unpleasant.

"There's more to courtship than kissing, Your Grace. A great deal more."

And how Philippe wanted to share that great deal more with her—though not if she pined for another.

"Harriet, have you been practicing on me?"

She folded the rag and began working the conditioner into the leather.

"Not entirely. I know kisses mean little, and I also know yours were meant only as friendly flirtation. I have enjoyed your kisses, but you see how it is with Papa. He's failing, and being female, I cannot run this business on my own, at least not to appearances. My best hope for keeping Papa happy and a roof over my head is to find a man who thrives around horses and coax an offer from him."

She sounded as if she'd enjoy emptying the muck cart on Philippe's boots nearly as much as she'd enjoyed his kisses, though her logic was unassailable: Harriet loved horses, she loved her father, and she'd sacrifice even her happiness to see to the welfare of both.

Though Philippe was not, by any stretch, a man who thrived around horses. "I have enjoyed your kisses as well, Harriet."

"That's the problem, then, isn't it? If my kisses are merely sweet and friendly, I must be doing it wrong. I'm twenty-eight years old, and I've spent much of those twenty-eight years watching happy couples ride, walk, and flirt their way up and down the bridle path. You've kissed me more than anybody else has. What am I doing wrong?"

He'd kissed Harriet exactly once—well, one and a half times, if a kiss to the cheek counted. Philippe took heart from her admission, though she'd also apparently kissed that rascal with the beautiful eyes.

The one who, like an utter gudgeon, had left Harriet Talbot all alone on the bridle path.

"You shouldn't have to win a man's notice, Harriet. He should notice you out of his own perspicacity. You are a treasure as you are, and offering a fellow favors he hasn't earned won't lead in the direction you deserve."

Harriet dragged the saddle into her lap, flipped it over, and applied the rag to the panel. "How can anybody, no matter how perspicacious he is, notice me when I'm either marching around behind a horse, or wearing the plainest habits I could find the time to sew? I smell of horse, I haven't any fancy jewelry, and my only dowry is this property."

"I like the smell of horses." Philippe could shower her with jewels and had no need of her land, though clearly, the horses came first with her.

She shot him a sidewise glower. "Lavelle, you are not helping."

How he hated when she used his title. "Pretty frocks matter to some, jewelry to others. Are those the sort of men you want to attract?"

"Women are supposed to look like women, not like stable boys. I understand that."

She sounded so aggrieved, and Philippe wasn't much pleased with the conversation himself.

"Give me some time to think about this," he said. "I've never much considered how ladies go about... being ladies."

"I'll finish the saddle," Harriet said. "You'll want to get back to the Hall, so you can prepare for dinner tonight."

Being the duke meant Philippe had nothing to do in preparation for his guests. At the Hall, they only dressed for dinner on Sundays, a custom the late duke had started that Jonas had approved of.

"Are you trying to get rid of me, Harriet?"

She ran the rag around the edge of the cantle. "You'll want a soaking bath. Riding can leave one sore."

Well, yes. A single hour in the saddle had been enough to remind Philippe of the peculiar affliction that was saddle soreness.

"I'll take my leave of you, then, though I'll need my jacket."

"Your—? Oh, sorry." She rose and shrugged out of his jacket, passing it to him without meeting his gaze. "You'll do it, though? Teach me about... flirtation? I can't ask anybody else."

"You've mentioned that." Philippe wouldn't *want* her to ask anybody else. "I will certainly accede to your wishes, but the matter will take some thought. I'll see you at dinner."

He'd arrived to the property with every hope of stealing another kiss, most likely in parting. Now...

"You could kiss me good-bye, Philippe. For... for practice."

Which he apparently needed, if his initial efforts had struck Harriet as merely friendly. He picked up her hand, kissed her knuckles, and got a taste of sheep grease and beeswax for his efforts.

"A significant part of attaching the interest of most men," he said, "is acting as if they haven't attached yours. All quite silly if you ask me, but I'm told that's how the game is played."

He bowed and stalked off, taking minuscule comfort from the fact that Harriet looked disappointed.

* * *

"Your mind is not on the game, my friend." Ramsdale moved his queen. "Check."

Talbot scowled at the board. "Checkmate, my lord, and my apologies. You are entirely correct that my thoughts are elsewhere this evening. Did His Grace seem distracted to you at dinner?"

Ramsdale began returning his pieces to their starting positions.

"Entertaining does not appeal to Lavelle. He says he feels as if he's impersonating his father or older brother when there's company at the table." He'd said this once, shortly after Lord Chaddleworth's death, but Ramsdale saw the same subtle self-consciousness whenever Lavelle played a ducal role.

Talbot swirled his brandy. "His Grace is a damned fool, if your lordship will pardon some direct speech."

"A fool for seeing the ghost of his father and brother lurking in corners? My own departed sire sometimes plagues me similarly." Though mostly as a bad example. How much worse must it be when the ghosts had been beloved paragons?

"The late duke was a good sort," Talbot said. "He paid fair wages, appreciated a job well done, and was loyal to those who were loyal to him, but if His Grace hadn't ignored his own children, Chaddleworth might not have felt compelled to be the best at everything he turned his hand to."

The black pieces were sorted out, all in their rows. Ramsdale started on the white pieces. "You're saying Chaddleworth sought his father's approval?"

"He lived for his papa's approval. Poor lad detested dogs, but because his father adored those great slobbering Danish hounds, Chaddleworth had to adore them. Philippe, being the spare, did a better job of going his own way—then."

Philippe seemed to be treading in a circle, from what Ramsdale could see. "Were you there when Chaddleworth died?"

Talbot cradled his brandy in a palm thick with calluses. "Half the shire was there. Everybody else had sense enough to just trot through the damned gate. Chaddleworth insisted on having a go at the stile, though it was damned foolishness on a green colt in boggy footing. His father had leaped that stile not a month past, but with a seasoned jumper on a dry day. One of the stupidest accidents I've witnessed in all my years as a horseman."

The details of the tragedy had never been bruited about. Even from Lavelle, Ramsdale had heard nothing more than *these things happen* and *such a shame.*

"Foolish young men with more pride than sense tend to have stupid accidents. Had Chaddleworth been drinking?"

"The weather was raw. Of course he'd been nipping from his flask."

Ramsdale knew huntsmen who'd stash full flasks in at least four pockets before shouldering a fowling piece. They would mostly tramp about the moors or quietly drink to the sunrise in grouse blinds. He expected equestrians to be more prudent. "Was Lavelle there?"

"The present duke was merely a lad. He had sense enough to stay home when the weather was dirty, though I'm sure he's regretted that."

Ramsdale sipped fine brandy, while Talbot's logic sorted itself out. "Because, like every other person plagued with a conscience, Lavelle thinks if he'd been there, his brother would have been more careful, more concerned with setting a sensible example."

"Chaddleworth loved his siblings. Of that I have no doubt." A concession, not a compliment.

"What happened to the horse?"

Talbot shifted on his chair. "The old duke wanted him shot, which would have solved nothing. Wasn't the horse's fault, and that colt was special to my Harriet. She'd started him under saddle, raised him from a foal. I bought him back for an exorbitant sum—His Grace did not want to sell me that damned horse—and passed the beast on to an earl in Surrey who stands him at stud. A fine, handsome bit of horseflesh, overfaced by an ignorant, drunken fool."

Talbot remained a horseman, to his creaky, aching bones.

"Lord Chaddleworth's death is not what took your mind off the game tonight."

Talbot shifted again, as if the thickly cushioned seat were a hard plank. "I've been a bit foolish myself."

"Haven't we all?" Lavelle was being foolish as well, and not merely because he hadn't laid his brother's ghost to rest.

"His Grace—His Current Grace, Philippe—asked me to polish his riding skills."

"I did wonder if he'd make good on that threat. I gather that's where his afternoon rambles have taken him?"

Talbot held out his glass. "Perhaps a bit more of this excellent brandy, my lord?"

Ramsdale took the empty glass to the library's sideboard and poured a generous portion. "Does it help?" he asked, passing Talbot his drink.

"Nothing helps, but drink means the pain doesn't matter as much. I got to thinking about your remarks the other evening."

"I was loquacious, at least by my own standards. Which remarks?"

"About Harriet and His Grace."

"The same Harriet and His Grace who spent a long, convivial meal pretending to ignore each other?"

Half of Talbot's fresh serving disappeared. "You noticed that?"

"Lavelle usually has the cordial nobleman impersonation down to a fine art. Tonight, he was barely sociable, and I have occasion to know he esteems Miss Talbot greatly,"—Ramsdale lifted his glass a few inches— "as do I."

"To my dear Harriet." Talbot sipped this time. "She's a countrywoman, not raised to split hairs when it comes to propriety. If Lavelle should offer her an arrangement, she'd be foolish to turn him down. The result for her would be a lifetime of security, even if His Grace set her aside after a few years. A father has to be practical, and nobody in this shire would think any the less of her for finding favor with the duke."

Well, no, they wouldn't. The average smallholder was no high stickler, and Lavelle would be discreet.

Then too, Talbot's chess skills might be in decline because the man could hardly see the chessboard. If Harriet had to look after a blind parent, she'd do well to supplement her resources with coin from the ducal coffers.

What a quagmire.

"Have you conveyed your sentiments regarding Lavelle to your daughter?" And would Harriet be insulted by her father's opinion? Outraged? Hurt? Ramsdale accounted himself an adequate judge of men, but without the first insight regarding women.

"I have not. When Lavelle came around asking for my help with his riding, I refused him, knowing Harriet was His Grace's only option, unless he wanted to admit defeat before he started. One can't teach a duke to ride without being in the same arena with him."

"I see." And in the same barn, and the same saddle room. "Lavelle claimed he was brushing up his riding so that he might send you some business. He'll brag of your establishment to his London friends, once he's capable of hacking out with them."

Except, Lavelle didn't exactly *have* London friends. Ramsdale's association with the duke dated from public school, where they'd both been far ahead of their peers in Latin and French and thus had needed an advanced tutor in the person of Professor Phineas Peebles.

In London, Lavelle was plagued by sycophants, toadies, and

matchmakers.

"Given how those two were acting at dinner," Talbot said, "I doubt His Grace will persist with the lessons, or that Harriet will be faced with an offer of ducal protection. I suppose that's for the best. She's a good girl, my Harry."

About whom Talbot should be worried, for that good girl had no husband to provide for her after Talbot's death.

"I have an idea," Ramsdale said. "I doubt either Lavelle or Harriet would be comfortable with a liaison, and their demeanor at dinner suggests their feelings are already engaged, do they but know it. I'll just give the situation a gentle nudge at the proper moment, and all will come right."

Talbot peered at him. "Choose your moment carefully, my lord. I can't have you young fellows fighting any duels over my Harriet. She'd finish off whichever one of you was left standing."

"A sobering thought. Lavelle and I are good friends. We'll not be fighting any duels. Shall I have the carriage brought around for you?"

Talbot scooted to the edge of his seat, braced himself on the arms of the chair, and pushed to his feet. "Please. Do you know what troubles me most, your lordship?"

Ramsdale knew. "Your daughter."

"A father worries about his daughter, of course, but Harriet has taken over the whole job at the stable. It's as if she doesn't realize that one bad fall, one kick, one rambunctious two-year-old, and she could be more incapacitated than I am. She loves the horses, but I wish she had a choice. I took risks, and I'm paying the price for that, but they were risks I chose. I fear Harriet sees herself without options, and that's not right."

Ramsdale held the door for Talbot. "I will consider it my happy privilege to see to it that Miss Talbot has at least one very attractive option other than whatever offer Lavelle might eventually make."

* * *

Rain could ruin a harvest, and yet, Harriet prayed for rain.

Her daft challenge to Philippe had changed everything, and with each passing day, Philippe seemed less Harriet's friend and more her ducal neighbor. Rain would have meant the day's lesson was canceled and allowed Harriet twenty-four hours to ponder the mare's nestmuddle she'd created.

"You have made remarkable progress," she informed her pupil as the second week of lessons drew to a close. "Let's change the routine today and enjoy the bridle path."

Philippe—who had taken over grooming and saddling his mount at the beginning of the week—gave Matador's girth a tug.

"I am ever your obedient servant, madam. If you say that Masticate and I are ready for that adventure, then ready we shall be."

Perhaps in the relative privacy to be had under the oaks, Harriet might renegotiate the terms of her compensation—or collect her first payment.

Jeremy had saddled a youngster for her, a leggy bay gelding rising four. Orion was willing and athletic, but lacked confidence. Matador would be an excellent partner for him on an outing beyond the safety and predictability of the riding arena.

"Your riding has improved day by day," Harriet said as their horses ambled onto the bridle path. "I will understand if you regard your instruction as complete."

Philippe made an elegant picture, even on an unprepossessing fellow like Matador. The dignity of the drum horse shone forth when a duke was in the saddle, and Philippe was a meticulous groom. Matador's long mane lay smooth and shiny against his neck. His tail shone nearly white in the afternoon sunshine.

"My lessons complete?" Philippe replied. "When this is our first outing beyond the nursery? Come, Harriet. You can't be so eager to cast me aside as all that."

The words carried a flirtatious meaning, but Philippe wasn't smiling.

"Are you teasing me, Your Grace?"

He ducked beneath a branch at face-smacking height. "I'm by no means competent on horseback, Harriet. Cantering circles on a leash, trotting over poles… I was a better rider at age ten than I am now. Perhaps other interests demand your attention?"

Now he smiled, but not with his eyes.

"I am busy. You know that. I think we've walked long enough. Let's trot, shall we? Your job is to match Matador's pace to Orion's without either walking or cantering."

That was a fine exercise for taking up half a mile, and Philippe's ability to rate his horse's paces improved over even that short distance. They came to a bridge, and Harriet brought Orion down to the walk.

"They might want a drink," she said, steering her gelding to the bank of the stream. "Orion needs a chance to regain his wind."

Philippe guided Matador to the stream bank as well. The larger horse slurped at the water, then pawed, making a great splashing mess. Orion danced around, while Matador, having come across a means of entertaining himself, took up pawing with the other hoof.

"Shall we cross?" Philippe asked, while Matador continued to churn the water.

"I suppose we'd better." Harriet sent Orion into the stream, and he obligingly waded across and leaped up the opposite bank.

Matador splashed away.

"Kick him, Philippe. Get his attention."

Philippe gave a stout nudge with his heels, and Matador whisked his tail. "He's like a university boy with his ale." Another, harder kick merited a double whisk of Matador's tail, but then Philippe added a tap to the quarters with his crop, and Matador deigned to toddle into the stream.

"That's better," Harriet said. "He's usually quite well behaved when reminded of his duties. I recall once—"

The churning resumed, and Matador snatched at the reins. Philippe snatched back and tried another kick.

Matador's right shoulder lowered as he braced himself on three legs and used his right leg to further stir up the water.

"Philippe, get off!"

"I'll not be unhorsed in the middle of a damned—"

"He's getting down to roll in the water. Get off!"

Had Harriet not seen the same scenario result in injury, she might have been amused. Philippe kept his head, though, and leaped out of the saddle just as Matador's forehand went down, followed with a heavy splash by his hindquarters.

The horse was under saddle, and this behavior was both dangerous and ill-mannered.

"Get up," Philippe growled, unlooping the reins from Matador's head. "Get up now, you wretched, rude, naughty excuse for a retired plough horse."

Matador's bulk was sufficient that the saddle hadn't yet been soaked, but if the dratted beast rolled, he'd likely break the tree, ruin the leather, and—

Philippe delivered a side kick to Matador's shoulder, enough to get the horse's attention, not enough to hurt. "On your feet, or so help me, I'll see you made into dog collars and ladies' reticules."

The kick was unexpected, clearly, for Matador's head flew up.

Philippe glowered at the horse, eye to eye. "I said *now*."

Matador braced on his front legs, then stood, shook hard, and followed Philippe from the stream as docilely as a footman toting parcels for the lady of the house.

"Butterball used to attempt the same stunt," Philippe said. "And then, having thoroughly soaked his girth and ensured the damned thing was loosened by the wet, he'd kick out, buck, swerve, and otherwise get up to dirty tricks in an attempt to dislodge me."

Philippe took the girth up two holes.

Matador grunted.

"I have no sympathy for naughty boys," Philippe said. "My valet will have an apoplexy when he sees my boots, and that is entirely your fault."

A halfhearted swing of a sopping tail was Matador's reply, enough to send droplets directly into Orion's face.

"You handled that well," Harriet said as Philippe led Matador to a sizable rock several yards upstream.

"Thank you." He swung into the saddle. "Shall we be on our way?"

They trotted, they cantered, they observed the rule about always walking the last mile home. The entire time, Philippe's conversation was limited to civilities, and his riding was punctilious. Matador had sought to test his rider, and Matador had failed.

The weather, as if responding to the mood of the outing, shifted from sunny to overcast, and then the breeze picked up.

"Rain on the way," Philippe said as he assisted Harriet from Orion's back in the stable yard. "I'd best return to the Hall, lest I get another soaking."

She should make him look after his horse, she should make him kiss her. "If the rain continues until tomorrow, then your lesson will have to wait."

They stood as if prepared to share a dance, while Jeremy led Orion and Matador into the barn. Philippe's eyes gave nothing away, not relief, not irritation.

He was very much the duke, and while he was an impressive duke, this display of his titled self-possession also made her sad. Where was her friend, and why had he gone away? Had her honesty about the situation at the stables chased him off?

Papa *was* failing, and Harriet *was* without any means of keeping the stables going on her own. She either married someone who could manage the stables or she... the alternatives were too bleak to consider.

"If the weather is foul tomorrow," Philippe said, "then I will pay a call and take tea with you. We will flirt."

He made flirting sound as if it involved balancing ledger books or liming the jakes.

Harriet stepped back. "Will we?"

"I always pay my debts, Harriet, and you asked that in exchange for these riding lessons, I acquaint you with the means by which women attract the notice of men they fancy. My riding has progressed, and you are due payment in the coin of your choosing."

A raindrop landed on his cheek. Harriet expected to watch it freeze before her eyes. "Philippe, are you angry?"

"Vexed."

He was furious. "Over Matador's misbehavior?"

He propped his foot on the edge of a water trough and unbuckled a spur. "What possessed you to put me on a horse named *Killer*?"

If he'd leveled a curse at her, Harriet could not have been more horrified. "I never did."

"Matador, from the Spanish verb *matar*," he said, unfastening the second spur, "to kill, hence the term as used when playing ombre and related card games."

What had this to do with a naughty horse? "I was unaware of the meaning. The horse came to us already named, and the only card game I know is piquet, which I learned from my mother." Papa hadn't the patience for card games, or perhaps he could no longer see the pips.

"The horse," Philippe said, leaning close, "shall henceforth be known as Gawain."

Gawain, the chivalric ideal, defender of women, and a great healer. *Well.* "That is a fine name. I can hang up your spurs for you."

"I will decline that offer. Thanks to my untrustworthy steed, the spurs straps need conditioning. I bid you good day."

He bowed quite formally and tromped off, boots squeaking with each step.

The sight should have been comical. Harriet stifled the urge to run after him and instead went into the saddle room and cleaned every piece of gear hanging on the wall.

* * *

As soon as Philippe gained the bridle path, he took off the boots that would soon give him blisters. Then he threw them, one at a time, at the nearest oak and muttered every English, Latin, and French curse he knew while searching the undergrowth for his wet boots.

Most un-ducal of him. Wet boots would cause his valet to have an apoplexy. Missing boots would likely result in giving notice.

When Philippe had retrieved his footwear, he took off his sodden stockings, stashed them in the boots, and marched in the direction of the Hall. By the time he reached home, he was soaked to the skin—for, of course, forty days' worth of rain had fallen in the space of an hour. He'd also cut his foot on some thorny weed growing where it had no business growing.

"I do believe you are bleeding on Lady Ada's carpets," Ramsdale remarked.

The earl stood on the third step of the main staircase, glasses perched on his nose, a book in his hand.

Philippe handed his boots, spurs, hat, and gloves to a silent butler. "They are my carpets, in point of fact."

Ramsdale came the rest of the way down. "So they are. Are we now bathing out of doors? You could not be more wet."

"Ramsdale, I'm in your debt for pointing out what I might never have noticed. I am indeed more than dampish. For that reason, I will now take myself upstairs and soak in a hot bath."

Philippe headed for the stairs, and Ramsdale fell in step beside him. "Don't suppose you took a fall? Landed on your head?"

"That is not humorous."

Except… it was. To anybody whose brother had not suffered a fatal fall, the comment was clumsily humorous.

"To see His Grace of Lavelle looking like a stray cat caught in a storm is hilarious," Ramsdale said, ascending the stairs with Philippe step for step. "You might have sent for the coach."

"Sent whom? The Talbot grooms are worked to exhaustion, and my lessons only put their schedule further behind. Besides, I was wet before Harriet and I even returned to the barn—or my boots were."

"Your boots are ruined."

"Our friendship might soon follow."

Ramsdale paused on the landing. "I can be packed and down the drive in the next hour, but if we're to have a grand row, let me say first that it's lovely to see you for once not acting like the damned duke."

Part of Philippe longed to toss Ramsdale down the drive, and his horse with him. That sentiment was so unworthy that Philippe sat on the steps, where he'd no doubt leave more wet on Lady Ada's carpets.

"I am being an ass. I apologize."

Ramsdale took the place beside him, as if peers of the realm routinely perched on stairways. "Your riding lesson put you in a temper. I almost forgot you had one."

So did I. "The perishing horse decided to roll in the stream." What a ridiculous moment that had been. Philippe bellowing at a ton of mischievous equine, boots soaked, horse splashing merrily away.

"I hope you delivered a sound spanking. No animal under saddle should behave thus."

Philippe's breeches were chamois, and when wet, they clung and chafed in uncomfortable places. "I applied my boot sparingly to his shoulder, once, but Ramsdale, I wanted to kill that horse."

"Ah."

"I wanted to end its life. On the instant, over and over. If I'd had a gun—a gun that hadn't got a soaking—the beast would be cantering across the clouds."

Ramsdale took off his glasses and polished them with the lace of his cravat. "You were angry, understandably so. When was the last time you used foul language and truly meant it?"

The day my brother died. "Not recently."

Ramsdale tucked his glasses away. "You were overdue. I daresay the horse isn't much the worse for the occasion. A few stripes from the crop on a hide thick with a winter coat probably didn't make much of an impression."

"One should never strike an animal in anger."

Ramsdale passed Philippe a silver flask. "Then one dropped his riding crop in the stream."

Well, no, actually. Philippe hadn't lost his grip on his crop. "I delivered a kick to the beast's shoulder, which seemed to offend his dignity more than anything else. What is this?"

"A medicinal tot. Drink up, Your Grace, lest you take a chill. Did the horse even notice that you'd kicked him?"

When a rider fell, he was typically offered a nip from the nearest flask. Philippe had not fallen—from the horse—but he'd lost his temper, which was worse in a way.

"Gawain was affronted. Not sporting, to kick a fellow when he's down."

"I daresay Gawain's grasp of Gentleman Jackson's rules of the ring is somewhat rusty, else he'd not have decided to indulge in an impromptu bath while under saddle. Leave some for me. The day has taken a turn toward winter."

The brandy helped. Sitting on the stairs to review the incident with Ramsdale helped too. "What would you have done in my place? Harriet had little to say once I was back in the saddle. Not a suggestion or a scold." Though she'd had a compliment, and she'd not made light of the potential danger.

"I'd likely have taken my crop to the ruddy beast, because what he did was dangerous and unmannerly. What if he'd tried that mischief on a less experienced rider? What if he'd got up to his tricks when Harriet wasn't on hand to ride for help if you'd been injured? You can't countenance dangerous behavior in an animal that large, or the beast will end up in the knacker's yard."

A valid point. "Jonas would have laughed and made a great joke of the whole thing."

"And the next time Jonas needed his mount's respect," Ramsdale said gently, "what do you suppose that horse's response would have been?"

Philippe lacked the fortitude at the moment to leap that hedge. "Ada will kick me for getting the damp on her carpets. I'm for my bath." He rose, and Ramsdale did likewise.

"The lessons must be progressing if you're hacking out on the bridle path."

"The lessons are progressing." While Philippe's attempt to woo Harriet had gone absolutely nowhere. Tomorrow, he'd advance that cause, and to blazes with hacking out on the bridle path.

CHAPTER SIX

Harriet was nervous, for she'd set out the good china for the second time in less than a month. His Grace of Lavelle had come for tea, and Papa had chosen today of all days to accompany the Earl of Ramsdale to watch some three-year-old filly run a match race in the rain.

That nobody thought Harriet required more than servants to chaperone her with the duke felt like more of an insult than a compliment.

"More tea, Your Grace?"

"No, thank you. The biscuits were quite good."

"They were fresh." Harriet stuffed one in her mouth, because that comment was the farthest thing from flirtation. She dipped the remaining half biscuit in her tea and then realized what she'd done and set it uneaten on the saucer. "Excuse me."

Philippe took a biscuit from the tray, broke it in half, dipped a flaky corner into Harriet's tea, and popped the biscuit in his mouth.

"Scrumptious," he said, lowering his lashes. "Delectably sweet and very satisfying."

He chewed slowly, all the while treating Harriet to a coy half smile of the eyes. Her insides went melty, and her brain—well, she hadn't a brain when Philippe looked at her like that.

This was hopeless. The man she loved saw her as only a friend— present farce notwithstanding—and the man she needed to marry would sell their best stock to any strutting lordling with coin and always smell of the stable.

"You are being ridiculous, sir."

He finished his half biscuit. "I'm flirting, Harriet. You are not flirting back, and nothing I've tried today has inspired you to even make the attempt. That's a very pretty frock. Did you wear it for me? Wardrobe is one way a woman practices her wiles on a fellow."

The pretty frock was Harriet's best, the only new dress she'd had time to make last winter. On this chilly day, exposing so much of her décolletage had been an impractical choice.

She plucked a plain wool shawl from the back of her chair and wrapped herself in it. "I don't want to talk about my frock. I haven't any wiles, and I've asked you to address that lack, not strut your manly wares before me to no purpose."

Oh heavens, she was cross with herself and taking it out on him. This whole, doomed scheme had been her idea, and only a bad rider took her own mistakes out on a hapless mount.

Philippe dunked the second half of his biscuit and held it up to Harriet's mouth. "I'm trying, Harriet, to instruct by example, much like when you climb aboard Gawain and make him appear to be every sculptor's perfect equine model. You *show* me what my objective is. Have a nibble."

His tone was so reasonable. He coaxed rather than commanded, but Harriet had had quite enough of biscuits and tea. Time to end this interlude on a positive note, regardless of her blunders and wayward notions.

She appropriated the treat from him and held it up to his mouth. "Your turn."

The duke covered her hand with his own, bent his head, and took the sweet from her, his lips brushing over her fingers.

"You have wiles, Harriet Talbot. You have endless wiles."

Harriet had an endless ache that was equal parts longing, frustration, and despair. She rose, keeping the duke's hand in hers, and took the place beside him on the sofa.

"I do not have endless patience," she said. "My objective is to learn how to go on with a man I esteem. Show me what comes next."

Philippe kissed her knuckles, one by one, and she realized he'd chosen to come for tea precisely because nobody wore gloves when food was served. He'd thought that far ahead, or probably hadn't even had to think. He'd shared many a biscuit with many a woman, and thus he knew what he was about.

Harriet got him by the hair and shifted him, the better to kiss him.

"I thought you wanted to learn flirtation," Philippe said, pulling back two inches. "Flirtation requires patience."

"Training horses requires patience, drat it. Enough drooling on my hand. Kiss me."

Oh dear. Oh heavens. His expression went from surprised, to affronted, to something Harriet didn't recognize but found both fascinating and masculine.

"A gentleman never argues with a lady."

Philippe scooped her into his lap, and what happened after that was a combination of kisses, caresses, rustling fabric, and lost wits.

This, this *passion,* was exactly what Harriet longed for, and Philippe was who she'd longed to share intimacies with, and yet, everything was all wrong too.

"Stop thinking," Philippe said. "Stop analyzing and labeling as if you're watching a new prospect go under saddle."

When would she have this opportunity again? When would she have privacy—true privacy, not simply a stolen moment in a saddle room—with the duke? When would she be free of the demands of stable boys, customers, horses in training, and riding students?

"You're thinking, Harriet," Philippe said, his hand gliding up her calf. "Your thoughts drum as loudly in your head as the rain beating on the windows, and that is no way to show a fellow that you fancy him."

Not a fellow—Harriet fancied *Philippe.* She'd worn her best pair of silk stockings for him, but they were only stockings. From the knee up, she was bare beneath her skirts.

"Be with me, Harriet," Philippe said, punctuating his words with a kiss. "Put all else aside and please be with me now."

His tongue danced across Harriet's lips, she gave chase, and then he opened his mouth and invited her to devour him. In the back of Harriet's mind, the voice of reason insisted that Philippe was *demonstrating* passion for her, manufacturing actions and sensations in response to Harriet's demands rather than out of genuine attraction.

This was not what she wanted, and yet, it was as close as she was likely to get—ever.

Philippe's hand slid higher, above Harriet's knee, and abruptly, she faced a choice.

When approaching a jump on horseback, the likelihood of clearing a sizable obstacle increased when the horse had forward momentum. A trot was all very fine for popping over a low hedge or a small crossrail, but the canter and the gallop were better gaits for bigger challenges.

The problem with a headlong approach to a jump was that the rider had a much smaller window of time in which to adjust the horse's stride, assess the footing, or gauge the best moment to give the hands forward. The decision to attempt the jump or change course arose in an instant.

That instant was embodied for Harriet in the moment when Philippe's hand glossed over her thigh, and he rested his forehead against hers.

"Say what you want of me, Harriet. I'm yours for the duration. You need only command me."

Was he hers, or was he saying what a man did when a woman was about to invite him to compromise her? Hers for the duration of a stolen interlude? For a few weeks?

"Don't stop," Harriet said. "I know only that I don't want you to stop."

* * *

Philippe wasn't sure he *could* stop. After years of trying not to notice Harriet *in that way*, years of telling himself that he'd ruin the friendship if he attempted a romance, years of forbidding himself from even improper speculation…

He had Harriet in his lap, demanding that he become her lover. She squirmed, her weight pressing on Philippe's arousal, which seemed to bother her not one wit.

"Harriet, we need to—"

"Don't you dare stop, Philippe. I've waited years, spent forever in that dusty arena going in circles…"

"We need to slow down." Rate their paces, conserve their passion for more than a short gallop. "Sit up, my dear."

She peered at him, blue eyes brilliant and determined, then she scooted higher in his lap. He set her aside and tried to find a coherent thought or two, because Harriet was depending on him to make this interlude go well.

Despite the clamorings of conscience, stopping was out of the question. Harriet would regard a refusal to leap into intimacies with her as a rejection.

"We have time," Philippe said. "We should make the best use of it." For when would he ever again find Harriet Talbot in skirts? If polite society were sensible, they'd dress ladies in nothing but riding habits, where both underskirts and breeches put all intimate decisions in her hands.

But no, fashion dictated that a properly dressed woman have not even clothing to protect her.

"I'd prefer a bed," he said. "Your bed."

Harriet took the pin from his cravat and set it aside. "My bed is little more than a cot. I've slept on it since early childhood. We'll use the guest room."

Why was she sleeping on a damned cot? "Lead on, my lady." Philippe assisted Harriet to her feet, and she allowed it, which was encouraging. They traversed the corridor hand in hand, Harriet leading, and came to a room Philippe hadn't seen before.

A lovely bedchamber, all flowers and light, not a speck of dust to be seen. The quilt, curtains, carpet, and upholstery were spotless and united by a theme of irises—purple, yellow, cream, and green—that was echoed on the pitcher and basin on the bureau.

"For London guests," Harriet said, "who prefer not to stay at an inn, though we haven't had any of those for several years."

The nicest room in the house went empty. "Move your things in here, Harriet. This should be your room now."

"But the guests—"

He took her in his arms. "Can stay at the Hall. Hospitality is only one of a duke's duties, and heaven knows we have the room."

"Thank you."

She rested her cheek against his chest and went still in his embrace. The headlong impulsivity over the tea tray was replaced for Philippe by a sense of protectiveness that eclipsed anything he'd known in his ducal role. He managed his family's assets, oversaw the estates, waved his title about among polite society, and appeared for state functions.

All of which was mere duty.

With Harriet in his arms and the bed two yards away, duty paled compared to his determination to be what she needed, even if she wanted him only to appease her curiosity and then go duking on his way.

"You must help me," he said, kissing her ear. "We've a lot of clothes to deal with, and I'm all thumbs."

She peeked at him. "You want my clothes off?"

"Mine too."

Harriet considered this and apparently found it a fair bargain. "I would like to see you in your glory. You're very fit."

He was also still a trifle sore, but it was the familiar soreness of the regular equestrian, not the beginner's agony.

"Then I will go first. If you'd help with my sleeve buttons?"

He held out his wrists, and she unfastened his cuffs. "Now what?"

"Now you unbutton what's buttoned, untie what's tied, and then I'll do the same for you."

This wasn't necessary. Lovers intent on sharing intimacies often merely pushed clothing aside or undressed as quickly as the situation allowed.

For Harriet, haste would not do—not yet. Philippe stood quietly while she undid his cravat, peeled his coat from his shoulders, and then relieved him of his waistcoat.

"My turn," he said, turning her by the shoulders. By twisting and arching, Harriet doubtless could have unbuttoned her own dress—the buttons weren't that close together—but Philippe enjoyed being her lady's maid.

He learned more about her with each piece of clothing that came off. She preferred buttons to hooks, though they were more expensive. Buttons were easier when a lady had to dress herself. Her chemise was so thin with age as to be nearly translucent, but the embroidered hem of delicate violets was in perfect repair. She wore jumps—country stays— that laced in front, which meant Philippe could watch her face when he untied the bow and worked the panels loose.

"This is not a steeplechase, Harriet, where you must clear every obstacle once the starting gun has sounded. We can turn back any time you choose."

"Said the man still wearing his shirt, boots, and breeches."

Harriet had a marvelous figure. This had for the most part escaped Philippe's notice over the years. He'd been too busy appreciating her humor, her affection, her warmth and friendship. But then, clearly, Harriet herself took no notice of her feminine attributes, which was likely why flirtation hadn't come her way in any quantity.

Philippe sat on the bed to pull off his boots and stockings. "My offer stands, Harriet. Don't do this because you've dared yourself to leap the hedge. Do this with me because it's what you want."

He'd dodged the obvious challenge: Do this with me because I am *who* you want. Maybe soon, maybe after today. Not now. When he made her an offer, he'd do so as a man confident in the saddle, however long that took.

She started on the buttons of his shirt. "Are you nervous, Philippe?"

Dukes were never nervous. "A little. I don't want to disappoint you."

Harriet smiled, a familiar, mischievous, Harriet smile. "We are of the same mind, for I have a similar concern. I'm the beginner here, and—"

Philippe rose and pulled his shirt over his head. "This is part of being lovers, Harriet. The newness and adventure. Courage and trust come into it, or they should."

Perhaps this was why Philippe had given up on mistresses, affairs, and flings. Without the courage and trust, the encounter was no more interesting than what went on in the breeding shed of any stable.

"Is this how you go on with London ladies?" Harriet asked, unfastening the first button of his falls.

She'd tried for a flippant tone, but Philippe heard the uncertainty. "There haven't been any London ladies for years, Harriet. Nor Berkshire ladies, Kent ladies, or Paris ladies. They all wanted to bed the duke, and he's a tiresome fellow whose company I would like—at least in this—to escape."

He hadn't put that logic together previously, hadn't worked it out.

Harriet wrapped her arms around him. "I was right to worry about you. I'm sorry, Philippe."

He was aroused—he was all but skin to skin with Harriet, and he'd been honest: no ladies for years.

He was also touched. Harriet had *worried* about him. She'd known that being the duke was a burden for him, when everybody else—probably even Ramsdale—envied him the title and felt free to turn that envy into jokes and innuendo.

Philippe let himself be held, let himself bask in the pleasure of an intimate embrace with a lady—perhaps the only woman on earth—who would rather he wasn't the Duke of Lavelle, but merely her dear companion, Philippe Ellis.

"Let's to bed, before you take a chill," he said, smoothing a hand over a derriere that had sashayed through his dreams for the past two weeks.

"Your breeches," Harriet said, stepping back.

"Are about to come off." He finished unbuttoning his falls and stepped free of his clothing. Nature had been kind to him, giving him proportions that went well with a delight in physical activity. He was muscular and well proportioned—enough women had said as much—

and he was grateful for his good health.

Harriet wasn't looking at his brawn or his build. "You desire me," she said with a small frown. "We've barely kissed, and there you are, as randy as any three-year-old colt."

"And now," Philippe said, tossing the covers aside, "my challenge and delight is to ensure that your desire for me is equally evident." He bowed and swept a hand toward the bed, a ridiculous gesture when a man hadn't any clothes on, but he made Harriet smile.

"I can assure you, that challenge is easily met," she said, bouncing onto the bed. "This is a lovely mattress."

Any mattress Harriet Talbot graced would be lovely. Philippe climbed onto the bed and positioned himself on all fours over her.

"You are lovely. You are scrumptious, delectable, fascinating..." He punctuated his description—this was not flattery—with kisses, and Harriet retaliated by running her hands all over his back. Her fingers and palms were callused, her touch sure.

No wonder the horses loved her, because that touch was confident and lovely.

Philippe waited for some awkwardness to creep into the bed with them, some sense of incredulity to be sharing intimacies with his friend Harriet, but no such convenient hesitation obliged him.

She switched to caressing his chest, exploring his muscles and bones, brushing a thumb over the hair of his armpits, then over his nipples.

"You are thorough in your investigations, madam."

Her hands went still. "I'm not supposed to be? Am I to lie here with my hands at my sides, sighing at regular intervals?"

This was bravado, and Philippe loved her for it. "You are to make a banquet of me. You are to indulge your every fantasy, your wildest curiosity, and not allow me to leave the bed until your dreams have come true."

What twaddle, though he meant every word. His dreams were certainly coming true—almost.

Harriet did sigh at regular intervals, and her hands ventured lower to caress Philippe's backside, his hips, and then to more intimate territory.

"So soft," Harriet muttered, running her fingers around the head of his cock. "Like a horse's nose."

Philippe laughed, and Harriet smacked his chest. "How will I look Gawain in the face now?" he asked. "The damned horse has a nose the size of Hyde Park."

He kissed Harriet, for making him laugh, for driving him daft. She arched up, her breasts to his chest, and Philippe went on a mission to pleasure those breasts. Harriet's sighs became moans, pants, and muttered orders, until her chemise was lost among the covers, and Philippe was confident she did, indeed, desire him as much as he desired her.

"Now comes the fascinating part," he said, spooning himself around her. "This is where you trust me, Harriet."

She twisted to send him a rumpled glower over her shoulder. "What was all this other? I thought you were rather enthusiastic about—"

He wrestled her back into his arms. "I was and am interested, as are you. Interested is a fine beginning, but we're about to move on to fascinated." If not obsessed.

Because surely, after an encounter like this, he'd be more than her friend? More than just the man she could trust with her intimate education?

She fit him wonderfully, though Philippe could feel some caution in her, some worry. He shifted back enough—a few inches seemed like half the width of the bed—to rub her shoulders.

"Do you ever get sore from the riding?" he asked.

"Sometimes, if I'm on a horse that's too narrow or too broad, if I work too many youngsters in hand. That feels good."

She made no mention of Philippe's obvious arousal tucked between her legs. He moved on to caressing her back, then to her hips and her backside.

"That should not feel so good," she said as he gave a firm squeeze to rounded muscle. "But it does. Nobody touches me, you know? Papa has to keep his cane on hand at all times, and it's hard to hug somebody when you're afraid of him toppling at any moment."

What a metaphor. Philippe kissed her nape. "I can imagine."

She prattled on, about the challenge of being a woman in a man's role, riding the hedges between eccentric, quaint, and scandalous, about wishing she'd been the son her father had wanted and needed and always feeling as if she were falling short.

He gathered her close. "Harriet, you do not fall short. You could never, ever fall short. I respect you above all others and always have."

She shuddered in his arms, though when Philippe kissed her cheek, he tasted no tears. The rain had slackened, and Harriet too had become more relaxed. Some burden she'd been carrying, some tension, had finally left the bed.

Philippe drifted his hand lower, over a flat, smooth belly to soft curls, and then to intimate flesh. Harriet lifted her knee, and he touched heaven. He went slowly at first, listening for bodily hesitation Harriet might be unwilling to speak aloud. He explored, he teased, he soothed and teased again.

When Harriet had settled into a relaxed rhythm, he grew serious. A few minutes later, she was thrashing against his hand, clutching at his hip, and breathing hard, and then she became wonderfully frantic, a woman in the throes of both satisfaction and surprise.

When the storm passed, she rolled over and wrapped herself around him. "Hold me."

Philippe *was* holding her, every inch of him plastered to every inch of her. He held her more tightly. Desire was a demon galloping in his blood, and yet, tenderness soothed that savage beast. Harriet, his Harriet, was warm and naked in his arms, and she'd found her pleasure, well and truly.

"Harriet?"

She kissed his chest.

He waited for the words of affection and wonder, words that confirmed they were not merely friends and would never again be merely friends. Her breathing slowed, a soft breeze against his chest. She nuzzled his throat and tucked her leg over his hips.

Then she was asleep.

* * *

In the week after taking tea with Philippe, Harriet started her ducal student over low jumps and on the basic lateral movements. He wasn't a beginner, but rather, an experienced rider regaining his skills. In her opinion, Philippe had more natural equestrian talent than his brother, Jonas, had had, though Philippe lacked Lord Chaddleworth's outgoing nature.

Philippe was quietly confident, in the saddle and elsewhere.

Not so, Harriet. She was all at sea, waiting for Philippe to invite himself to tea again, or waiting for him to declare that the lessons had achieved their purpose. Lord Ramsdale had started coming along, perching himself on the rail and calling encouragement or making jests as the mood took him.

Even that, Philippe bore with equanimity.

"The harvest ball is tomorrow," Philippe said as he swung down from Gawain's back. "You will save your supper waltz for me, please."

Harriet had used Philippe's cravat pin to secure her stock tie every day for the past week. Today was no different, and still, he hadn't noticed. If a man could misplace a gold pin so cavalierly, perhaps he could *take tea* with just as little thought.

"Half of polite society is in Berkshire this time of year," Harriet said. "Surely a more eligible lady will claim your supper waltz?"

"That's the beauty of the ballroom," Philippe said. "In that one preserve, the gentleman gets to choose. He needn't wait for the lady to show him her favor."

That comment had hidden meaning Harriet was too exhausted and bewildered to parse. She'd spent her free time moving into the spare bedroom, dodging her father's pointed questions about where they'd house guests and what was wrong with the bedroom she'd slept in since leaving the nursery twenty-some years past.

Harriet had held her peace, though Papa had deserved at least a scolding.

"Some other lady will have to waltz with you, sir. You'll want to walk Gawain up and down the lane before you put him up. Winter coats take longer to dry, and that was a fine session you put in over the jumps."

The compliment had no visible effect. Philippe ran his stirrups up their leathers and loosened Gawain's girth. "As you wish, but if I don't waltz with you, I won't waltz with anybody, save my sister, with whom I must open the dancing."

He led Gawain away, and Harriet remained in the arena, feeling as if she'd lost some gladiatorial match.

"He rides as if born in the saddle," Lord Ramsdale said, striding up from the rail. "Truly, you have worked a miracle."

"Phil—His Grace has worked the miracle. He has faced his demons and ridden them down. He's more than prepared to hack out in Hyde Park if he chooses to add that to his social schedule."

Hyde Park was doubtless full of earls' daughters who had more than one nice dress to their names.

"So why don't you look like a riding instructor who's proud of her pupil?"

Why didn't Ramsdale look like a lord? He wasn't blond and slim and polished. He was dark and muscular—as was Philippe—and those characteristics did not entirely ruin his pretentions to grace. What rendered his lordship something of an impostor in fine tailoring was his voice.

Ramsdale's voice was as dark as his countenance, all rumble and growl. His was an eloquence suited to pronouncing dire judgments on hopeless miscreants, for issuing challenges on the field of honor, or reading tragic poetry.

Harriet had the sense he liked his voice, liked being able to open his mouth and speak darkness into any conversation, and yet, she liked him. Ramsdale was kind to Papa without being condescending, and he was, in a backward, subtle way, tolerant.

"I am very proud of His Grace," Harriet said as that good fellow led Gawain down the lane. "I wish he were more proud of himself."

"Dukes are supposed to be arrogant, not proud. I think that duke is smitten and knows not what to do about it."

"Phil—His Grace would never be arrogant." Though he could be exceedingly hard to understand.

Ramsdale glanced around and leaned nearer. "Miss Talbot, did I, or did I not, hear him announce that he'd waltz with you or no one?"

"Look down your nose at me all you wish, your lordship. You should not have been eavesdropping."

He straightened. "That's a handsome pin you're using to secure your stock tie. I recall giving Lavelle one exactly like it on the occasion of his investiture."

Men. "If you have something to say, my lord, please be about it. Your missishness is keeping me from my responsibilities."

"Good God, no wonder he's in love. In all the world, the word missish has never been used to describe the Earl of Ramsdale. You may account me impressed."

In love? Philippe? Harriet was torn between a desire to swat his perishing lordship with her crop—which he'd doubtless find hilarious— or to take off down the bridle path at a hellbent gallop.

Which would not do. "Be as impressed as you please. I have work to do."

Ramsdale stepped close and put a hand on her arm. "I am trying, in my bumbling way, to matchmake, you daft woman. Lavelle stares off into space for half the evening and barely touches his breakfast. He bolts luncheon so he might be punctual for his lessons, and one must repeat pleasantries to him twice before he realizes he's being spoken to."

Oh, Philippe. "Because his brother died at this time of year, my lord. The duke and Lady Ada are haunted by tragedy in autumn, and when the leaves fall, they recall their brother falling as well."

Ramsdale's gaze narrowed, and still he did not move away. "By damn... by damn you have the right of it, but not the whole of it. Lavelle goes quiet and mopish every autumn, but he's not moping this year. He's brooding. Why won't you waltz with him?"

Philippe was coming back up the lane, and in the stable yard, Jeremy held a new horse, a mare who'd been taken out of training by an injury and who was now sound enough to complete her education.

"Why are my decisions any of your lordship's business?"

"Because your father and that lonely duke are my friends," Ramsdale said gently. "Because I esteem you greatly, Miss Talbot, and think you'd make a very fine duchess. You come from an old, respected family, your father is a gentleman, you're not without an inheritance, and your land marches with the ducal estate. Why shouldn't you waltz with Lavelle?"

Harriet could have stood against scolding, lectures, high-handedness, or even rudeness. Ramsdale's kindness made her throat tight and her eyes sting.

"When I was attending tea dances, the waltz was not yet popular, my lord. His Grace will look a fool if he tries to waltz with me, for I don't know how."

Didn't know how to flirt, didn't know how to sew the fancier riding habits, didn't know the latest dances. Didn't know how to keep her miseries to herself.

Ramsdale kissed her cheek and winked. "As it happens, I am very proficient at the waltz. I will await you on the side terrace as the ball gets under way. While His Grace is opening the dancing, I will instruct you on the very simple exercise known as the waltz. Name your firstborn son after me, and I'll consider our accounts squared."

He was making a jest, and being generous. "One lesson won't be enough."

"Bollocks, Miss Talbot—if I might be excused for departing from missish vocabulary. The waltz is based on three simple movements, and I could show them to you right here and now, except this footing would be the devil to dance in and Lavelle would skewer me with his ducal glower. You find me tomorrow as soon as you arrive, and I'll have you dancing like a duchess in ten minutes flat."

Harriet should say no. She should laugh and offer a witty riposte, except she knew less about witty ripostes than she did about waltzing.

"His Grace is looking splendidly thunderous," Ramsdale said, patting Harriet's arm. "Promise you'll meet me on the terrace."

"I'll meet you, just to be free of your meddling, my lord." And to learn how to waltz.

Ramsdale kissed her cheek *again*, lingered over her hand, and generally comported himself like an ass, and yet, he'd given Harriet hope.

While Philippe put up his horse, bowed his farewell to her, and gave her not even a backward glance.

CHAPTER SEVEN

Philippe had not wanted to believe his eyes. He'd been behaving like a good student, walking his horse as Harriet had told him to, while Ramsdale had literally hung on her arm, taken liberties with her person, and kissed her in public.

Twice.

Harriet—who suffered no foolishness from anybody—had smiled up at the earl as if he'd promised to grant her every maidenly wish.

And now, as the line of guests outside the ballroom doors stretched down the steps and out into the receiving hall, Philippe must again behave like a biddable gentleman when he wanted instead to kick fragile heirlooms.

Or a certain earl's backside.

Philippe longed to believe anything other than mutual attraction explained the affection Ramsdale had shown Harriet the previous day. And yet, Ramsdale's overtures made a bleak kind of sense.

Harriet had been *practicing* on Philippe. She'd never represented anything to the contrary. In the long week since that wonderful interlude in her guest bedroom, she'd not so much as patted Philippe's cravat. She had nattered on about his riding position, gradually raised the crossrails to the dizzying height of two and a half feet, and congratulated him effusively on being able to ride as well as a ten-year-old boy.

Did she even realize that was *his* cravat pin mocking him from beneath her chin every day?

Like a gentleman, Philippe had not assumed that one liberty granted meant others were expected.

Because they weren't.

"Your Grace, good evening!" Lady Ambrosia Warminster offered her gloved hand, sank into a slow curtsey, and came up, eyelashes batting away.

"My lady, a pleasure," Philippe said, the same as he'd said a hundred times in the past hour. "I'm so glad you could join us." Though she must have traveled half the day to accept what Ada had doubtless intended as a courtesy invitation.

"I anticipate nothing but joy this evening, particularly if you'll join me on the dance floor, Your Grace. A lady mustn't be forward, of course, but I do so love to waltz."

Other guests in line were smirking at this forwardness, and a month ago, Philippe would have yielded his waltz. Give the woman a bit of what she wanted and then disappear among the wallflowers, bachelorhood intact.

Philippe dropped her hand. "You dare me to deprive an entire shire's worth of eager bachelors of the opportunity to stand up with you, my lady? I could never hold my head up in society if I should be so selfish. Ah, Mr. Stolzfuss and Mrs. Stolzfuss. I hear your filly did quite well in the rain last week."

Lady Ambrosia went smiling on her way—she had dozens of titles to chase after if that was her game of choice—while Philippe greeted more neighbors and willed the line to end.

The Talbots were among the last to arrive.

"My friends," Philippe said, shaking Jackson Talbot's hand. "A pleasure to see you both."

He bowed to Harriet and maintained his composure by a slim thread. She wore a new dress, a soft brown velvet trimmed in red piping that revealed to the entire world the lush perfection of her figure.

"Harriet looks a treat, don't she?" Talbot said. "Resembles her dear mother more each day. Come along, Harry. A man must find some fortification for socializing in a crowd this size."

When had Talbot become so oblivious to manners where his daughter was concerned? Philippe possessed himself of Harriet's hand as she half-turned to follow her father.

"Miss Talbot," Philippe said. "You're looking very well." Delectable, radiant, *beautiful*. "I don't believe I've seen that frock before."

Oh, that was original.

"I restitched one of Mama's dresses."

"Harriet," Talbot barked, leaning heavily on his cane. "I need to get off my damned feet."

Harriet snatched her hand away.

"Mr. Talbot," Philippe said, "surely you don't begrudge me a moment to appreciate the beauty before me?" A moment to work up the nerve to ask Harriet what exactly Ramsdale meant to her?

For Philippe could not believe that the woman who'd admitted him to her bed a week ago felt nothing but friendship for him. She could have easily shared that experience with the earl if he was her choice, and Harriet—Philippe's Harriet—wasn't a woman who proceeded by indirection or intrigue.

"You flatter me, Your Grace," Harriet said, smiling graciously. "I'll wish you a pleasant evening and see you in the ballroom."

She curtseyed, he bowed, and away she went, Talbot leaning on her arm.

The line eventually dwindled, and Philippe vowed that next year, the harvest ball would instead be a picnic. Papa and Jonas had loved all the folderol and pageantry, but Philippe's slippers were already pinching, and the evening had barely begun.

"Has Lord Ramsdale come down?" Philippe asked the first footman when the final guest had been greeted. Crewe had been with the family for ages, and counted as an ally.

Unlike a certain earl.

"Indeed, he has, Your Grace. He's taking the air on the side terrace, where the other guests have yet to intrude."

"I'll fetch him inside," Philippe said. "Lady Ambrosia requires a consolation earl for the opening set." And the dancing would not start until Philippe signaled the musicians.

He slipped down the footmen's stairs to the corridor that led to the side terrace, which was dimly lit to encourage guests to tarry in the better-illuminated back gardens. Philippe at first didn't see Ramsdale, though he should have been hard to miss.

The earl stood in the shadow of an overhanging balcony, a woman before him.

"Had I known what treasures those riding habits kept hidden," Ramsdale said, "I'd have forbidden you to wear them years ago."

"My lord, no man tells me what I might or might not wear."

That was Harriet, and she was being playful—flirtatious even.

"Somebody ought to provide you some guidance," Ramsdale said, standing much too close to her. "Your papa is preoccupied with working you to death, but I daresay some changes are in the offing that will redound to your everlasting joy. Are you feeling more prepared to face the crowd inside? I, for one, would rather tarry out here under the stars."

What manner of discussion was this, and what *changes* did Ramsdale refer to?

Harriet went up on her toes and kissed Ramsdale's cheek. "I am much fortified by your company, my lord, and while I too would prefer the quiet of a pleasant autumn night, we've been away from the festivities too long."

She hugged him—purely, openly hugged him, and Ramsdale sneaked a kiss to the top of her head.

"Then let's away to the ballroom, my dear. Before you know it, the evening will be over and all our tribulations behind us."

Ramsdale offered his arm with a gallantry Philippe hadn't seen from him in London and escorted a beaming, beautiful Harriet down the path that led to the back gardens.

Philippe took a solitary bench at the edge of the terrace and watched Harriet and her swain as they joined other couples strolling beneath the torches.

In the past five minutes, nothing had changed. Philippe was still the Duke of Lavelle.

Ramsdale was still his best friend.

Harriet was still Philippe's... more than his best friend. His dearest friend, his almost-lover on one very special occasion, and the woman for whom he'd climbed back onto a horse. She had given him something important over these past few weeks, made him take stock of his life and his priorities.

She was truly his friend, and if Ramsdale was her choice... so be it.

Philippe rose, affixed a gracious smile to his features, and returned to the house. Jonas would have laughed, or taken charge of the situation with a combination of charm and influence Philippe would never claim and no longer wanted.

The way forward was clear, and a duke might hesitate to take it, but as Harriet's friend, as the man who loved her dearly and wanted only her happiness, Philippe knew exactly what he must do.

* * *

"Your Grace is having a bad ride," Harriet said, trying to keep the consternation from her voice. "They happen. Sometimes we're tired and don't realize it. Sometimes the horse is out of sorts. You must not take it personally."

Gawain was being contrary, which made no sense, though often a horse grasped emotions a rider was trying to ignore. Philippe had been courteous and pleasant through the grooming and saddling, but from the first moment he'd set a boot in the stirrup, he and Gawain had been having a difference of opinion.

While he and Harriet had had... not even a difference of opinion. Ever since the ball last week, her friend Philippe, her lover Philippe had disappeared. The Duke of Lavelle had taken his place, and the loss cut her to the heart.

"Let's try a few jumps, shall we?" Philippe suggested. "Gawain needs to work out some fidgets."

Gawain wouldn't know a fidget if it had been braided into his tail. "You want to jump today?" Harriet asked. "I was under the impression you dreaded work over fences."

Philippe patted Gawain's neck. The horse switched his tail and stomped at imaginary flies. "Gawain is a trusty fellow. We've managed adequately thus far. Perhaps he's bored and seeks a greater challenge."

At the ball, Philippe had partnered a different woman at every dance. That was polite behavior for a host, of course, but why did all his partners have to be beautiful, fashionable, and from the best families? Was that Philippe's idea of a greater challenge?

"Gawain is no longer young," Harriet said, dropping a rail from the nearest jump. "He can start out with a modest effort and work his way up, the same as he always does."

Harriet was no longer young, no longer a girl. She ought to have the backbone to simply ask Philippe why, when the supper waltz had come around, he'd merely suggested that Ramsdale stand up with Harriet, while Philippe had partnered some Amazonian creature who appeared to use shoeblack on her hair.

"Trot this rail a few times," Harriet said, stepping out of Gawain's path.

Philippe and Gawain bickered their way over the low rail three times, though Gawain never quite refused. Philippe's timing was off, though, and that was unusual.

"Raise the damned bar," Philippe said. "Gawain isn't paying attention."

This, in fact, might have been true. The lesson horse's greatest woe was boredom, and trotting crossrails was tedious in the extreme. Harriet added a second jump, raised the bar on it a few inches and silently willed the horse to settle to his work.

Gawain seemed to have forgotten where his feet were. He took off too close to the first jump, then too far away. He ignored the second jump until the last moment, then charged through the line as if the horses of hell were trying to steal his dinner.

"Your Grace, I think that's enough for today. Sometimes, the best you can do is put the horse away and hope for a better ride tomorrow."

"He's being contrary," Philippe said, trotting Gawain in a circle that included a small, ponderous buck. "Raise the damned bar, and we'll end on a good note if I have to toss him over the jump myself."

On the next circle, Gawain kicked out, but he was such a large, well-padded animal that even this misbehavior posed no danger to the rider.

"You haven't jumped more than two and a half feet," Harriet said. "Are you sure?"

"For heaven's sake, Harriet. How many times have you told me that it's easier to jump three feet than two?"

There came a time to raise the bar, and no instructor knew for sure when the pupil was ready. Philippe wasn't riding well today, but then, perhaps *he* was bored—ready to be through with his instruction even.

"That's three feet and three inches," Harriet said, moving the rail upward. "Gawain can handle that height easily. Try it at a forward trot."

Philippe adjusted his reins and guided the horse in a circle, but as Gawain came out of the circle, he broke into the canter. Harriet kept her peace, rather than hollering adjustments when Philippe might already be coping at the limit of his abilities.

"Drat you," Philippe yelled as Gawain sped up.

Oh, no. Oh, dear angels. "Ride around!" Harriet called, heart sinking. "Pull him in a circle!"

Philippe ignored her, though he wasn't in position. Gawain took off in a mighty leap half a stride too soon. He also chose to jump a good foot too high, and in the middle of his airborne arc, he twisted his back, sending Philippe flying into the dirt.

The duke landed in a heap, a puff of dust rising around him. Jeremy, who'd been wheeling a load of muck to the manure pit, came clambering over the rail, and Harriet ran the width of the arena to kneel in the dust beside her duke, and still, Philippe did not move.

* * *

"You're an idiot," Ramsdale said, pacing before the breakfast parlor's fire. "A very great idiot, and if you don't soon show some sense, I will decamp for London and let all and sundry know that the Ellis family has fallen prey to a strain of lunacy."

Philippe was not an idiot, unless being in love qualified. "You must do as you see fit, Ramsdale, though I'm sure the Talbots will miss you. I'm for a walk."

"What you call a walk these days would cross half of Spain. Why not ride with me? Everybody falls off from time to time—everybody—and we get back on, Lavelle."

Being angry with Ramsdale was difficult when the earl was determined to be so loyal, and in truth, Ramsdale had done nothing wrong.

"I've had that discussion with Miss Talbot," Philippe said. "She was desperate for me to get back on the horse, but my mind is made up. Horses are dangerous and smelly. They attract flies and drain a man's exchequer. I'm done with horses."

In truth, Philippe missed his rides with Gawain, and if anything plagued his conscience, it was the look of reproach in the beast's eyes as the stable lad had led him away from Philippe's last lesson.

"For reasons beyond my humble ken," Ramsdale retorted, "I'm sure Miss Talbot has missed you, but you haven't so much as paid a call on the Talbots since you took a tumble."

"Miss Talbot is quite busy. Perhaps you hadn't noticed how hard she works to keep her father's stables in business, but I won't bother Miss Talbot when she has other tasks to see to."

Leaving the lady to her horses had been rather the point. A clean break, cede the field, stand aside so that two people in love might find their happily ever after—or whatever version of love one of Ramsdale's nature ascribed to.

Harriet would *pity* Lavelle if he explained that he'd had aspirations in her direction, and her pity would have unhorsed his pride more thoroughly than Gawain had tossed him backside-first into the dirt.

No need for messy explanations or awkward scenes.

Like this one.

Philippe patted his lips with the serviette. "We have few beautiful days left before winter arrives. If you should take the bridle path in the Talbots' direction, please give them my fondest regards, but don't expect to see me on horseback ever again."

Philippe had hiked the bridle path in both directions for miles. His steps always took him past the Talbot property, and most of the time, he tarried behind the hedges as Harriet rode one horse after another, coached the grooms, or stood by while her father and a client watched sale stock put through their paces.

Ramsdale visited Jackson Talbot frequently—or Jackson and Harriet, both.

Soon there wouldn't be enough leaves left to conceal Philippe's spying, and that was for the best. Regardless of how a rejected swain behaved, a duke did not lurk in hedgerows.

"If you're determined to tramp over half of Berkshire, I'll tramp with you," Ramsdale said. "We should pack some comestibles, for the pace you set leaves a man peckish."

"I'm paying a call on my nephews," Philippe said. "By this time next year, they'll be at public school. I'm their guardian, and a consultation with their tutor is in order. You'd be bored witless."

A local widow had presented Jonas with twins before Jonas had completed his university studies, and they, along with two girls—one each in Kent and Sussex—were Philippe's responsibility. He'd looked in on the boys within two days of returning to Berkshire, but not since.

They were lively, dear, and he missed their high spirits.

"I forget how many little darlings Chaddleworth left you. Three? Six? It's a wonder he didn't work his wiles on Miss Talbot, though I suppose he knew you'd hold him accountable for that folly."

Philippe set aside half a plate of hot, fluffy eggs. "Ramsdale, are you trying to get yourself evicted? One mustn't speak ill of the dead."

"Admitting the truth is not speaking ill, and your sainted brother was a hound. Thank God, you never sought to emulate him in that particular."

Just the opposite. Philippe considered that insight as he finished a lukewarm cup of tea. "Perhaps I did learn from my brother's bad example. If you're intent on burdening me with your company when I visit the boys, then meet me at the front door in fifteen minutes."

Ramsdale took the place at Philippe's right and appropriated the unfinished plate of eggs. "You are daft, hiking all about the shire at a time of year when the weather changes by the minute. We could ride the distance in a quarter of the time."

Well, yes, they could, and a pleasant hack it would be. "I tried getting back on the horse, and despite Miss Talbot's best efforts, I failed. A fool persists at a doomed endeavor, a wise man gives up and accepts what cannot be changed."

Ramsdale gestured with his fork. "Very profound. Perhaps you should make that the family motto. These are superb eggs. You will please not hold supper for me. I'll be dining with the Talbots this evening, for Mr. Talbot and I have much to discuss, and I'll wish you the joy of your perambulations."

This casual announcement, made between bites of egg—bites of Philippe's eggs—was a death blow to Philippe's faint, ridiculous hopes where Harriet was concerned. Ramsdale planned to closet himself with Jackson Talbot. Given what Philippe had witnessed the night of the ball, the agenda for their conversation was all too easy to imagine.

"I'll wish you a pleasant day and let Lady Ada know you won't be joining us this evening."

At least Ramsdale had spared Philippe the necessity of asking an old friend what his intentions were toward a dear friend.

A dear, much-missed friend. Who'd almost become Philippe's lover… and his duchess.

Breakfast with Ramsdale was sufficiently unsettling that even walking five miles to call upon the widow and her offspring wasn't enough to raise Philippe's spirits. He went two miles out of his way to pick up the bridle path on the return journey, and there he found a measure of peace.

Jonas might well have seduced Harriet.

Jonas might have been up to eight by-blows by now, had he lived.

Jonas should have known better than to attempt that damned stile, but at Philippe's last riding lesson, he'd finally gained some insight into his brother's life and death. Riding was a risk, but the greater risk was in living a life without challenge, a life that refused to grapple with the difficult questions.

Besides, the first thing Jackson Talbot had taught Philippe long ago was how to take a fall safely, and Philippe had learned that lesson well.

If Philippe loved Harriet—and he did—then her happiness mattered more than his own. If Philippe loved Ramsdale—and he more or less did—then honor demanded that Philippe not question his friend's claim on the lady's affections.

That conclusion wasn't ducal, wasn't even particularly gallant, but simply where common sense and honor led.

Philippe had traveled a mile down the bridle path when he spied a riderless horse cropping grass beneath a stand of oaks. The bay gelding's reins were drooping over its neck, which was bad news all around. A hoof could get caught in those reins, a leg tangled.

"Halloo, horse," Philippe said as he approached the animal. The last thing a loose horse needed was an excuse to spook. "Having a light snack, are we?"

The horse's head came up abruptly, and it dodged off a few paces.

"You're a fine, big specimen," Philippe said, "and you look familiar, but you're not too bright a fellow if you intend to jaunt off across the countryside with your reins dangling."

The horse took another mouthful of grass, keeping an eye on Philippe all the while.

This could go on for the rest of the day, until the horse either galloped off down the bridle path or stepped on a rein and fell in a heap. A day that had begun sunny and mild was turning overcast, and Philippe was still several miles from home.

Several miles from anywhere, given that this little corner of Berkshire was more woods than cultivated land.

"You've had your snack," Philippe said, walking right up to the horse. "Time to be a good boy and tell me what you've done with your rider."

In the face of confident handling, the horse stood docilely. Philippe got the reins sorted out and took stock of the surrounding terrain. No coat of sweat suggested the gelding had galloped any distance, but a relaxed trot with time for the occasional graze could still cover five miles in an hour.

Philippe examined the saddle, lifting the flaps and peering behind the cantle. A stylized coat of arms had been burned into the leather beneath the offside flap—a ram's head, caboshed.

Unease wafted on the freshening breeze. Philippe got a firm grip of the reins, because he was about to shout at the top of his lungs and the horse would doubtless startle.

"Ramsdale! Ramsdale! Where the bloody hell are you?"

CHAPTER EIGHT

The Talbot conveyances were aging but well maintained. Harriet had finished the last ride of the morning when the ancient coach rumbled around from the carriage house, Jeremy at the ribbons.

"Is Papa going somewhere?" Harriet asked, shading her eyes to peer up at the groom.

"Aye, miss. Got a note from the Hall, and said to have the carriage ready at noon."

The coach mostly collected dust. If Harriet had errands to see to, or the housekeeper or cook needed to attend the market, they took the dog cart. But then, clouds were gathering and the wind had picked up half an hour ago.

"Have you any idea where Papa's off to?"

Papa himself came thumping down the steps from the front porch. He'd troubled over his appearance, combing his hair, donning his top hat, and wearing a pair of clean gloves. He dressed thus for services and for calling on his banker or his solicitor.

"Has Ramsdale bothered to come by yet?" Papa asked. "His lordship assured me he'd be here well before noon."

"I haven't see him. Are you and his lordship paying calls this afternoon?"

Papa pretended to inspect the coach, though at this distance, he was unlikely to see details. "Aye, we're off on a business appointment."

Harriet had been preoccupied lately—missing Philippe, wondering what she might have done differently at his last lesson, wondering what in blazes had gone amiss between them—but her father's sheepish expression got her attention.

"Where are you going, Papa?"

"To see a man about a horse."

When Harriet's mother had been alive, that phrase had been a euphemism for everything from a trip to the jakes, to a ramble down to the village tavern, to an actual transaction involving an equine.

"With Lord Ramsdale?"

"Aye, if he'd deign to keep his appointments. He should be here by now."

"Let's sit on the porch while you wait for him," Harriet said. "Jeremy, you may walk the lane a time or two while my father and I await his lordship."

Papa's ascent of the steps was uneven. He used his right foot to gain a stair, then brought the left even. Up with the right, even with the left.

"Your hip hurts," Harriet said. "You will take some willow bark tea tonight if I have to pour it down your throat myself. Am I to know the nature of your business appointment?" For the past year or so, she'd lived with a gnawing fear that Papa would sell the stable. She wouldn't miss the endless work, but she'd miss the horses.

She'd miss knowing she had a livelihood very much, and in a hopeless way, she'd miss knowing she had an inheritance to bring to any union.

Not that she'd be marrying anybody. Philippe had obliterated any schemes in that direction. He'd given her some lovely memories, along with an inability to consider making similar memories with any other man. Ever.

Ramsdale was a keen horseman, had means, and had visited the area often. He might well be accompanying Papa to a call on the banker in Reading.

"Where exactly are you off to, Papa?"

"Please do not think to intrude into the financial aspects of running this property, Harriet," Papa said. "I can't stop you from taking the horses in hand, and I mean no criticism of your domestic skills, but I am the owner, and you are my daughter. I'll manage this stable as I please."

Harriet had ridden many—many—a fractious horse. When a beast ten times her size decided to turn up sullen and contrary, she knew better than to allow its bad behavior to upset her. She corrected the horse's errors firmly but without rancor and offered it a chance to do better next time.

She ought to have reminded Papa of his manners long, long ago. "When I inquire as to your destination, I am hardly wresting the ledgers from your grip. If you're making decisions that affect me, then I have a right to know of them."

Though as to that, Papa's entries in the ledgers had become all but unreadable. Harriet had taken to reconstructing the monthly figures by virtue of studying the tradesmen's bills, the wage book, and the receipts herself.

And those figures were sometimes discouraging.

"I provide for you more than adequately," Papa replied, "and no daughter of mine will presume to insert herself into a domain wherein for nearly forty years I have—"

Harriet rose, because her own hips ached, because her heart ached, and because *Papa was wrong.*

"I am your daughter," she said. "Also your barn manager, trainer, chief groom, breeding consultant, groundskeeper, hostess, nurse, veterinarian, foaling expert, assistant farrier, equine dentist, harness repairer, and— because you are too stubborn to purchase a pair of dratted spectacles— also your eyeglasses. I have long since intruded into the male sphere, and you were the first to boost me into that saddle. You own this stable, you do not own me."

"Harriet Margaret Talbot, you will not take that tone with me."

The coach had lumbered down the drive and with it went the last of Harriet's self-control.

"I am tired, Papa. I stink of horse all the time. I no longer have a nice pair of boots because the sand in that arena has ruined them all. I spent so much time repairing bridles, saddles, and harnesses last winter that I have barely anything decent to wear to services. I haven't embroidered a pretty handkerchief since Mama died, and now you are about to sell the stable that I have all but married myself to. The least you can do is warn me."

The jingle and creak of the wagon faded, and a cloud of dust slowly dissipated over the drive.

Harriet made unruly horses, cheeky grooms, and presuming customers mind their manners with her. Why hadn't she demanded the same respect from her own father? Like Gawain with an inconsiderate rider, she should have tossed Papa's high-handedness to the dirt long ago.

Papa rose shakily, balancing both hands on the head of his cane. "I am taking on a partner, Harriet. Lord Ramsdale has funds to invest, a sharp eye for young stock, and a fine appreciation for a well-run operation. You have nothing to say to it. We're meeting with the solicitor this afternoon, if his lordship hasn't cried off."

A partner.

Harriet did most of the work and much of the worrying that kept the stable from failing, and Papa was *taking on a partner,* everything but the handshake already in place.

"I see."

He brushed a glance over her. "What do you see?"

"I see that I am through being helpful, biddable, good-natured, meek, and dutiful. I see that this operation has been well run for the past five years because I've run it, despite your insistence on selling good horses to bad riders. Despite your unwillingness to expand our breeding program. I wish you and his sharp-eyed lordship the joy of your partnership. I'm off to see about finding a partner of my own."

She passed him her riding crop, sat long enough to remove her spur, and tossed her gloves at his chest for good measure.

"Harriet, where are you going?"

"To the Hall. I've tried being patient. I've tried being a *good friend,* being understanding, and tolerant, and saintly, but it won't wash, Papa. Philippe owes me—and Gawain—an explanation, at the very least, and I intend to have it, even if that means I never set foot in the Hall again."

Papa thumped his cane against the porch planks. "The damned man took a fall, Harriet. Leave him his pride and let good enough be good enough."

"Good enough is *not* good enough," Harriet said, marching down the steps. "A cot that grew too small fifteen years ago isn't good enough. Waltzing with the earl isn't good enough. Selling a gorgeous mare to that bumbling toad Dudley isn't good enough. And kisses and pleasure aren't good enough either."

Papa waved the crop at her. "Young lady, you will control your words lest I—"

"I'm not a young lady, Papa. At my age, Mama had a ten-year-old daughter and had less than ten years to live. Philippe will listen to what I have to say if I have to kick, buck, snort, strike, bite, paw, clear the arena, and—who on earth is that?"

The bridle path curved around the Talbot pastures and paddocks, and for much of the year, the way was shrouded in greenery. As autumn advanced and the leaves fell, riders traversing the path became visible, mostly for the simple fact that they were moving objects against a backdrop of fixed trees and fences.

Somebody was coming around the curve at a dead gallop.

"He's going to take the stile," Papa said. "Going to aim that beast straight for our lane."

The rider's form was excellent. He stood in the stirrups, balanced over the horse's withers to free its back from his weight, hands moving to follow the rhythm of the horse's head. He wore neither coat nor hat, which made his horsemanship only more evident.

"They make a handsome pair," Harriet said, then an odd shiver traveled over her arms. "That's Philippe, Papa. That's Philippe, and that gate is nearly four feet—"

For a silent eternity, Harriet's heart went airborne, three-quarters of a ton of fear, hope, and admiration soaring with Philippe's horse.

"Well done!" Papa exclaimed when the horse landed as nimbly as a cat and cantered on around the far end of the arena. "Foot perfect and right in rhythm."

"But, Papa, *that's Lavelle*. His Grace promised me he'd never sit a horse again, and he just cleared a four-foot gate at a gallop and made it look easy."

Papa sat back down, using his cane and the table to brace himself. "Well, then, the duke must want to talk to somebody rather badly. Do you suppose it could be you?"

"I certainly want to talk to him," Harriet said, taking off at run for the stable yard.

When she got there, and Philippe had leaped from his heaving horse, Harriet didn't say a word. She simply hugged him, and hugged him and hugged him, until he put his arms around her and hugged her back.

* * *

"What were you thinking," Harriet shouted, once the stable lad had led Ramsdale's horse down the drive. "Jumping an obstacle like that on a horse you're not familiar with? You fell not two weeks ago, before my very eyes and over a smaller jump in good footing. You could have been hurt. You could have been killed! Philippe, you c-could have been k-killed."

She went from shaking him—or trying to—to squeezing Philippe so tightly he could barely breathe.

"That gelding is nothing if not athletic," he said, speaking as calmly as he could when his lungs were ready to burst. "We hopped a few stiles in the last mile, and I knew he was up to the challenge, but, Harriet, it's Ramsdale who's taken a fall. He said he was merely winded, but I know he took a knock on the head, and I fear a worse injury."

"Hang Ramsdale," Harriet retorted, pulling back but keeping a good grip on his arms. "You rode like a demon, Philippe. Like a winning steeplechase jockey when you swore to me..." Her eyes, which had been filled with concern, narrowed. "You swore to me you were done with horses forever. You had tried and failed, and nothing I could say, threaten, or promise would change your mind. You *gave up.*"

Jackson Talbot thumped down the porch steps. "What's all this about? Good form, Your Grace. Harriet, let the man go."

"Send the lads to assist Lord Ramsdale, Papa. He's taken a fall, and I will not turn loose of His Grace until I've had an explanation."

Talbot's eyebrows climbed nearly to his hat brim. "Ramsdale's taken a tumble?"

"I left him sitting beneath an oak where the bridle path, the woods, and the stream all meet east of here," Philippe said. "He seemed right enough, if a bit dazed, but the clouds are gathering, and he's miles from shelter."

"And you left him your coat," Harriet said. "What if it had started to rain, and you on a strange horse, in bad footing, no coat... I taught you better than this, Philippe."

She was scolding him, also stroking the lace of his cravat and calling him Philippe.

"You are concerned for me," Philippe said.

"Of course she's concerned," Talbot said. "Else she'd not be so ill-mannered as to use your Christian—"

Harriet left off petting Philippe's chest and faced her father, hands on hips. "Hush, Papa. I can speak for myself. Your business partner is sitting beneath a tree nearly three miles away, possibly addled and injured and storm on the way. Hadn't you best concern yourself with *him?*"

Philippe slipped an arm around Harriet's waist. "I'd be obliged if you'd send Ramsdale some aid, Talbot. I can continue on to the Hall, but your property was closest to his mishap, and I'd hoped to count on my friends for assistance."

Harriet stiffened beneath his arm.

"Of course," Talbot said. "Cooper! Hitch up the dog cart. Tell Jeremy to put up the coach and get word to the solicitor that I'll have to reschedule my appointment. Lerner, you go down the bridle path on horseback. Earls can't be left out in the wet or they grow contrary."

A raindrop landed on Philippe's cheek in the midst of Talbot's stream of orders.

"You come with me," Harriet said, wrapping an arm around Philippe's waist and urging him in the direction of the barn. "I have a few things to say to you, and I want to say them in private."

Philippe had things to say to Harriet as well—a question to ask, rather. They left Talbot barking more instructions to the grooms as the raindrops organized into a cold drizzle. Some considerate soul had lit the stove in the saddle room, though, so it was warm, which—now that Philippe was no longer riding at a gallop—felt good.

Harriet's hug, when he'd dismounted had felt wonderful.

"What did you want to say to me?" Philippe asked when Harriet had closed and locked the door. The look of her—hems wrinkled, the toes of her boots dusty, braid coming a bit undone—warmed his heart.

"I've missed you." They spoke the same words at the same time.

"Ladies first," Philippe said, gesturing to the worn sofa.

Harriet took a seat, very much on her dignity. "Can you, or can you not, acquit yourself adequately on horseback?"

"*That's* what you wanted to ask me?"

She nodded, gaze solemn.

Philippe took the wing chair—he did not dare sit beside her—and now, when his arse was planted on a flowered cushion, he felt as if he faced an obstacle too high and wide to negotiate confidently. He could continue to dissemble, to stand aside for true love, or he could trust Harriet with the truth.

"I can acquit myself adequately on well-trained mounts," he said. "I have had the benefit of good, patient instruction, and my skills rest on a solid foundation."

Harriet bent to unlace her boots. "You rode like Lord Dunderhead's incompetent twin at your last lesson. What was that about?"

The sight of her removing her footwear—her old dusty boots—was distracting. "I saw you with Ramsdale, Harriet, at the ball. He's clearly smitten, and I'm happy for you. I hope he offers for you and spares me the burden of calling him out."

She set her boots aside. The soles and the uppers were coming apart near the toes, a common injury to riding boots.

"Ramsdale is smitten, and you are happy. What about me, Philippe?"

She was not happy, but beyond that, Philippe dared not venture. "You are Harriet, my dearest Harriet, and if the earl is your choice, then I owe you both my best wishes."

But what if Ramsdale was *not* her choice? A chat on a secluded terrace wasn't the same as an afternoon spent without clothing on a wide and comfortable bed.

"Did it not occur to you, Your Grace, that I might have required some practice at the waltz? London ways are slow to catch on in the country, and I've been too busy waltzing with equines. Ramsdale was instructing me, or humoring me. I wanted to do you credit when I stood up with you, and then you couldn't be bothered to ask for my supper waltz."

This was... this was very bad, and possibly wonderful.

"You never granted me your supper waltz. I assumed Ramsdale—"

Harriet smacked his arm. "Why must you assume *anything* when I'm right here, where I've always been? If I'm your dearest Harriet, you can ask me. You can simply put a question to me—not to Ramsdale, or Papa, or Gawain, for pity's sake." She jabbed her thumb at her chest. "Ask *me*."

Do you and Ramsdale have an understanding? But that wasn't what Philippe wanted to know. Understandings were private and not exactly binding.

Do you love me? She'd say yes. That question was almost cowardly, because he knew she'd say yes.

So Philippe aimed his courage and his heart at the most important challenge he'd ever faced. "Will you marry me?"

Harriet sat very tall, and very still, like a skilled whip at the start of a carriage race. "I beg your pardon?"

"I love you. I have always loved you, and when I finally set aside the notion that I must martyr myself to my brother's sainted memory, or to the title, or to polite society's inanities, I see that you have always been in my heart. You have never treated me as anything less than your honored friend. You have had faith in me and been patient and kind, and then I kissed you, and... God, Harriet. I do know what it's like to take a bad fall."

She put a cool hand to his temple. "Does your head pain you?"

"Not in the least. Twenty years ago, your dear papa made sure I knew how to take a mere tumble into the sand. My heart pains me. I saw you with Ramsdale, overheard your conversation with him, and realized you would be better off with a man who could ease your burden here, not take you away from who and what you love."

She was frowning at the worn carpet, and frowning was bad.

"You appeared to return his affections," Philippe went on, "and it's as if the breath left my body and hasn't returned. I can't think, I can't sleep. I am nobody's Philippe. Nobody's friend. Nobody's dearest anything. I ceased in some vital way to function, as if I left the best of me in the sand of your riding arena."

Harriet drew her feet up and wrapped her arms around her knees.

So much for the efficacy of an impassioned proposal, and yet, affection for her—bottomless, admiring, desiring affection—welled in Philippe's heart. He would always love her, and that would always give him joy and cause him an awful ache.

"Say something, Harriet. You told me to put my question to you, and that means you owe me an answer."

She turned her face, resting a cheek on her knee, her expression cross. "I'm making up my mind, choosing my words, trying to train myself out of a bad habit. If I'm to answer with anything other than 'Yes, Papa,' or 'Of course, Philippe,' this will require some effort on my part."

Philippe wanted desperately to kiss her, but she'd probably whack him, and then he'd want to kiss her even more.

"Tell me if you'll be my duchess," Philippe said. "We can sort the rest out from there."

Her glower became ferocious. "No, I will not be *your duchess.*"

* * *

Harriet was angry, and not with herself. Papa's decision to take a partner—meaning to bring a titled lord with money into the business, because what mattered hard work and loyalty—and the notion that Philippe had fallen on purpose at his last lesson left her upset in ways too numerous to list.

She and Philippe had much to sort out, but as with any spirited mount, she would begin as she intended to go on.

"A duchess is not a prime filly," Harriet said, "to be owned by this or that lordling, raced by this or that stable. She's a person married to a man who has a title. If I marry you, we will be husband and wife, but I hope I don't consider you *my duke.*"

Philippe stared across the room, at the rack of saddles and bridles neatly arranged on the wall. "Is that a yes, Harriet, or a no?"

She dropped her knees and smoothed her skirts. She'd told Philippe to ask her, but the habit of answering for herself would take some time to develop.

"I love you," she said, taking him by the hand, and drawing him to sit beside her. "You have been in my heart forever too, and when you took me to bed... I will never be the same, Philippe. I like that. I like that I chose to share that with you, despite propriety, despite common sense. I want to marry that man, the one who can inspire me to reach for my heart's desire, to step off the bridle path and gallop the fields and forests."

Philippe slipped an arm around her shoulders. "I want to be with the woman who gave me the confidence to get back in the saddle, and to pitch myself from it. The woman who made me think about whether I'm living my life, or trying to live my brother's. I'll never be an avid horseman, Harriet."

"I'll never be an avid duchess."

He took her hand. "Fair enough. I'm not an avid duke, and with you, I'll never need to pretend otherwise."

The rain began to beat against the windows in earnest, and Harriet tucked closer to Philippe's warmth. "You needn't be an avid horseman either, Philippe. I'll be an avid wife, though."

"I will be a passionately avid husband."

He kissed her, and what happened next had to qualify as the fastest disrobing of a woman in a riding habit in the history of equitation. Philippe made a bed of wool coolers before the parlor stove, and amid the good smells of leather, horse, and hay, Harriet made the decision to anticipate her vows.

Two hours later, a sopping, irascible Earl of Ramsdale had been retrieved by the grooms, and Philippe was passing out toddies in the Talbot family parlor.

"A toast," Ramsdale said, "to new ventures succeeding beyond our wildest dreams."

"To new ventures," Philippe said, lifting his glass and smiling at Harriet over the rim.

She'd requested that they not announce their engagement until Philippe had told his sister. Philippe had inquired whether Harriet wanted him to observe the protocol of asking her papa for permission to court her.

"You can ask Papa for permission to court me," Harriet murmured as Papa and the earl began bickering about repurchasing Utopia from Lord Dudley, which they'd both agreed was a fine idea.

"And if he says no?" Philippe asked.

"He won't. He wants to be asked, though, included in the discussion. I know this, because I'd stopped including him in matters relating to the stable. I didn't want to bother him, he probably didn't want to bother me. I see that now."

"I'll bother you frequently, Harriet," Philippe said, "and I'd rather not have a long engagement."

"What are you two whispering about?" Ramsdale groused.

"Breeding stock," Harriet replied, which retort had the earl and her papa looking perplexed, and Philippe grinning.

As it happened, the firstborn child of the Duke and Duchess of Lavelle arrived a scant eight months after the wedding and, true to Harriet's promise, was named after the Earl of Ramsdale.

Lady Seton Avery Ellis rode like a demon and waltzed like a dream, but that's a tale for another time.

As for the Earl of Ramsdale... his happily ever after lay in the direction of a long-lost Italian manuscript that scholars claimed held arcane secrets for capturing the affections of another. Ramsdale certainly didn't believe in Cupid's arrows or Aphrodite's potions... and yet, he fell in love anyway.

And fell very hard, indeed, which is also a tale for another time...

THE END

To my dear Readers,

I love a horsey tale, so thanks for indulging me in this one! For those of you who wondered, Andrew, Lord Greymoor, owns the farm in Surrey where that colt with the big nose stands at stud. Lest you think I'd make you wait forever for Lord Ramsdale's happily ever after (he says it feels like forever), **The Will to Love** is included in the October 2017 anthology, **How to Find a Duke in Ten Days**. (Excerpt below, because Ramsdale insists, politely of course.)

My most recent full length Regency novel was **Too Scot to Handle**, the second book in the Windham Brides series. **No Other Duke Will Do** (November 2017) is the third story in that series, and my first romance set in Wales—but not my last!

Because the Duke of Haverford is also a very persuasive gentleman, I've included a sneak peek from his courtship of Miss Elizabeth Windham.

If you'd like to stay up to date with all of my new releases, sales, and special deals, but you aren't keen on receiving yet another newsletter, please considering following me on Bookbub. If you're more the newsletter type, I only publish those when I have illustrious doin's to pass along, and I will never convey your information to third parties, ever. Sign up here: graceburrowes.com/contact/. For more information about any of my books, visit my website at graceburrowes.com.

Happy reading!
Grace Burrowes

From **The Will to Love** by Grace Burrowes in
HOW TO FIND A DUKE IN TEN DAYS

The Earl of Ramsdale has run an advertisement seeking assistance with the translation of his uncle's will. Ramsdale hopes that document can point him in the direction of a long-lost manuscript, the Duke's Book of Knowledge. Alas for the earl, his quest is off to an inauspicious start…

The scholars who responded to the advertisement proved a shabby lot. Two reeked of mildew, two could not fumble through a single sentence of Uncle's codicil, and the fifth wanted a sponsor for yet another expedition to plunder the Nile.

Time was running out, and defeat was unacceptable.

"Have any more responses come?" Ramsdale asked his valet when the Nile explorer had been sent on his way.

"Not a response per se," Pinckney said, tidying tea cups and saucers onto a tray. "There is a gentleman below stairs who said he'd wait rather than make an appointment. Tidy young chap, relatively speaking."

"Tidy and skinny, I've no doubt."

The afternoon was gone and so was Ramsdale's patience. "Send him up, but don't bother with another tray. I doubt he'll be staying long."

Pinckney used a small brush to dust the crumbs from the table onto a linen serviette. "And will you be going out this evening, my lord?"

Ramsdale had been ruralizing in Berkshire for the past month, being a doting godfather to a friend's infant daughter. Had a fine set of lungs on her, did his goddaughter.

Pinckney withdrew, and Ramsdale gathered up what passed for his patience as a slim young fellow was admitted by the footman.

"My lord." The scholar bowed. He had a scraping, raspy voice. He also wore blue-tinted spectacles that must have made navigating after dark difficult, and in the dim light of the sconces, his countenance was very smooth.

Too smooth. "Have you a card?" Ramsdale asked.

The scholar's clothes were loose—probably second- or third-hand castoffs—and his hair was queued back and tucked under his collar. He passed over a plain card.

Phillip Peebleshire. *Ah, well, then.*

"You look familiar," Ramsdale said.

"We are not acquainted, my lord, though I have tutored younger sons from time to time."

Probably true. "Well, have a seat, and lest you think to impress me with your vast qualifications, let's begin by having you transcribe a few lines from this document."

Of the two seats opposite Ramsdale's desk, Peebleshire took the one farther from the candles. Ramsdale passed over Uncle Hephaestus's first codicil—there were nine in total—and Mr. Peebleshire took out a quizzing glass.

"I have paper and pencil," Ramsdale said, "or pen and ink if you prefer."

"This codicil," Peebleshire read slowly, "is made by me, the undersigned testator, Hephaestus George Louis Algernon Avery, being of sound mind and composed spirit, as witnessed in triplicate hereto, and does hereby revoke any previous codicils, but not my will, which document is dated—"

Ramsdale plucked the document from Peebleshire's pale hands. "You can translate at sight?"

"The legal documents all tend to follow certain forms, my lord. The vocabulary is limited, until you reach the specific bequests and conditions of inheritance. A modern holographic will written in such arcane language is unusual, though."

"My uncle was an unusual man." Generous, vindictive, devious, and merry. In life, Ramsdale hadn't known what to make of him. In death, Uncle had become purely vexatious.

Ramsdale repeated the exercise with the second codicil—the only one he himself had muddled through in full—and again, Peebleshire translated accurately at sight.

Bollocks. Ramsdale rose and took a candle from the branch on his desk. "What compensation do you seek for your services?"

Peebleshire named a sum per page—shrewd, that—as Ramsdale lit several more branches of candles around the room. The wages sought were substantial, but not exorbitant for a true scholar.

"How quickly can you complete the work?" Ramsdale asked.

"That depends on how much of it there is."

Uncle's will ran on for thirty pages, and the codicils for another sixty. As near as Ramsdale could fathom, seven of the codicils were rants against the established orders at Oxford and Cambridge, with much ink spilled casting aspersion on the reputation of one Professor Peebles.

"Nearly a hundred pages," Ramsdale said, "and I also have correspondence Uncle wrote to various scholar friends. Can you translate French?"

"French, German, and all of the romance languages, Greek, Aramaic, Hebrew, Latin. My Coptic is less reliable, and I am not confident of the Norse languages. I'm gaining proficiency in spoken Arabic, but the written language is a challenge."

If that recitation were true, Ramsdale would have to admit to surprise. "Then you are clearly qualified to meet my needs," he said, "but before we discuss the rest of the terms, I have one more question for you."

Because Ramsdale had lit every blessed candle in the room, he could see his guest well. Peebleshire sat forward, apparently eager for the work.

"What is your question, sir?"

"How will I explain to your dear papa, that his darling offspring has taken to parading about London after dark in men's clothing, Miss Peebles?"

Read on for an excerpt from
NO OTHER DUKE WILL DO!

Julian, Duke of Haverford, is hosting a house party for the sole purpose of finding a husband for his sister. Elizabeth Windham has been sent to the same gathering for the sole purpose of finding a husband... though she insists all she's truly interested in is locating a good book in Haverford's vast library collection....

"Miss Windham, good morning," Julian said.

The lady was Miss Windham now, not Julian's Elizabeth of the towering oak and summer sunshine, not the charming phantasm of his dreams, and yet he wanted to kiss her again. She wore a simple green dress that hinted at the curves beneath, especially as she strode across the library and began wrestling with a window.

"Lady Glenys must instruct the footmen to open these windows each evening after the card parties break up," she said. "The cigar smoke isn't good for the books or the portraiture."

"The footmen should also be soaping and oiling the window hardware," Julian replied, reaching past her to shove the window open. Cool air bearing a hint of the sea wafted into the room and blended with the scent of lily of the valley on Miss Windham's person.

Julian moved away lest he stand about like an idiot, his nose pressed to Miss Windham's neck.

"I've come to find a book to take with me to our picnic across the lake," she said, surveying rows and rows of literature. "I finished the three you lent me."

"You'd rather spend this afternoon here with the books than socializing on the lakeshore. You love books." And Julian loved knowing this about her.

"I love what books can do," she said, moving to another window. Julian let her struggle a bit, because he liked the lines of the dress from the back almost as much as he did from the front.

Almost. The window gave and she moved to the next.

In defense of his dignity, he opened the two windows on the far side of the fireplace rather than again assist the lady.

"Books," she said, dusting her hands, "can reach from beyond the grave and provide comfort and knowledge from somebody long dead.

Books can instruct and entertain, they can—well, you must treasure them as I do, for you've amassed a fortune in books."

Julian had no fortune whatsoever unless acres of Welsh countryside counted. "The first Marquess of Haverford was a bibliophile, and his descendants have maintained and added to his collection as a family tradition. I doubt many of these books have been read since my father's birth."

Elizabeth would read them, though. If she were his duchess, winter by winter, shelf by shelf, she'd learn the depth and breadth of all three of the collections. Julian would learn too, for she'd read to him, and he to her.

And then they'd read to their children.

"You do not behold your library with any joy," Elizabeth said, when all the windows were open. "Or perhaps, like me, it's the prospect of the afternoon's activities that dims your pleasure in the day. Do you realize that all of the coachmen, footmen, grooms, and porters who came with your guests are idling about the carriage house, the attics, and the stables when they ought to be assisting your own staff?"

"I've been too busy with the bachelors and young ladies idling about to notice the outer reaches of my domain doing likewise." Too busy noticing the exact rhythm of Elizabeth Windham's strides.

She had a vocabulary of walks. In the out of doors, she moved quite freely, and inside the house, she could set a good pace too. She also had a ladylike saunter suitable for strolling the gardens or accompanying another guest into the breakfast parlor.

"Have a word with your butler, and get the idlers off their backsides," she said, swiping a finger over the bottom of the marquess's portrait. "As soon as this party concludes, you will have his lordship's portrait cleaned, please."

"Yes, ma'am." Yes, Your Grace, for truly, Elizabeth Windham was meant to be a duchess.

"Tell me about Mr. Sherbourne. He was intent on making an entrance in the breakfast parlor this morning, and your sister says he might not even have been invited."

Sherbourne owns my soul. "I can guarantee you he wasn't invited, for no acceptance of an invitation has shown up in my correspondence, and he'd best not be directing mail to my unmarried sister. If she invited him personally, he still has no excuse for arriving a day late."

Elizabeth took a window seat, sunshine slanting over her shoulder and making the simple green gown shimmer like new leaves in a morning breeze.

"I told Lady Glenys that," she said. "I gather she's been too overwhelmed planning this event to keep track of every detail. You must be certain to praise her for how smoothly she handled Sherbourne's arrival at breakfast."

When was the last time Julian had praised his sister for anything? "Who praises you, Elizabeth?"

"You said you like my kisses."

Didn't see that one coming. "I adore your kisses. Let's find you another a book, shall we?"

The library door stood wide open, the windows stood open, and from down the corridor, Julian heard the last of his guests finishing their breakfasts. He held out a hand to Elizabeth and she joined him between the bookshelves.

His kissed her, or she kissed him. The undertaking was gratifyingly mutual.

In the first instant their kiss proved to Julian that dreams and recollections did not match reality. Elizabeth Windham put together two concepts that in Julian's experience had no connection. She was both sweet and fierce, attractive in her soft curves and tender overtures, and compelling for the sheer determination of her grip on his arse.

She hauled him closer and her tongue danced across his mouth. He reciprocated, and a stolen kiss became an utter rout of his self-restraint. Julian backed Elizabeth up against the shelves—biographies, the last rational corner of his mind noted—and drew her as close as a man could hold a woman.

She held him even closer and wrapped her leg around his thigh. Elizabeth would delight in pleasures taken amid the scent of books and forever after, Julian would look more fondly on his collection of biographies.

The lady eased her mouth away and rested against him.

"The door is open," she whispered.

Julian's first thought was, "The door to opportunity…" but reason returned in the next moment. The door to the library stood open, assuring that sensible people would commit no improprieties therein. He and Elizabeth were not visible from the corridor, of course, but one of them really ought to move.

He was a duke, the host of the gathering, and responsible for protecting her reputation. All of that was very true, but what inspired Julian to prudence was a nascent erotic interest that needed only a hint of inspiration to become obvious arousal.

He eased away, even as he stole a parting kiss. Elizabeth looked as tidy as a dowager's sewing box, while Julian felt as if he'd fallen headfirst from the mighty oak. Rather than stare into her eyes, his gaze landed on the books behind her.

"We've upset the biographies," he said, taking another step back. "Some of those volumes recount the illustrious doings of my ancestors."

She turned, presenting the elegant line of her shoulders and back, and began setting the books to rights.

Saved by the books, Julian thought, forcing himself put more distance between himself and the nape of Elizabeth Windham's neck.

DESPERATELY SEEKING SCANDAL

THERESA ROMAIN

CHAPTER ONE

*If a gentleman wishes to catch a lady of good fortune, he will need good fortune
himself. There is no creature so suspicious as a wealthy woman, especially if she is
not beautiful. Any male attention is regarded as suspect.
And rightly so.*
Vir Virilem, *Ways to Wed for Wealth*

Rushworth Green, Berkshire

She was certain now. The man was following her.

Ada had suspected it when the fair-haired gentleman regarded the
milliner's shop window far longer than a man normally would. Now that
he was waiting for her outside of the confectioner's, pretending to hold
a conversation with Ada's groom, she was certain of his ulterior motives.

When one was the sister of a duke who had recently wed in scandal,
alas, one constantly encountered people with ulterior motives. When
she'd been the sister of an unwed duke, it had been the same. Four
years ago, when she'd had a London Season and was known to have a
substantial dowry—ditto, ditto.

Her brother Philippe's recent marriage to Harriet Talbot, the daughter
of the estate's former horse master, had only reminded the *ton* that Lady
Ada Ellis existed. That she had been jilted four years before. And that her
thirty thousand pounds were yet unclaimed.

To avoid gossip, she now ducked into shops that she didn't need to visit.
She eyed each stranger warily. Unsettling though such preoccupations
were, she almost welcomed the break. She'd already spent hours today
poring over accounts. Numbers that had always added up before, this

time refused to obey. She had to have them in perfect order before her brother returned from his honeymoon trip, so he'd keep her on as steward.

"Been shopping today, my lady?" said the confectioner.

"I...have." She looked at her empty hands. She didn't need a thing in the world, but there had to be *some* reason for her to come to Rushworth Green. "I'm looking on behalf of my brother and his wife. When they return from their honeymoon travels, Her Grace will want to change the house to suit her tastes."

Until the words came out of her mouth, she hadn't realized they might be true. But the notion made sense. Every Duchess of Lavelle for hundreds of years had added on to or altered Theale Hall, while every duke oversaw the land and the tenants.

And the dukes' spinster sisters... what became of them?

Ada wrenched her mind away from that question. "Mr. Porter, do you recognize that man speaking to my groom?"

"To your horse, rather? He's staying at the White Hare, my lady, with his younger brother. Gave his name as Goddard."

"Goddard?" She didn't recognize the name, though reporters at scandal rags adopted outlandish pseudonyms. There was no way to know a Jones from a Finkleworth.

She turned away from the shop window toward the counter. "Thank you, Mr. Porter. A dozen caramels, please." She stripped off her gloves and tucked them away. If one had to be trapped in a shop by a man who was almost certainly a London reporter, that shop might as well be one that offered sweets.

Porter's round, ruddy face settled into its familiar smile lines as he counted out the paper-wrapped candies. He had known Ada almost since her birth, and he had never discouraged her fondness for confections.

Once she paid, she took the folded paper sack from the confectioner, opening it at once. Butter! Sugar! The smell alone was heaven.

The mysterious man was still outside. Ha! He met her eye through the shop window as Ada peered at him. Then he had to look away and act innocent, holding forth about halters or the horse's conformation or whatever it was. Her groom Fowler looked bored, good man.

Oh, never mind this. Ada could stay in the shop forever and eat caramel candy, or she could exit the shop and still eat caramel candy and also find out who this strange person was. Folding over the top of the sack again, she bade good-bye to Porter and marched out of the shop, candies in hand and skirts in a whirl of blue-striped muslin.

Walking up to her bay gelding, Equinox, she greeted Fowler as he held the horse's bridle and that of his own mount.

"You have been making a friend," she said to her groom.

Fowler, a thin and grizzled man of middle age, looked uncomfortable. "An acquaintance, my lady."

"Indeed. And who might this acquaintance be?" She lifted her brows, looking down her nose at the stranger.

"Colin Goddard, my lady." The man in question swept a bow. He was handsome, annoyingly so, with the sort of waving gilt hair that gentlemen disordered and arranged for maximum appeal.

"Colin Goddard, what business have you with my groom?"

"None at all. I was just admiring your horses."

Fowler made an indescribable noise. Equinox snorted, bobbing his head. The gelding was an impatient fellow who didn't like to be kept standing. The gray cob, Fitzhugh, looked up the high street with a mild and curious eye.

"I see," said Ada. "And now that you've admired them, do you plan to make your way through the village and look into more shop windows? Or would you like to have a caramel candy"—she shook the paper bag— "and tell me for which periodical you write?"

"I certainly wouldn't decline a candy." The man dared grin, the sort of smile that said, *I'm charming and I know it.* "I hadn't better do anything more, for the sake of my reputation."

"Nonsense. It's my brother's reputation you have in mind."

"Lady Ada, I—"

"There, see? If you were merely smitten by my horses, you wouldn't know my name."

"Curses. You are too sly for me." He shrugged, taking a candy from the bag. In its little paper twist, it looked like a fat butterfly.

"Fowler, you have one too." Ada held out the bag. When the gelding stretched his neck, she rubbed his velvety muzzle. "None for you, Equinox, though you shall have an apple once you're back in your stall." He was as fond of sweets as Ada, but she had seen his teeth stuck together with treacle once before, and she wouldn't repeat that experience for anything.

Ada unwrapped a candy for herself, tossing the twist of paper back into the sack. Burnt sugar, smooth stickiness, rich butter coated her tongue. Porter was a wizard.

A light autumn breeze tickled her cheeks; dry leaves scudded by along the packed-dirt road. For a moment, Ada sucked at the sweet, considering. "All right. Mr. Goddard—is that truly your name?"

At his lazy nod, she added, "Very well, then. Mr. Goddard. Tell me why you're here and what you hope to gain."

"I'd not hoped to benefit from such frankness."

She ignored the curious glances of the villagers passing by along the sleepy high street. "I'm twenty-four years old, wealthy, plain, and cynical. Frankness is my finest attribute."

"I should never call you plain."

"No. You never should. It would be rude."

She *was* plain, though, and his candied words didn't change that. Long face, dark brows. Light brown hair and the family's gray eyes. Wide mouth, rangy figure, small feet. She seemed put together from pieces of entirely different women. It had been amusing, in her only London Season, to watch the portraitist try to turn her into a conventional beauty. In the end, he had slapped laurels on her head and draped her in a toga, declaring her far too rare to have a more usual sort of portrait.

"I'm a reporter, as you guessed," he said. "But I'm not seeking a story about your brother."

So. He was hungry for more pieces of her family, was he? Since scandal writers had made a meal of her eldest brother's death, scraps of privacy were all that remained. She could spare no more.

"Fowler," she said, "will you walk Equinox and Fitzhugh up the high street and back? They appear impatient."

Fowler shot a pitying look at Goddard. "Yes, my lady."

As soon as they had retreated a few steps, Ada rounded on Goddard. "So." She made her voice heavy with disbelief. "You're not interested in the Duke of Lavelle's marriage."

"Not at all."

"Not even though it was to the daughter of our former horse master." Harriet was a gentleman's daughter, but that was not how her background had been reported in the press.

"A matter of complete indifference to me, I assure you."

"You came all the way to Berkshire—"

"It's not *that* far. Only a few hours in a mail coach."

"—for what, then? To eat candies given you by a stranger?"

"Unwise of me," Goddard granted. "I ought to have asked if you'd done something horrible to it."

"I didn't. So what's the reason you're following me about?"

He eyed her. His was the sort of assessing attention that a man might give a horse for sale, not the sort a man gave a woman he found attractive. "It might be for a story about you."

The candy caught in her throat. Her stomach rolled. Could he know about Lord Wrotham's visit to the area? She had only just got the letter two days ago. "I could thwart you, then, simply by leaving your presence."

"I'd stay in the inn and haunt you every time you came into Rushworth Green."

Ada tapped at her chin, considering. "That would be annoying. I suppose I could bribe you to leave."

"What would keep me from returning for another payment?" He grinned. "Not that I would. I'm just mentioning it as a flaw in your plan."

He reached for another caramel. She batted his hand away. "I could," he drawled, "speak to the people in the village. Or the dukedom's tenants."

She looked at him coolly. The Lavelle-gray eyes were a formidable weapon when employed properly. "Is that a threat?"

"Only if you are threatened by having people talk about you." He smiled disarmingly. "Look. Lady Ada. I don't need your help with this, but it would be easier for us both—and more pleasant—if I had it."

"And what is 'this'?"

"The sort of story that will make my career. And it just might make you happy too."

He looked so pleased with himself, but not in a way that raised her hackles. It was a sort of excited surprise, like the contents of his own mind were an unexpected delight.

By this time, the groom had returned with the two horses. Behind Goddard, Equinox investigated the man's hat with curious nibbles.

Fowler coughed. "My lady, would you like me to get the constable?"

"No need," Ada decided. "Mr. Goddard hasn't done anything wrong. Yet."

"I would never!" Goddard managed to look wounded. "I'm an honorable man."

Tucking the little paper sack under one arm, Ada took out her gloves and pulled them back on. "Because following a woman around is exactly what a gentleman would do?"

"It is if he intends to write a story about that woman."

"Also not what a gentleman would do." She checked the fit of her gloves, not wanting to look at the reporter again quite yet.

Goddard traveled with a brother, Porter had mentioned. And Goddard said—though it could be a lie—that he didn't care about her brother's marriage. Certainly it was true that he didn't adopt the sly nudge-wink manner that men often did when the subject of Lord Wrotham, that jilt, came up around Ada.

She might be able to make use of this visitor, just as he hoped to make use of her.

Her curiosity was piqued.

She turned away, letting Fowler hand her into the sidesaddle on Equinox's back. She took up the reins in one hand, regarded the little sack of candies dubiously—then tossed them down to Colin Goddard.

"Don't regard that as a posy or anything of the sort," she informed him. "I am at home to callers tomorrow from two o'clock to three. You may call then and explain to me what you have in mind."

"Thank you, my lady." When he bowed again, he swept off his hat with all the swagger of a Royalist Cavalier.

Reporters. She rolled her eyes. "And if I don't like it, I *will* call the constable."

That brought him up short. "But I haven't done—"

"Mr. Goddard. Do you really believe the family of a duke needs a reason to have someone removed from their presence?"

It was a good parting line. As Ada wheeled Equinox about and set him on the road back to the ducal seat, followed by Fowler on his cob, she wondered if Goddard was watching her ride off.

She decided she didn't mind if he was. For the past four years, Lady Ada Ellis had been buffeted by one loss after another.

Now she just might have a chance to strike back.

* * *

Colin wasn't about to miss the chance to speak with Lady Ada Ellis in a situation other than a few stolen, tense moments in front of a confectioner's shop. At half one the following day, he left the room he had rented for himself and Samuel at the White Hare, bidding his brother ring for whatever he might need.

He made his way to Theale Hall on foot, sixty percent to save the hire of a horse and forty percent to survey the grounds of the stately home.

One approached the ducal seat by way of the stables, a practical touch that he approved. Of course, these were no mere stables: They were great long rows of ruddy-gold stone with large windows. The frames and muntins were painted a crisp white, as if they belonged to houses. Likely, the Lavelle dukedom's horses lived better than many Londoners.

A circular drive connected the stables to the great house itself, a decorative rectangle of the same red-gold stone topped with a city of gables and slates and chimney pots. Unlike a London mansion, though, to which one often had to skip up a flight of marble steps before deigning to knock at the door, this one had a subdued entrance. No steps, just a jut of stone into which a set of rich brown double doors were set. From behind the edge of Theale Hall, a dower house peeked its smaller stone face.

At five minutes of two, Colin stood before the front door of Theale Hall. He had brushed his hat, donned his best clothing. When the butler opened the door to him, he doffed his hat.

"Lady Ada is expecting me," he said with more certainty than he felt. The lady had been prickly the day before, but not, he hoped, completely set against him.

The butler showed him not into some frothy parlor all done up in flowers and silks, but into a study. A masculine room, all wooden shelves and ancient oils and beautifully bound volumes. The air was scented with leather and lamp oil and the faint, musty smell of old paper.

"Lady Ada." The duke's sister was seated behind a desk half the size of Colin's room at the White Hare. "This is where you welcome your social callers?"

She pulled off a pair of gold spectacles and blinked up at him. "This is where I spend most of the hours I pass indoors." Blotting a page in a large ledger, she slid it to one side of the desk. "Thank you, Chalmers. We won't require any refreshment."

"We won't? Are you sure?" Colin asked. "I think I might require something."

She leveled at him the sort of look a barmaid offered when her arse had been pinched one time too many.

"Fine," he sighed. As the butler left them alone, he dropped into a chair across the desk from her. As he leaned against the back, he groaned a little. Sturdy leather, supple as cloth, with upholstery as comfortable as an embrace. It was a good life, being a duke's sister. Or simply visiting her for a while.

She steepled her hands. "I learned a bit more about you, Mr. Goddard. You truly are a writer for hire. And at present, you work for... *The Gentleman's Periodical.*" She spoke the words slowly. They were weighty to her, though he didn't know why.

"A tone of surprise, Lady Ada? I would not dare lie to someone so formidable."

"Formidable? Honestly." She took up a quill and penknife. "You might as well call me plain and frightening and be done with it."

Why she called herself plain, he had no idea. She wasn't beautiful in the way of painted portraits and marble-carved statues. But she looked like no one else he'd ever seen in the world, and that was surely the opposite of plain.

"Frightening, I will grant you," he said with mock sincerity. It didn't fool her for a second, for she shook her head.

"An attempt at flattery? How transparent." Thumb against the end of the quill, she shaved a perfect sliver from its nib. "Do tell me about your work."

It saved my life, he could have said. He'd been born to gentry, but his father was too fond of the bottle and the dice. The family lost their land, then their money—and when the influenza swept England in 1803, his parents lost their lives as well. Colin had been fifteen then, his younger brother only ten and troubled by a condition that kept him out of the public eye.

Boys' tricks helped them survive for a time, as they eked out a living in the village their father had lately served as clerk. Both bright, the brothers would perform feats of recitation, memory, and mathematics for anyone who would give a coin. Through the new clerk, they sometimes reviewed books and documents from the occasional London publisher. With Samuel's aid, Colin eventually struck up a correspondence with one—a Botolphus Bright, who published a daily broadsheet—and asked for employment.

I don't hire writers. I buy pieces, had replied the editor. *What do you have to offer?*

The brothers scrawled a criticism of humorous writing in a tone so dry as to parch his fingers. "I never read anything so ridiculous," said Bright when offering publication, and that was how the brothers were able to have meat again. They abandoned their village life for London and never looked back.

That had been ten years before. From the daily broadsheet, Bright had moved up in the world, and he now published the monthly *Gentleman's Periodical* of which Lady Ada seemed so fond. It was an upstart publication, aping the established and respected *Gentleman's Magazine* in every way except for being established and respected. But it was profitable enough. Bright had never yet hired the Goddard brothers, but Colin was determined that would change. If he played his cards right, the decade of piecework and scrambling for every coin would end in the security of an editorship.

But there was no way Colin would tell all of that to Lady Ada. "What if I make things up to impress you?"

"What if you do? I shall probably spot it. I'm not at all bad at telling when someone's lying."

"Really? Let's test that. At some point before I leave, but only once, I shall tell you a lie."

She held up the quill, gave a satisfied nod, and set it and the penknife aside. "That was it right there. You intend to tell me far more than one."

"Curses. In that case, there's at least one more for you to catch."

"Lucky me." She toyed with her spectacles, flipping the stems out, then folding them again. "Very well. So. You work for *The Gentleman's Periodical*, a blight on the occupation of writer, a waste of rag for paper, and a shameful end for every bit of ink spilled."

"Um."

"Instead of on dits, you deal in *on-demandes*, a spate of posed questions that have nothing to do with reality, but avoid libel because they make no assertions."

She was right. It had been one of Colin's most brilliant ideas about five years before. If one merely asked a question, the answer could be anything. *Did the Prince Regent marry a French woman in secret? Does the owner of Tattersalls sell the meat of ill horses to the city's most expensive butcher shops?*

The questions page was instantly popular. Bright had granted reluctantly it had saved the periodical more than once from financial failure.

Lady Ada was not an enthusiast, it seemed. Colin could guess why. After the accidental death of her elder brother four years before, the questions page had made a meal of the circumstances of his death. Issue after issue, the public couldn't get enough of scurrilous suppositions about the death of a duke's son and heir.

That was one of the times Colin's questions had saved the *Periodical*. Lady Ada's gray eyes were frosty, as if she were reading this thought right out of his brain. He held himself still, refusing to fidget.

She leaned forward, holding his gaze. "Were you responsible only for yourself, Mr. Goddard, I should make you eat the most recent issue of *The Gentleman's Periodical*, then have you booted out of the house before you finished chewing. But you are not, are you?"

Colin turned his head, eyeing her aslant. "Where do you get your information?"

She shrugged, unbending a fraction. "London is only a few hours by mail coach, as you say. Even less time when one sends an express. And when you stay in the White Hare in the village, learning more about you is a matter of giving a half crown to the innkeeper or sending him a haunch of beef."

Inwardly, Colin cursed the resourcefulness of the wealthy in general, and Lady Ada Ellis in particular.

She added, "You are the sole source of care for your younger brother, who is not and never has been well."

That was putting it a bit strongly, but it was the way most people thought of Samuel. "Remember how I said you were frightening? That understated the matter."

"For the sake of your brother"—she softened—"I will not toss you out on your ear. Family must be cared for."

He drummed his fingers on the arm of his chair. "Thank you? I think?"

"Oh, you definitely want to thank me. You are here to catch yourself an editorship, is that right?"

"I'm here to write," he said smoothly. Another lie—well, more of a dodge.

"Tell me, Mr. Goddard, what *do* you plan to write about? And why must it involve me?"

"It needn't, though it'd be better with your help. I have promised my editor half a dozen pieces in a series on how a plain, ordinary sort of person might catch a wealthy spouse."

The series was inspired by the recent marriage of a horse master's daughter to the Duke of Lavelle. Had it happened in London, it would have been the talk of the *ton*. Instead, their quiet Berkshire nuptials merited only a sniffing mention in the society papers—and a few questions in *The Gentleman's Periodical.*

That was good. Less competition for Colin. He'd intended to stalk the duke and duchess for scandalous tidbits, but when he arrived in Rushworth Green to find Their Graces abroad for a honeymoon journey, it occurred to him that the duke's sister could work as well for his purposes.

"Oh dear." Lady Ada's lips pressed together, holding back a smile that fought to escape. "And how am I to help with that? Not to be caught, surely."

"I would never presume to that degree. Instead, I thought you could tell me about your brother's courtship of the former Harriet… Tallboys?"

"You know quite well it was Talbot," she said serenely. "And you told me yesterday that you weren't interested in writing about them."

"You weren't keeping track of my lies then," he said. "That was a good one. I told it well, didn't I?"

She fixed him with a silvery glare. "I'm not a humorless woman, but I don't think your immorality is as funny as you do. Sorry I can't be more obliging."

The lift of her brows niggled at him, and before he could think better of it, he leaned forward. Too far forward, almost in her face. "Lady. Ada. Ellis. Sister to a duke. You can afford anything you like, and so you need never reckon the cost of morals."

She snorted in his face as if she were her long-nosed gelding. "Do I not?"

"Honor. Ethics. Whatever name you want to put to the notion of taking one's pay where one can, never knowing where the next coin will come from—but knowing that it will never come at all without the work of one's mind and one's hands, and sometimes of one's body."

She swept him with a curious gaze, but said nothing. The word *body* echoed in the air, making him feel naked. And not the good sort of naked that one became with a lover. This was simply bareness.

He drew back again. "Pretend I never said any of that, if you wish."

"No, I don't think I will." She continued watching him, her expression unreadable. "You finally said something that was meaningful to you. Not many people are so frank with me."

His shoulders were tense within his inexpensive blue coat. "Ah, well. Honesty is the one thing I *can* afford, I suppose."

"There. That was a lie too. Your face went all twitchy."

"I...meant that, sincerely. I was merely twitchy at the realization that there's not much I can afford, especially when up against a foe such as yourself."

"Flattery again? You need some new tricks, sir." She held up a hand. "Please don't think that I misunderstand you. I know that I am privileged because of the circumstances of my birth. I must do my best to earn the moral right to my good fortune."

"Morality again," Colin sighed.

"Yes. Morality again." A smile touched her lips. "So. I want to be left alone, and you want to mock my family for coin."

"Not exactly," he hedged.

"But close enough?"

"Close enough," he allowed.

Frequent missives for two to four weeks, he had promised Botolphus Bright. They could appear in serial form in the magazine for months, at the end of which time the articles could be collected into a small pamphlet and sold for twopence.

Bright wouldn't allow him to write under his own name, but that was all right. Colin had already picked a name under which the series would appear. *Vir Virilem*. A virile man. The outlandishness made him laugh.

Lady Ada had sharpened a quill. She had blotted a ledger. She had folded and unfolded her spectacles, and now she seemed at a loss what to do next. "I could have you thrown out of town, but I think you'd come back. And I am not unfeeling. I know that you seek betterment."

"And you seek?"

"At this time? With you? A bargain."

Innnnteresting. He shoved at the edge of the desk, tipping the chair onto its back legs. "Let me hear the terms before I agree."

"Of course." She hesitated, then leaned forward. "Beginning this evening, and for the next fortnight, a certain person will be visiting the area. He intends to buy horses of Talbot and Ramsdale, who hold a partnership in the horse farm that adjoins my brother's lands."

"How am I to help with that? Do you wish me to arrange for this visitor's murder? Skewer him with a quill, or whatnot?"

She didn't turn a hair. "He doesn't deserve such a clean end. Mr. Goddard, this visitor is Lord Wrotham, the heir to the Baddesley earldom. Four years ago, we were betrothed. Scandalous talk related to my eldest brother's death—in large part, the clever *on-demandes* from your delightful publication—led his lordship to break the engagement."

She looked so calm, so sober—but a muscle twitched in her jaw. She was gritting her teeth on some deep emotion. Anger? Sadness? He couldn't put a name to it. But the one that washed through him, he recognized as guilt. Or its cousin, shame.

"He wasn't worthy," Colin said. Hoped. Wished.

"At this point in time, I'm inclined to agree. However, he still holds the opposite view. And as he is newly wed, I will be obliged to host him and his new bride with a smile on my face."

Colin sucked in a sharp breath. "My sympathies. That's going to be difficult."

When the smile spread over her features, it was of the sort that would strike fear into any man who wasn't an ignorant fool. "That's where you can help. Mr. Goddard, for the next fortnight, you are to be madly in love with me."

He blinked.

"Because you are so deeply infatuated, you will spend the two weeks as I choose," she went on. "And how convenient! You will be living the life you wish your readers to experience through your work. If you are caught out by Wrotham as a fraud, you lose. If you surrender before the fortnight is up, you lose. But if you survive the two weeks, you win."

"What do you mean by surrender?"

"That you allow a breach in your character. For example, if you attend a formal dinner party in a borrowed set of my brother's clothes, and you must fawn over me, and instead, you communicate in any way that you would rather not."

He had to be missing something. "Fine clothes? Twenty-four dishes served to me by a servant? Goodness, I can't imagine how I will bear it."

Again, that little shrug. "Fine talk. Do you accept?"

"Do I? Of course. I can't believe you're offering me this chance." He held up a staying hand. "So when I win—"

She laughed.

It was more disconcerting than anything she could have said, but he soldiered on. "When I win, you will give me any information I need to complete the series of articles for *The Gentleman's Periodical*."

Fire sparked in her gray eyes. "If you win, Mr. Goddard, I will help you write them myself."

"It's a bargain," he said. "When shall we begin?"

"Why not at once?" She rang for the butler. Behind that wide, long desk, she sat back in her chair and folded her hands.

"Chalmers," she said when the butler appeared, "please show Mr. Goddard up to a guest room, where he might change into some of His Grace's spare clothing."

Colin bounced to his feet.

"From..." Lady Ada eyed Colin, her gaze lingering on his chest, then thighs. "Two seasons ago, I believe. And alert Cook that we will be adding one to the party dining here today."

"Very good, my lady," said the butler.

Too right, thought Colin. Two weeks to live the high life and to end by cementing his and Samuel's future at *The Gentleman's Periodical*?

This would be very good indeed.

CHAPTER TWO

*When one moves out of his or her class to attempt to snare a wealthy mate,
awkward situations will inevitably arise. To show one's awkwardness will make one
an object of pity. To hide it, and to act at ease with whatever arises, will make one
an object of respect.
Better yet, it will irk the jealous and insecure.*
Vir Virilem, *Ways to Wed for Wealth*

This dinner would be awful, and he was sure Lady Ada had planned it
that way. Colin was going to kill her.

Though not until after he completed his articles.

The duke's clothes from two seasons before were made for a tall man
of athletic build who delighted in bespoke tailoring. Colin was physically
fit enough; one didn't live in London without pounding the streets half
the time. But the duke was several inches taller, Colin guessed, from
where the seams hit. The buckskin breeches that ought to have fit like
paint were too high at the waist and too baggy at the knee.

The coat was another matter. Colin suspected this one hadn't
belonged to His Grace since the duke was a youth. The butler, Chalmers,
had helped Colin shrug into it, but as a result, his shoulders were drawn
together, his arms awkwardly restricted. By drawing in a huge breath,
then holding it, he was able to do up one button and somewhat hide the
terrible waistcoat the butler had also foisted upon him.

"Why does the duke still own this clothing?" he grumbled, tugging at
the bottom of the too-short coat.

"Her ladyship encouraged him to, as she thought it might serve some purpose," said the butler. "Which it now has." He packed Colin a trunk of similar clothing to take back to the inn with him.

Colin would be damned before he'd wear clothes of Lady Ada's choosing again, but he had to admire the lady's style. So, he was forbidden to display the smallest amount of displeasure? Fine. Good. He'd show her just how delightful he could be despite wearing the coat of a boy and the breeches of a Goliath.

Because there was one thing for which she hadn't accounted: He couldn't afford to give up.

* * *

Ada watched Colin Goddard closely as the other guests arrived. Would he be boorish and vulgar to try to embarrass her? She almost wished he would, so she could have him tossed out of her house.

Her brother's house, that is. Ada was in charge only by chance, and her borrowed power wasn't real.

But it must have been good enough for Goddard and the story he hoped to sniff out, because he wasn't boorish at all. He wasn't exactly polite either, not in a deferential way. But he was *charming*. He was charming in the way that only people who are utterly at ease can be charming, unconscious of themselves, their whole attention given up to the interest and comfort of others. In the too-tight coat and not-quite-fashionable accent, he chatted and laughed with all of the neighbors.

"I'm a writer," he explained, "staying in the area. As Lady Ada and I have been acquainted through her brother"—oh, he was a slippery one!—"she invited me to dine tonight. Unfortunately, I'm not an elegant fellow, so she offered to help me out."

"Wouldn't say she'd done you any favors!" bellowed Squire Martin, a ruddy man with a luxuriant mustache and almost no hair on his head. "Should've let you wear your own kit. No need to stand on ceremony with friends."

And just like that, Martin was in Goddard's pocket.

Curses. She hadn't accounted for the common masculine dislike of elegant clothing.

Perhaps the female guests would be more skeptical of this unknown writer. Besides the Martins, there were the Ponsonbys, the vicar and his wife; the local schoolmaster, a Mr. Johnson; and the headmistress of the girls' school, a widow named Mrs. Semple.

Just as she had invited Lord and Lady Wrotham upon learning of their stay in the area, she had added Colin Goddard today. The timing was fortunate; with Goddard, the number of men and women would match. Ada would not be superfluous.

Old Mr. Talbot had been invited, as usual, but he was frail and crotchety and missing his daughter—Harriet, the new duchess—too much to attend. Ada would have a basket packed for the old gentleman later.

She hosted these dinner parties every month, a tradition she'd carried on from the time of her parents. As the heart of the Berkshire economy, the old duke and his duchess had thought it important to maintain connections with the appendages: church, schooling, horse-training. Farmers and tenants were welcomed during open days and the annual harvest ball. Would Harriet and Philippe keep up these traditions?

It wasn't Ada's business to know or care, but she cared nonetheless.

While the locals trickled in at whatever early time their feet or horses carried them over, Lord Wrotham and his lady wife arrived precisely at the appointed hour.

When Samuel Johnson created his dictionary in the previous century, he surely foresaw the existence of his lordship in the definitions of punctilious. Scrupulous. Meticulous. No attention was overlooked by his lordship—and no trespass either. He was a handsome man of about thirty years, with brown hair and a long, narrow nose. His clothing was expensive but not flashy, beautifully tailored.

Reluctantly, Ada admitted that he cut a fine figure. She was glad she'd donned a new gown, one in shades of cream and white, all dotted over with silk embroidery and finished with a lovely trim of twining vines in the same silk. Colin Goddard, who was looking as ridiculous as Ada had hoped, cast her an appreciative look that had her stomach in a flutter.

All part of the act, she reminded herself.

Lady Wrotham looked near Ada's age, twenty-four or thereabout. She had a crown of blond braids, sparkling brown eyes, and a pleasant smile. Ada had intended to dislike her, but she couldn't manage the feat.

"Thank you for the invitation," the viscountess said, introducing herself as Serena. "I wouldn't have felt right about being so near Wrotham's old acquaintances and not paying my respects."

From the frank look she gave Ada, it was clear she knew exactly what sort of acquaintances Wrotham and Ada had been. From her smile, it was clear that she hoped to set it behind them. Ada was willing. How long ago that betrothal seemed now.

Through the numerous courses of dinner, as they sat around the table in proper man-woman-man-woman fashion, Colin Goddard kept his dinner companions smiling. He kept firing heated glances in Ada's direction. A particular favorite of his was to sip at his glass of wine, then look at her over the top.

Over the top indeed. Well, she'd asked for it. And Wrotham, stick-stiff and serious, was noting these attentions with a grave expression that gave Ada a lowly sort of satisfaction. *Just because you didn't want me doesn't mean I'm unappealing. Unattractive. Unlovable.*

Even if the proof of this was false, nothing of the sort, she found herself forgetting… almost. Goddard was a most convincing actor.

After the last dishes had been removed, the women went into the drawing room—but just barely had Ada settled next to Serena Wrotham when the men filed into the room as well.

"Couldn't stay away any longer," said Goddard blithely. "Port and politics have nothing on you ladies." When he fired another lovesick look at Ada, Lady Wrotham looked at her knowingly.

"Shall we have cards?" Ada asked. "Or a dramatic reading? Mr. Goddard, as a writer, surely you'd enjoy reading aloud to us all."

He hitched at his ridiculous huge breeches. "I'd make a dull job of it," he said. "I never can do justice to another man's words. But if you'll allow me to mangle them a bit, I could monologue for you."

Putting a hand to his heart, he intoned,

"My mistress' eyes are like a stormy sea;

Coral is far more red than her lips' red;

Her breasts are darker than a blond lace be;

If hairs be wires, brown wires grow on her head."

Ada's cheeks flamed. "That is horrid. You should apologize to William Shakespeare right now for treating one of his sonnets so."

Goddard bowed. "As long as the lady doesn't ask me to apologize for sincere words, Mr. Shakespeare may have my heartiest plea for pardon."

What a flirt he was. *Stop pretending,* she wanted to say. *Never stop pretending,* she wanted to say too. Lady Ada Ellis, daughter and sister to Dukes of Lavelle, had never been the sort of woman with whom men flirted outrageously.

Goddard contorted a few more poems for the group's amusement, then the Ponsonbys and Martins settled to cards while Lady Wrotham played several pieces on the pianoforte. Beautifully, of course. When her husband joined his voice with hers in a duet, Ada had to look away for a moment, studying her ringless hands with fierce determination to hold back tears.

Lord and Lady Wrotham were well suited, and that was a fine thing. Ada neither missed him nor regretted him. No, she regretted the four years that had passed—that she had allowed to pass—without another journey to London, another Season, another suitor. Grief for her eldest brother's sudden death had brought her home; her father's death the following year had kept her here. But why did she stay here so constantly now? The dukedom needed her, she thought, in her brother Philippe's absence.

Maybe that was only an excuse.

She kept a polite smile on her face for the remainder of the evening. The Ponsonbys were the first to depart, as usual; the vicar was an early riser. Squire Martin had more than once fallen asleep in his cups in the armchair before the drawing-room fire, but tonight his wife elbowed him out of a drowse and hurried him along. The Wrothams and teachers left with gracious thanks for a fine evening too, and before the sun had fully sunk sleepy below the horizon, Ada was alone.

Wait. Why was she alone? Where had Goddard got off to?

He wasn't in the dining room drinking port. He wasn't in the chair before the fire, and he certainly wasn't hiding beneath the pianoforte or behind a potted palm.

Ada found Chalmers and asked him whether he'd spotted their wayward guest. With a pained expression, the butler directed her ladyship to the study.

The study? Where a hungry sort of reporter could make a meal of the dukedom's accounts? Could browse through Ada's favorite books, or crack open the seals of her correspondence?

She strode down the corridor to the study, picking up speed. She was almost at a run by the time she reached the familiar old door and wrenched it open.

"Ha!" She sprang into the room, prepared to catch him doing something inappropriate.

But he wasn't. He'd shrugged out of the tight coat—she couldn't blame him for that, since Philippe hadn't worn it since he was fifteen—and was sitting in waistcoat and shirt-sleeves on the desk, flipping idly through a poetry book she'd left out.

At her dramatic entrance, he looked up mildly. "Hullo. What a lovely noise that was. Feeling rambunctious, are you?"

She sniffed, drawing herself up straight. "You're meant to leave with the other callers, Mr. Goddard, not go prowling around the house."

"Ah, my manners went begging." He sat in her favorite chair before the fire, the one in which she'd been planning to sit, and stuck out his legs, slinging one ankle over another.

"They have. You shouldn't sit in the presence of a standing lady."

"I know. But I behaved myself *so* well this evening, wouldn't you say?"

"Better than I expected. I'm becoming familiar with your wiles, though."

"Say it isn't so! Doesn't familiarity breedeth contempt, or so goes the old saying?"

"That depends on the one with whom I'm becoming familiar." She slid around the desk to scan its surface. Writing implements. Paper. The ledgers were tidied away, and she couldn't tell whether he'd opened the desk's drawers to get at them.

"So suspicious," he said. "I do have a code of ethics, of sorts. If it's closed, I don't open it. If it's on a shelf, I don't take it down."

Mollified, she left the desk—though not before snapping up the book he'd been paging through. "An unconventional code for a reporter." She found another chair, wrenched it over to the fireplace and stuck it beside his. "I wonder if it puts you at a disadvantage."

"Maybe so. But that's my problem, isn't it?" His calm was unfailing.

She tried to reply in kind. "The neighbors hadn't had such a nice time in a while. I thank you."

His grin was pure wickedness. "And what about Lord Wrotham? We put his nose out of joint a little."

"A very little. It is an uncommonly large nose. I did like his wife, which I wasn't expecting to."

"He doesn't deserve her."

Ada looked at him curiously. "You take my part with admirable prejudice."

"I didn't like him. I'm glad you didn't marry him."

"I came to the same conclusion soon after he jilted me. If the only thing he wanted of me was my family's good name…"

"Then he was a fool."

Ada smiled. "Spoken like a man who recently fabricated a shocking alternative to one of Shakespeare's sonnets."

"You weren't shocked at all. You liked it. Shall I finish my recitation? I only did the first four lines of the poem. The next bit is meant to be about your cheeks not being rosy, or your breath not being like perfume, but I can make it much more enticing."

"Ah… that's all right."

He shrugged. "For the best, since your cheeks *are* looking rosy right now. Embarrassed? I was only doing what I promised. I'm besotted with you, or don't you recall?"

"Believe me, I haven't forgotten a word of our earlier conversation."

He nodded at the book she held. "You're holding that so tightly your knuckles are going white."

She released the book as if it were a hot poker, letting it thump to the floor. "I always hold books like that when I come upon someone flipping through them unexpectedly, thus violating his professed code of ethics."

"I did not. You left it open on your desk, which meant it was all right for me to look through it." He hesitated. "It's not in English, is it?"

Her brows lifted. "No, it's not. Couldn't you tell? It's German poetry."

He shifted in the chair, drawing his legs in from their sprawl. "I wasn't aware it was possible to write a poem in German. An argument, yes, but a poem?"

"A few people have managed it over the years. I've been reading this one so long, it's more of an old friend than a mere book by now." And she'd dropped it on the floor, poor book. She bent to pick it up, dusting off its binding of faded red morocco leather.

"Why this one?"

She smiled. "It was the only book small enough to fit into my pocket and hide from the governess."

"Your governess wouldn't allow you to read poetry in German? Strict woman."

"She was German," said Ada, as if that explained everything, and Goddard laughed.

"I was never encouraged to read much," she added. "Numbers were my particular gift, and therefore I had to work with them."

Numbers, numbers. Ever since she'd joined Philippe for his childhood lessons from their governess, the family had made it known that Ada had a head for numbers. And so she did. A column of numbers was as easy for her to read and make sense of as a page of words.

But it was words, twisting, mysterious words, that Ada really loved. One couldn't jot columns of numbers at random in one's bedchamber when the lights were low. But one could write—and hide the pages, knowing that disappointment and punishment would follow if they were ever found. Her observations ran toward the ordinary and wry: on which days the governess's breath smelled like whisky, or how much less time the lower housemaid took to change the linens on her own, as opposed to when one of the footmen helped her behind a closed door.

Such observations were not encouraged. Whenever she'd spoken of them, the conversation had been turned toward numbers again.

"Dear me. Are you a mathematical genius?" Goddard adopted a tone of mock distress.

"That's putting it too strongly. But I had a knack for addition. And because it came easily, I had to learn more and more maths."

"So you *are* a genius. And here I sit in your presence. I knew I felt a warm glow."

"That's the fire, thank you very much. And I have a talent for maths, but that doesn't mean I enjoy the subject."

"Don't you?" He looked genuinely interested.

"I manage my brother's estate in his absence, and I keep the accounts. It's... all right. But it's not for me—does that make sense?"

"Maybe. But why do you spend so much time on it?"

She thought about it. "Just this: I want to help my brother, but I know anyone with a decent head could do this work just as well. If he ever chooses to hire a steward, he won't need me at all."

Recently, Philippe had been dropping hints that he wanted to do just this. *You should go to London, Ada. We should hire someone to do this, Ada. You can't be wanting to spend your life doing this, Ada.*

No, she didn't. But what else *was* there for a spinster with no other family?

"Sisters aren't kept around because of the good they can do," Colin Goddard said. "Or so I've gathered. I never had one myself."

She traced the tooled shapes on the tiny poetry book's binding. "Why would one keep a sister around, then?"

"Because a brother loves her and wants her to have a safe and comfortable place to live." He leaned forward, took up the poker, and jabbed it into the glowing coals a few times. "Though that's only a guess.

I'm much more diabolical. I keep my brother around because he's a workhorse and I can take advantage of him."

"I sincerely doubt that." When he sat back again, she said, "You tore a strip off me earlier with all your talk about morals and privilege."

"Is that what I did? I wondered why a feeling of unaccustomed power was coursing through me. Now I know."

"Yes, that was it. And I let you because I didn't know if it was worth punching back. So to speak."

"Of course it was! I've been told before that my face is very punchable."

He had a winning way, she could not deny it. That smile, that comfort in his own skin. It made one want to stick to his side and tell him everything. She wondered if this talent had led him to writing, or if it had been the other way 'round.

"It wasn't your face, but the words coming from it. However, if I engaged in every argument someone wanted to foist upon me, as the sister and representative of the Duke of Lavelle, I'd never get anything else done."

His waving hair glinted in the firelight. "What a contentious life you lead."

"You have no idea," she said dryly. "But you'll be pleased to know, I'm sure, that I like you more than I expected to. You were ridiculous this evening, but you acted with decency."

"Thank you." Somehow, from his seated position, he managed a servile bow.

"Which is why *I'm* going to tear a strip off *you* before we go any further with this bargain of ours."

He snapped upright. "Ah. It's about the writing again, isn't it? Why does this bother you so much, Lady Ada? If you're not hurt, why not let me benefit?"

She chose her words carefully, like picking her way through a quagmire. "Because it does hurt. Scandal devoured my eldest brother's memory. It brought me the humiliation of a jilting. And now it dogs my remaining brother."

The *on-demandes* after Jonas's accidental death had been brutal. *Was Lord Chaddleworth's fall truly an accident, or did he arrange it to cover his despondence? Was it because of debt? An illicit love affair?* Could she have met the writer of those questions, she'd have given him answers that he wouldn't forget for a lifetime.

Jonas's death was exactly what it had seemed. Horse plus man plus jump plus wall—plus muddy earth and not enough training—equaled a broken neck, unconsciousness, inevitable death. But because of *The Gentleman's Periodical*, questions that ought never to have been asked were then on everyone's mind. And from their minds to their lips was but a small journey.

Ada sighed, remembering. "Let me put a different perspective to you, Mr. Goddard. When you write about someone and collect your pay, do you ever think of what comes next?"

"Always. I think about spending it on bread and clothing and paying the rent on the rooms I share with my brother."

"Do not be deliberately obtuse."

He schooled his expression into one of greater seriousness. "You mean, I suppose, do I ever think of what comes next for the people my brother and I write about. No, I do not. I don't have time to. We have to find someone or something else to write about."

"You spread rumor and scandal for profit, never thinking about the pain caused by your written word. The strained marriages, the broken engagements. The friendships befouled by jealousy and doubt. Everyone you write about is a real person, but they are not real to you. As you just said, you don't have time to think of them as real. You don't think of them at all."

* * *

Her crisp, calm words were darts into the blithe armor with which he covered himself. With which he *had* to cover himself, to shift from one voice to another, one false persona to another. To earn the money that took care of himself and his brother.

"I can't afford to," he said. "The people I write about are those who can afford much more than I. But I am sorry for any pain I've caused you. I didn't do you justice."

He wanted to say more, but he clamped down on further apology. What good would it do for her to know he'd thought up the scandalous questions that had dragged her life askew?

She looked at him with those silvery eyes of hers, and something tight in her posture relaxed. "There you go, acting like a human being. What am I to do with you?"

"I have two ideas. First, you could call me Colin. And second, you could give me some clothes that fit properly, or else let me wear my own for the remainder of the fortnight."

A smile sneaked across her features, then vanished. "Yes to both. And you may call me Ada, since you are madly in love with me."

With that, she bid him good night. When she swept out of the study, leaving him alone, his heart was still stammering over her final words.

She was one to watch out for, was this Lady Ada Ellis. Frankness and humor and all that collected breeding—Lord have mercy, if he didn't feel himself going soft about the edges already. It would be only too easy to pretend to be in love with her. The difficult part would be remembering why he was truly here with Samuel: to take notes, to write their pieces, to make money, to leave.

He didn't realize until he was back at the White Hare that she'd never specified the favor she would claim of him if she won their bargain.

CHAPTER THREE

Alas, when one seeks to mingle with the upper class, one must adopt its more foolish trappings. Affectations of dress and behavior—such as the unaccountable fondness for equestrian sports—hold no purpose except to prove that one belongs in the company of the wealthy. For the wealthy, this is purpose enough.
Vir Virilem, *Ways to Wed for Wealth*

"Yes, you are going to ride a horse," Ada repeated. To Colin's ear, she sounded exasperated. "If you are besotted with me, then sometimes you will have to ride a horse."

"I can be besotted with you without being besotted with a horse." Colin thought this was a sturdy argument, but Ada was having none of it.

She continued her march down the row of stalls. "Gentlemen ride, especially in Berkshire. We're only a shout away from Ascot."

"I'll refrain from shouting."

She ignored this. "And you could be a gentleman, you know. If you chose."

This was so startling to Colin that he dropped his gloves. "Really?"

"Really."

Nudging the gloves with his boot, he tried to pop them into the air.

"Just pick them up."

"This coat is too tight." It was another borrowed garment, though this time Colin understood the need for it, since he owned no riding clothes of his own.

Ada pursed her lips. With a smooth gesture, she snapped them up and stuffed them into his hand. "And I'm the one wearing stays. Honestly."

She was a little flushed when she stood upright, which meant her comment was not an invitation to evaluate her appearance. But since Colin wasn't a gentleman, no matter what she said, he did it anyway. She wore a riding habit of a shade between blue and green that made her eyes look cool and bright. Her hair was tucked up beneath a little shako-style hat, setting off her graceful neck, her stubborn chin. She looked pretty and obstinate and confident and embarrassed all at once, and he could almost forgive her for her determination to seat him on a horse.

The stables were as well-appointed inside as the exteriors had led him to believe. They were scented pleasantly of straw and liniments and warm animals, though the odor of manure underlay it all. Still, it was much nicer than a London street, and he said so.

"The stalls are cleaned more often and more thoroughly," Ada replied. "Now. Will you choose your mount, or shall I choose for you?"

Colin stalled. "Surely there have been gentlemen since the beginning of time who have not known how to ride a horse."

"There have, but you are not to be one of them. We are going to ride horses and make ourselves visible as a courting couple."

"How unbending and obstinate you are. I'm not sure why I'm besotted with you."

Her brows shot up. "Perhaps you recognize your own qualities in me."

Despite himself, he chuckled. He enjoyed every minute with her, every spar and parry.

He did *not* enjoy every minute in the stables. But he could do this. It wasn't as if he didn't see horses every day in London. They were more common than dogs, pulling wagons and carts and carriages, being ridden or sold, pampered or abused.

But he wasn't usually so *near* a horse. When he rode in a stagecoach, the horses were outside, and he was within. And as he looked down the row of generously sized stalls, at the generously sized animals, his stomach rolled over.

This brown one here, with the black legs. It was much taller than a person, and should it choose to stomp on Colin's feet, his were outnumbered two to one. "Do you have a smaller horse?"

"I do. My mare, Atalanta. But she wouldn't hold your weight." An assessing look at Colin decided her. "No, you'd best ride Equinox."

Equinox was apparently the large brown animal Colin had just eyed with suspicion. "But I—"

"If you're my suitor, and we're going to convince Lord Wrotham that I don't give a snap for him anymore, then we have to ride. And we have to ride the bridle path that passes between the Lavelle property and the horse farm where he's buying new animals."

"Do you know for certain that he's there? Won't all our work be wasted if he doesn't see us?" He was trying valiantly to save himself and Equinox the indignity of being paired. "I know I agreed to the bargain, but this is a great deal of trouble to score off someone you don't care about anymore."

"It's not only that." She checked the fastening on the headpiece, then scratched behind the horse's ears. "I need to create an impression, whether he sees us or not. As long as *someone* sees us, word will get about."

"An impression. All right. Anything specific, besides the fact that you sit a horse far better than your poor swain, Mr. Goddard?"

"Rather." She counted on her fingers. "First, that I am not a retiring little snippet of a person who has never returned to London since being jilted. Second, that I'm not the sort of woman who has never since had a suitor. Third, that I'd never be content to spend my days with the numbers created by and for my brother's business interests."

"That's a lot to communicate in one ride. If I'm sifting through all the negatives properly, though, I might add that your description of yourself is far from the truth."

"It is *precisely* the truth. But for the two weeks you are here, it's not anymore."

He recognized this as an earnest plea for help, though Ada didn't speak those specific words. "What happens at the end of the two weeks? Should I propose and you refuse me in spectacular fashion?"

She looked startled. "I hadn't considered the best way to bring an end to the charade. Remiss of me."

"I'm sure I can think of something dramatic and stunning." He sounded blithe, didn't he? Yet, already he was dreading the end of these two weeks. The pretense of fondness for Ada was as comfortable as a warm cloak.

"So. Equinox." Colin eyed the horse. It eyed him back with a long-lashed eye of deepest brown. "Good name. Does he sleep half the day?"

"Horses aren't much on sleep, unlike the cats that roam around the stable. The cats catch mice sometimes, but they're most useful at lying around in sunbeams." She nodded at a gray tabby that was doing just that. "Equinox was foaled on the twenty-first of March, about six and a half years ago now. How could he be named anything else?"

"I should have guessed. The name makes perfect sense." Unlike the names of some racehorses, which seemed chosen at random from scraps of a torn dictionary.

"Go ahead, get to know him." Ada motioned toward the big brown horse. "I'll get Fowler. He can saddle Equinox for you."

Thus Colin was abandoned with a horse named after a day of the year. Sometimes his life was strange. "Hullo, horse. How are you?" He extended a cautious hand. The horse plunged his muzzle into Colin's palm, lipping at his gloved hand, then snorting an enormous warm breath of disappointment.

Ada approached with the wiry groom Colin remembered from their first meeting. "Equinox wanted a treat from you." She smiled, rubbing the gelding's long nose and finger-combing his forelock into place. "Maybe he remembers how you admired him in front of the confectionary shop in the village."

"I could admire him again if you wish."

"He'd much prefer you gave him something to eat. Here, make friends." As the groom began saddling the horse, Ada reached into a bin and held up a dirty glob with a stringy top.

"A... rock?"

She rolled her eyes. "You can't be *that* much of a Londoner. It's a beetroot."

Holding it by its top, she knocked it against the stall door to free the loose dirt. He recognized it, now that he knew what it was. The horse seemed to know what it was too. He stretched out his long neck, upper lip folded up as if he were shoving the earthy scent into his nostrils.

Colin held the vegetable by its greens and offered it forward gingerly. Long teeth bit through the beetroot as easily as Colin might chew a caramel candy. The horse displayed purple-stained teeth as he strained for the rest. Colin stepped back out of reflex.

"Don't tease him," said Ada. "May I?" When Colin nodded, she stood next to him and cradled his hand in hers, guiding it forward, upward, to be a vegetable platter for the gelding. With another crunch, Equinox took the rest of the root into his mouth.

With Ada's hand on his, the horse's teeth didn't faze Colin a bit. "Uh... thank you," he said. "Will—will he eat the greens?"

He sounded tentative. He hated sounding tentative. But he couldn't remember the last time someone had helped him with something so simple and everyday. *You can do this by yourself, but you needn't.*

"He'll eat anything," Ada said. "Here, lead him from the stall. Fowler, help Mr. Goddard mount while I saddle my mare."

The groom looked at Colin beadily. "If you'll come into the paddock, sir? We'll find a mounting block." He took hold of the gelding's bridle and led the horse from the stable.

Colin watched them walk away, man and beast. "All right, all right," he grumbled. "I'm besotted. And I'm going to ride a horse. Maybe I can take a few notes on the sort of horseflesh the wealthy keep. Stick it into an article sometime."

Ada laughed. "Only wait until the new duchess returns from her wedding trip. She and Philippe"—it took Colin a moment to realize he was hearing a duke's Christian name—"are traveling through Spain and Portugal with the express purpose of viewing the native breeds. Harriet is a genius with horses. There's nothing she doesn't know."

Marvelous. Add her knowledge of horses to Colin's and they'd still make precisely one genius. "And your brother?"

"Harriet got him to ride again after our eldest brother died in a fall. It took years, but he's as enthusiastic now as she is. She helped him realize how much he'd missed all things equestrian." Ada tilted her head. "Maybe that's part of why they fell in love. They're a little more complete with each other than either of them were on their own. Though that sounds sentimental, doesn't it?"

"It does, but then again, you're talking about a newly wed pair's love for each other. Sentiment isn't out of place."

Sentiment. Travels. Horseflesh. Borrowed clothing. Surely he had enough material for his first few pieces for Botolphus Bright. He tried to memorize every word that was passing, so he could tell his brother everything that evening.

"Go into the paddock, my admirer," said Ada, "and get onto the back of your horse. I'll join you as soon as Atalanta and I are ready."

"I should have suspected you wouldn't make these two weeks easy," Colin muttered. "But you needn't go out of your way to make them difficult."

Her expression was all sweetness and innocence. "Resourceful as you are, you wouldn't enjoy the game unless it was a challenge."

"I would never doubt that you were challenging."

She tsked. "I see. You are trying to bait me."

"Is it working? Have I got you hooked yet?"

"Possibly," she said. "But you'll have to catch me to know for certain." And looping her skirts up off the floor, she strode down the line of stalls.

* * *

"Don't go that way," Ada blurted. Her heart was in her throat, her stomach just behind it. "I changed my mind."

Colin reined in with creditable skill—though, as he'd never allowed Equinox above a slow walk, this wasn't much of a feat.

"What's wrong?" He squinted at the bridle path that unwound ahead of them, all shade-dappled and smooth. "Is it unsafe?"

How to explain? She was going to sound like a fool. She swallowed. Cleared her throat. Willed her insides back into their proper order. "No, it's a fine path. It's—there's a legend about it, that's all."

"Is there? Now I'll have to hear it." His hands went lax on the reins. Naturally, Equinox stretched his head down to crop some grass. "Since it seems my horse has stopped for a late breakfast anyway, I've nothing else to do." Colin looked delighted by the halt.

"Keep hold of the reins, even if you let him graze. If he takes it into his impatient head to bolt, you'll—"

"Fall off his back at once," Colin finished. "Let's not pretend I'm anything but dead weight in the saddle."

"Adoring, admiring dead weight," Ada reminded him.

"Naturally, all of that. So, what's the legend? It must be terrifying if you want to abandon your plans to trot me by the Talbot horse farm."

"I never planned for you to trot," she said. "I'm optimistic and hopeful, but not *that* much."

As Equinox stepped forward, finding juicy nibbles here and there, Colin fired a long-suffering look at Ada. He did take up the reins, she was relieved to note.

She guided Atalanta toward her stable companion, letting the fine-boned gray mare join in the impromptu graze. "It's silly. The old legend, I mean. It states that the first person to kiss you on the path by the light of the full moon is your true love."

He grinned. Already, she was sorry she had told him. "I see. And has this worked in real life?"

"My brother Philippe kissed Harriet Talbot," she grumbled. "You see how that worked out."

His smile grew. "You're afraid that if we ride the path together, I'll kiss you, and you'll be stuck with me for good?"

Her mouth opened.

"This is wonderful. I think I can set your mind at ease. First, it is daytime. Second, the full moon will not shine for several more nights. Third, when night falls, if we find ourselves on the path, I shall manfully avoid kissing you. Unless you think the path will exert an atmosphere so intoxicating that I will not be able to resist?"

She didn't know *what* she'd thought. Only that Colin Goddard plus bridle path plus legend was a combination likely to endanger her heart or her sanity. "Forget I said anything, Mr. Goddard."

"Call me Colin, please. Remember, you did agree yesterday. And I always go by Christian names with women who toss old legends at me as an excuse to get me alone to kiss them." He eyed her appraisingly. "Ah— *have* you ever been kissed on the path before?"

"On the path? What sort of hussy do you take me for? No, I've only been kissed on the lips." He smiled, and something unlocked within her.

"All right. Let's chance it." She nudged Atalanta with her heel. The mare flicked her ears, annoyed at having to stop eating, but obediently walked toward the path.

"There's no way I can kiss you if you walk off without me," said Colin. "This old fellow's going to graze until the next equinox. Oh, hullo! That did it." At the sound of his name, the gelding had picked up his head.

As Ada watched, he started after Atalanta. Colin held himself still in the saddle, looking uneasy. He was going to have the devil of a sore seat the next day.

They had the winding path to themselves as far as Ada could see. When the horses fell into step next to each other, she asked, "Will all of this go into one of your articles? The path and the legend?"

"And your stubborn insistence that I ride a horse? Yes, it might well. I'll work it up with my brother later this evening, once I'm back at the inn."

"Your brother would be welcome to come to the Hall. He needn't even pretend to be in love with me."

"He'd be yours in a moment, my lady."

"Just Ada," she mumbled. She was regretting all sorts of things about this ride now. Letting Colin into the stable, blurting out all that nonsense about how she'd drawn back from London society after Jonas had died and Wrotham had jilted her.

Except it hadn't been nonsense, and he'd known it. And he hadn't teased her, or mocked her, or done anything but look at her with blue eyes that seemed, somehow, to know what she meant.

"You are being ridiculous," she said crisply. "Do be serious. I recall that your brother is not well. Could he use help with the travel from the White Hare to the Hall? I could send a chair."

"It's not that sort of illness." Colin relaxed his hands on the reins. Equinox's ears pricked. He looked at Ada, then at Atalanta.

"Don't do it," Ada said. "Don't even think about it." At Colin's questioning look, she replied, "Equinox wants to unseat you. He's getting impatient with the walk."

"Don't tell me you want me to gallop."

"As much as I'd love to see it, no. Take up your reins—good, hold it firmly. Let him feel the pressure of the bit. Not hard, but unmistakable. You're in charge of him."

"Glad one of us thinks so," he muttered.

They had reached Ada's favorite part of the path. Other parts ran alongside pasture or hopped a burbling stream, and one could see half of Berkshire in such places. But here the bridle path was flanked by rows of ancient oaks, sturdy as walls and tall as church steeples. In summer, the trees cast cool shade, and the earth was soft with dew every morning. Even in these waning autumn days, as the trees dropped their leaves, the path was private. Here, there was no sound but the steady thump of hoof beats, the occasional trill of a bold bird's song.

Soon, they'd be coming upon the bounds of the horse farm, where Wrotham might be visible. They'd best look engaged as they rode. Delighted in each other.

She reintroduced the subject from which Equinox had distracted her. "Do you want to tell me how I can arrange for your brother to visit the Hall? Or do you want me to drop the subject?"

Colin looked more comfortable in the saddle now, settling into the horse's gait. "Neither one is necessary. It is Samuel's wish not to mix in public. He is troubled with..." He thought for a moment. "Within my family, we always called them twitches. Samuel's twitches."

"He's always had them?"

"He's always had some, since he could walk. They change over time, so he loses some and develops others. But usually he feels he has to move, or to make a noise, as you or I might feel we have to sneeze. He can't help it—or he can, but it becomes intolerable after a while. As you can imagine, it's embarrassing to him."

She had never heard of such a condition. "I wouldn't want to embarrass him," she said. "Please give him my greetings and let him know he is welcome at the Hall any time he would choose to accompany you."

"I'll tell him." Colin ventured a tug at the brim of his hat. "Thanks. He'll like that."

Perhaps this was why the brothers traveled together. If Samuel was embarrassed to be seen by others, he'd need to stay with his elder brother to maintain contact with the world. "Does he travel with you because he enjoys it?"

Equinox sneezed, shaking his head. Atalanta danced to one side. "We rely on each other," Colin said at last. "Whether we enjoy it or not."

"Brotherhood described with admirable conciseness," Ada said dryly.

"Do you miss your brother, Lavelle? Or is one permitted to miss a duke?"

"A sister is permitted, surely. And I would rather have him around than not, but I am used to being apart from him." She reined in, easing Atalanta over a stone-scattered part of the path. Here, it was brighter, the oak trees that had cradled the path giving way to hedges. Through gaps, she could see paddocks, grooms, horses being worked. Plenty of eyes to catch sight of the duke's sister on a pleasant ride with her admirer.

"Besides," she added, "a duke's household is full enough of servants that I am never by myself."

"That doesn't mean you're not lonely sometimes."

"No, I suppose it doesn't."

They finished their ride in a companionable silence—but Ada's thoughts roamed abroad even as she sat serenely on horseback. She'd known since the moment of meeting Colin Goddard that he had an ulterior motive for seeking her company. But did he have other motives too? Might he be fond of her for her own sake?

How could she know?

And why was she disappointed he hadn't even tried to steal a kiss?

* * *

In his room at the White Hare, Colin groaned as he eased himself into the steaming bath. A copper tub was usually a luxury, but if he hadn't been able to soak his sore muscles today, he'd be a piece of human hardtack in the morning.

The White Hare was a clean and comfortable inn, neither cheap nor costly. Of habit, Colin held fast to every coin he could, since one never knew when the next would come. Thus the brothers were in a small room under the eaves. The bedstead was hardly big enough for one, but Samuel preferred to sleep during the day so he could spend his waking hours away from curious eyes.

Just now, Samuel sat on the edge of the bed and laughed, head bobbing. "I knew you'd regret riding a horse."

"I knew it too, though I thought I'd be much worse off than this. A little muscle soreness isn't bad compared to being tossed on my backside."

It wasn't a *little* soreness. But a man had his pride, even with his brother.

He hissed, sinking more deeply into the water. Through the window, the sky purpled and bled into a sunset.

As Colin took hold of a cake of soap and a cloth, Samuel rose and paced back and forth across the room. Three strides this way, three that.

Five years Colin's junior, he was the darker of the two brothers, with puckish brows and the angular face of an ascetic. Like their father, Samuel got absorbed in his work to the exclusion of almost all else. For Samuel, the *almost* was conversation with Colin, his link to the world outside their room. For their father, it had been drink.

"You're invited to come to Theale Hall anytime you like," Colin told him. "Lady Ada asked me to tell you so."

"Did you tell her about me?"

"About your twitches? Yes, something of them. She said she wouldn't wish for you to be embarrassed, but wanted you to know you might come whenever you wished."

"She sounds nice." Nod. Nod.

Colin rubbed the cloth liberally with soap. "*Nice* is not what I would name as her defining quality." Proud. Intelligent. Appealing. Prickly. Those suited her better.

Pretty too. Warm. Unexpected.

"But she is nice," he agreed.

Samuel sat down. "We don't have to do this, Col. We could leave and write a different series instead. Bright will find something else for you to observe."

He had thought of that himself. But. "We need this," he said. "You and I. We've scrambled for the day's pay for years. With this series and a pamphlet afterwards, we'll have a steady wage. Bright promised."

More than a steady wage. Colin would become its co-editor.

Samuel's hands clenched, unclenched. "We've never gone hungry yet."

That was true. "And we won't. I'll make sure of it." He put a soapy hand out, palm up. Samuel pressed it—their old agreement, better than a handshake.

"Two weeks of pretense," Colin said, relaxing into the hot water. "Lady Ada knows what's going on. It was her suggestion. She won't be injured."

Samuel pulled back his hand, still looking doubtful.

"It'll be fine," Colin assured him. "Are you ready to take notes on the day?"

"Ready." Samuel rose to his feet and took up the portable writing desk with which he traveled. The brothers were always amply supplied with paper, ink, quills, and pencils—as well as a penknife, sand, and anything else that might be needed for the smooth transfer of ideas into the written word.

Samuel wrote with a beautiful hand. Colin could tell that, even though he couldn't decipher half of what his brother wrote, or what anyone else wrote. When Colin tried to read, the letters wiggled like the contents of a fisherman's bait bucket, altering and flipping. He knew it wasn't like that for most people, and no one but Samuel knew it was like that for him. He had a wonderful memory, and that was enough to get him by most of the time.

That, and Samuel's steady hand.

"The trappings of the upper class," Colin began. He held the cloth over his head, squeezed rivulets of warm water down. It felt like sensual fingers on his scalp, behind his ears, down his neck.

Kiss me on the path, he had wanted to tell Ada. *Or on the lips. Either one.*

She was a dangerous woman, with her listening ears and deep, wondering eyes. A man might confide anything in her, even the truth.

A man might fall hard for her, and not just play at being besotted.

Colin had shut his eyes. When they popped open, Samuel was staring at him. "Ready for more," he prompted.

So, on they went. Colin recounting the day, Samuel transcribing it. The brothers shaping witty, deathless prose—or at least prose good enough to earn their bread for another day, week, month.

They'd write the series, and then they'd return to London. Colin had promised to play the swain for only two weeks.

How far could he possibly fall in that time?

CHAPTER FOUR

An opportunity might arise to further one's relationship with the pursued—and if it
does, be prepared to take it.
Readers uncertain what is meant by "further one's relationship" might need
assistance beyond the scope of this guide. The author offers his sympathies.
Vir Virilem, *Ways to Wed for Wealth*

Colin should have learned his lesson from the *on-demandes* of *The Gentleman's Periodical*: The questions to which he didn't already know the answer were the truly troublesome ones.

How far could I possibly fall? was a troubling question, asked by a fool who'd thought his journey to Berkshire would be nothing but time to fill before he could return to the real life of London. To Bright's publication, and reporting on whatever the long-nosed editor thought would sell copies. And above all, a life of trickery. Endless trickery, from a writer who could hardly write, but whose livelihood depended on words.

Each day with Ada unspooled with startling ease and rightness. It was easy for Colin to forget that his every moment here was pretense—until he returned to the White Hare to share his observations with Samuel. The brothers turned them into pithy prose, written in Samuel's elegant hand.

Day by day, there was less that Colin wanted to tell Samuel, more that he wanted to hold back, to turn over in his mind and let it flourish there.

Much like a beetroot. Which, by the bye, he now fed daily to Equinox, who deigned to let Colin ride him when Ada deemed such pursuits necessary.

He still preferred to walk, though. As he went daily from the village to Theale Hall, sometimes he took the bridle path, which threaded alongside the Talbot horse farm for much of its length. Here, he indulged a bitter curiosity, peering over the hedges to spy upon—that is, observe—the noble visitors. Wrotham sat his horse with a skill Colin would never achieve. His wife looked at her husband with shining eyes such as had never looked upon Colin.

After several days of this, Colin could deny the truth no longer: He was jealous.

He was jealous not because he wanted Lady Wrotham, but because he wanted something as honest and sweet as she and her bridegroom possessed.

Everything Colin wore, said, did was some gradation of a lie. The only person who knew the full truth about Colin's identity—the writer of the questions that had split Ada from Wrotham, the fake suitor for a fortnight, the writer who could hardly read or write—was his brother.

The devil of it was, Colin's desire to be with Ada was honest. But that was the only bit that could be. She'd made a bad bargain with him, and he didn't intend to free her from it. She had asked him for two weeks of devotion, and she was going to get every minute of it.

He was selfish like that.

After a particularly trying day in which Colin had been asked to read everything from the names on horses' stalls to a soliloquy from *Hamlet*, he was out of reasons to demur and wanted nothing more than to walk away from words. He returned to the White Hare seething with frustration, and when Samuel asked for his daily report, Colin put him off.

"You recently arose, and it's growing dark. Let's get a lantern and go walking."

Samuel must have sensed the edge in Colin's mood, even if it didn't sharpen his tone, for he agreed. The innkeeper at the White Hare was willing enough to lend them a lantern, since they were always current with their bill, and within a few minutes of Colin's suggestion, the brothers were walking outdoors.

"Hardly needed a lantern," Samuel observed, "with the moon full tonight."

The full moon. That was right. He'd known it was coming up. "We ought to walk the bridle path," Colin decided. "There's a local legend about it. Might see a few young lovers doing their best to make that legend come true."

He filled Samuel in on the legend as Ada had told it to him, true love and kisses and all, embellishing it with comic details of his own battle to stay on Equinox's back as she had recounted the old tale to him.

Samuel laughed. "You didn't tell me any of that when it happened. Just that she'd demanded you ride horseback."

"I had my pride," Colin said loftily. To be more truthful, he'd had his awkward hopes even then—hopes that had only grown stronger each day since. Hopes of kisses from Lady Ada Ellis, hopes that she'd see him as something more than the interloper who threatened her family with scandal once again.

The brothers found the path, wide and well-kept. Samuel swung the lantern breezily in one hand, looking around with some curiosity. He sometimes fell into a crouch, walking half-bent over for a few steps. Since he preferred it when one didn't mention his twitches, Colin merely strode along at his side. He breathed deeply of the cool air.

"It hardly smells of anything here, have you noticed?" he asked Samuel. "Maybe horses, a little. No coal, no stink from the Thames, no fog. A night like this, with trees whispering alongside the path, is enough to make a man swear off London."

"It's too quiet." Samuel kicked at a dry leaf. "And the moon is too bright."

"Not hidden behind fog and smoke, you mean. It's a strange look, I agree." Certainly it was bright enough to spot giggling couples kissing by its light, if Ada's legend was widely believed. For now, though, the path was deserted, the silence broken only by the rattle of autumn's last leaves on mostly bare branches, the brothers' footsteps, the occasional whicker of a restive horse on the Talbot lands.

And then another set of footsteps, barely audible on the soft surface of the path. The approaching figure was hardly more than a silhouette against moonlit trees—and then it drew closer, falling under a spill of silver light, and revealed itself to be Lady Ada Ellis.

The three people stilled upon seeing one another, like butterflies pinned under glass.

"Ada." Colin spoke her name. He hesitated, caught between *ought to* and *wish*.

"Colin," she replied. She was bare-headed and gloveless, as if she'd walked out in a hurry, though she wore a pelisse, long and warm, over her gown. "And Mr. Samuel Goddard, I presume?"

Samuel broke the stillness at once. "Happy to meet you, my lady. Ah—I must be off." Half running in his crouch, he disappeared around a curve of the path. Taking the lantern with him.

And then it was just Ada and Colin and the moon. To Colin, woman and celestial object seemed equally lovely, far away, untouchable. How far apart were they? Maybe a half-dozen steps. Maybe fifty miles, the distance between where they each belonged.

"It's not safe for you to be walking out here alone," Colin said.

"It wouldn't be if we were in London, probably. But we're not."

"Yes," he said dryly. "Samuel and I were noting the differences. He did not find them to Berkshire's advantage."

"Did you?" She took a step closer. "Do you like it here?"

"Does it matter?"

Another step. "It matters to me. If you're my devoted suitor for two weeks—"

"Half that, by now." Too little time left.

"—I want you to be happy about it."

"You needn't worry about that," he said. "I can handle it right enough. Is it helping you?"

"What, not to have to stand alone while a man who once swore he'd be mine until death puts his arm around another woman?"

"Yes. All of that."

She closed the distance between them. "It is, actually. It gives me courage. I know if I were less prickly, I wouldn't have to bribe or browbeat people into helping me."

"Nonsense. If you'd like company walking back to your home, you may have mine." He offered his arm.

"I have no particular destination," Ada said, accepting his escort back toward Theale Hall.

"You didn't put it as if you were browbeating me," Colin added as they set off. "When we made the bargain, you called it just that. A win for each of us. It was very sensible."

"Oh, good. Sensible Ada." She sounded grim.

"If you'll forgive me for mentioning it, you are in an odd mood."

"I've forgiven you much worse than that. And yes, I am. I lost my eldest brother almost exactly four years ago, and today I visited his sons. They are twins, two of four he fathered on the wrong side of the blanket.

During the carriage ride home, I did a bit of addition and realized that I could easily have had a child or two of my own by this time if Wrotham hadn't jilted me."

The words were like weights on his shoulders. *Jilted because of what I wrote.* Somehow, he spoke in a light and teasing tone. "It's always maths with you, isn't it? Would you like that, having little Adas running about?"

"God help me if they were anything like I was as a child." She walked on a few more steps before she added, "It would certainly be a different sort of life. I don't know if I'd like it. I'm sure I'd like the children, but it would only have been a matter of time before I displeased Wrotham. He's so proper, have you noticed?"

Colin coughed. "Rather."

"If I'd married him, I'd have to behave perfectly all the time, or my husband would be displeased."

"He was never besotted with you," Colin pointed out.

"No, he wasn't," she sighed. "It would have been nice to pierce a heart or two as I wended my way through life, but it's a good life all the same."

"Totting up numbers again, my mathematical genius?"

"If I am, I'm fortunate that they're large numbers. My brother's wealthy, I'm wealthy, etcetera. But no, not just the numbers. I love the village here and the path. The horse farm makes for fine neighbors, and my brother is happily wed, and—"

"You could go on listing marvelous things for some time as I turn green with envy. Fortunately, you can't see my lovely color by night."

"I'm sorry, I didn't mean to be a braggart. I was trying to convince myself that I have everything a woman could want."

"Trying to convince oneself never works. I've tried it often."

"Oh? Of what does a handsome and amoral reporter need to convince himself?"

"Amoral, you call me? What a flirt you are." As she smiled, he considered his reply. A rush of wings in one of the trees lining the path made him look up. A bird tucked up for the night, chased away by their footsteps.

"I attempt to convince myself I have the nerve," he went on, "to pursue a new story or idea when I'm footsore. When I'm tired and my skin is thin, and the editor of *The Gentleman's Periodical* still won't take me onto his staff."

She tightened her grip on his arm, an annoyed reflex. "I will ignore your mention of the worst waste of rag since paper was invented. What helps you get your nerve back, if you can't convince yourself that all is well?"

"Sometimes, someone I care about has to do it for me."

"A woman?" Her voice was low, tentative.

He liked that she had asked. "There's not been a woman in London I particularly cared about for a long time. No, my brother is usually the one to knock sense into me. And sense it is to count your blessings and then keep putting one foot in front of the other."

"My brother isn't here. Who will knock sense into me?" Now she sounded teasing. He'd have to be a fool to mistake the tone.

"Well. I could do it." Obviously.

She slanted a look at him. "How would you do that? Would you recite another of your poems? Mangle a bit more Shakespeare?"

He had a good memory; once Samuel recited a poem or piece of prose, most of it stayed in Colin's head. "Since you asked.

"Let me not to a bargain with Ada
Admit impediments. Besottedness is not besottedness—"

"It's meant to be 'love,'" she cut in. "A word of one syllable. You're spoiling the meter."

"I have to put my own stamp on it, or you won't be impressed."

She looked thoughtful. "I have been impressed. Not by the poems, but by much else about you."

The air was cool and sweet and lovely. He drew in a deep breath of it, filling himself. "Have you? Yet you hardly know me."

"Do I not? I have seen how you treat your brother, strangers above your station, servants, horses. I've seen how you deal with me. We thought we'd have to be enemies at first, but here we are getting along fairly well."

He hadn't been prepared for her to notice so much; he hadn't expected her to be so generous. He wasn't sure how to fight her kind words.

"It was the caramel candies," said Colin. "I was yours from that moment." After a silence, he added, "What penalty will you demand if I fail to uphold my part of our ruse?"

"I don't know. I was sure I'd have you drummed from the county in disgrace."

"But now?"

"Now I know you have a feeling heart. And you're trying to help me. So if you do not succeed, it won't be because you haven't tried."

He couldn't have been more unsettled if she had arranged an audience for him with the queen. "I'm a real paragon," he said flippantly. "Glad you've noticed."

She made a little noise of exasperation. "If you were a paragon, I should never have managed a second conversation with you. And you'd never have wanted one. You're far better than that. You are real."

The simple words stung, sweetly. Words of one syllable, piercing his heart. He couldn't be flippant in response to this. He could only reply in kind, the words thick and difficult to pronounce, as they were drawn from so deep within.

"You are all I could want, had I the right to ask."

She slowed, digging the toe of her boot into the earth. "Don't tease me."

"I wouldn't dare. Not with an old legend keeping watch over us and the moon so bright overhead."

She gasped. "The full moon! I hadn't even thought about it."

"Really? You weren't strolling out here to claim a kiss from your true love?"

The moonlight was sufficiently bright for him to note the roll of her eyes. "Hardly. I was trying to escape my thoughts."

Funny, I was trying to do the same by walking out tonight. He decided to keep that to himself. "Anything in particular you want to share?"

"Most of them relate to you."

Another spear of pleasure. She was killing him by inches, and he had no defense against her.

Halting, he drew her to the edge of the path. It was relatively unshielded here, hedged and fenced and open to the sky. Cool moonlight spilled down like a waterfall.

"Old legends be damned," he said. "You know I have to kiss you now."

"You mustn't," she said weakly.

"Because?"

"It seemed like the sort of thing I ought to say." With her frank gray eyes, she looked straight through him. "But I think you must. As long as you don't kiss me on the lips, we'll be safe."

Safe? He hadn't been safe in years. Not since he first talked his way into a reporting job, betting his nerve and Samuel's skill against the world. Not since they were orphaned, alone with no one to depend on but themselves.

And certainly not since he'd stepped from a stage coach onto the high street of Rushworth Green. Since he'd laid eyes on a woman with gilt-brown hair and the sort of mouth that made one want to listen, dream, sin.

But under the quiet moon, hemmed in by patient hedges and a slow autumn breeze, he took Ada's hand in his. And for this moment, he felt safe.

He lifted her bare hand. Brought it to his lips. She smelled sweet and piquant, like a lemon tart.

Her eyes went wide. "You—"

"As you said, we'll be safe if we don't kiss on the lips. Surely the old legend didn't mean people had to be bound together when they only kissed on the hand. Why, that's just using good manners."

He'd left his hat back at the inn, and a nighttime breeze ruffled his hair. It tugged at hers too, light brown wisps soft around her face and silvered by moonlight.

With his thumb, he traced the winging line of her brow. Gently, he kissed that too, then kissed the other and drew her into his arms to kiss the side of her neck. Up its heated length, he pressed with lips and tickled with the tip of his tongue. When he reached her ear, he drew the lobe into his mouth and nipped.

"None of this counts, Ada," he murmured. "I know you don't want it to count."

Another spear, and not the pleasurable sort. She didn't want to tie herself to him. Or maybe it was just that she didn't want to tie herself to anyone. A jilted woman, a wealthy woman, a woman with so many blessings she'd practically walked a furlong while enumerating them— that sort of woman didn't need a man like Colin, even if she found a speck of genuineness within him.

But she needed kisses just now, of the sort that would make her quake and quail and shiver. And he needed to give them to her, needed whatever pieces of her she would allow.

Her pelisse covered her, neck to wrist, then fastened down the front with little hooks. Colin made it his mission to undo them. Then he found the hollow at her collarbone—yes, a kiss belonged there. Since she moaned, he gave her a second one. Up the line of her throat, more, and one for the sharp line of her chin. She was warm and lovely and so right in his arms, yet there was something so proud and untouchable in her spirit that he could have sunk to his knees before her.

So he did, heedless of the leaf-littered earth. As he knelt, he trailed his hands down her sides. Over the curve of hip, the line of thigh, the calf, the ankle. He paused at the hems of her pelisse, her gown.

"There are so many more places I want to kiss you," he told her. "And if we were not in the open, with moonlight like the light of a stage on it, I would try to persuade you. I'd draw up your gown and nip your ankles and tickle behind your knees until they went all loose and your eyes were dreamy—did you say something?"

"An incoherent noise of pleasure," she said, looking down at him with wonder. "Go on, please. After the knees?"

"The thighs next. The skin of the inner thighs is sensitive. Perhaps I'd lick you there, then blow over the place I'd licked to give you prickles of cool and heat. You might like the sensation."

"I might," she said faintly. "Why isn't there something I can lean against?"

"Lean against me." He rose to his feet, took her in his arms, and whispered into her ear. What he would do, had he the right. Were they alone, and in private. Were he hers for good and all.

Which of them did he torment more? He couldn't say. She was taut in his embrace, breathing harder than usual. He was erect in his trousers, which were uncomfortably tight. He could practically see her bared all over. If he shut his eyes, it could almost be real.

"You had best finish walking me home now," she said in a voice that was not steady.

"I had best." Reluctantly, he let her go. Formally, he offered his arm again. Determinedly, he forced down all that lust and longing—or tried to. They walked the remainder of the path in silence.

He bade her farewell before the door of Theale Hall.

"We're not on the bridle path anymore," Ada said. "So we're not bound by the old legend. You can kiss me on the lips now."

"Damned right," he growled. Taking her face in his hands, he pressed his lips to hers. Oh, they were everything: soft and sweet and welcoming and warm and trusting, so trusting, that he would do as he'd promised and no more. Just a sip when he wanted to drown in her.

He was unsteady on his feet as he stepped back, leaving her to enter that great old ancestral home of hers alone. Almost untouched.

He couldn't say the same for himself. Nothing was the same as he walked back to the White Hare, lost on the familiar route, seeing nothing of the silvery night. He was all in a whirl, off balance, and it was all due to her.

Somewhere along the path, he had lost his heart.

* * *

Ada wrapped herself in a dressing gown, then drew open the draperies, letting the pie-round moon shine into her bedchamber.

She curled up on the window seat, drawing her knees in. This was the sort of night she'd write about if she were a poetess.

The moon shines bright. In such a night as this,
When the sweet wind did gently kiss the trees
And they did make no noise, In such a night
Colin Goddard found the bridle path
And Ada sighed her soul toward where he stood…

Colin wasn't the only one who could contort Shakespeare for his own ends. *The Merchant of Rushworth Green*? It hardly had the ring of immortality to it.

Much as Ada loved words, she was no poetess. If she dug out one of her old diaries, she would fill it instead with wonderings. Was a kiss truly a kiss if it was not on the lips? What did it mean if it was?

At the end of the two weeks, how was she going to let him go? But what would he stay for? Much as he'd charmed the neighboring families, his life was in London.

One week left with Colin. He could leave anytime, really, with his ears full and pockets about to become so.

Maybe he would stay longer because he chose to.

Maybe he would stay until Philippe and Harriet returned? That would be another three weeks, if all went as planned. Where Harriet and horses were concerned, one must expect priorities to be shifted. But if there was anything Harriet loved more than horses, it was Philippe and home.

And what would there be for Ada to do, once His Grace and Her Grace returned from their travels and turned Theale Hall on its sleepy head?

She wouldn't wait for that. The following day, she would dissolve the pact she made with Colin. Let him stay or go, as he wished. And let him know that he had won not only their bargain, but a feeling from her that was too deep to name.

CHAPTER FIVE

As you carry on your courtship, do not allow your heart to be touched. The softer emotions have no place in a marriage for gain.
Vir Virilem, *Ways to Wed for Wealth*

The following noon, the message arrived for Colin just as he had descended the stairs of the White Hare. He had dressed in his own clothing—for once, thank goodness, and it fit like heaven—and was prepared to fortify himself with bread and tea before marching the familiar line of the bridle path toward Theale Hall.

"This just arrived from the Hall for you, Mr. Goddard," said the publican, a hearty, friendly man named Jarvis. "Her ladyship's groom brought it from her ladyship. Said she didn't need a reply by note, but that you could make it in person."

A dew of perspiration broke out on Colin's forehead as soon as Jarvis pressed the note into his hand. It was addressed to him, so he knew it read *Mr. Goddard*, but the letters all twined around as if Ada's handwriting were a living vine.

"Of course." He fired a confident smile at Jarvis. "Thank you. I'll just… have a look at it in private."

Which meant he'd have to have Samuel read it to him. Clutching the note in his fist, he climbed the stairs with considerably less brio than he'd thumped down them only a few minutes before. His brother had just gone to sleep, being nearly nocturnal, but he could wake up for a moment. It would take him far less time to wake, read it aloud, and go back to sleep than it would for Colin to flounder through it on his own.

But when he eased open the door of their shared chamber and took a look at Samuel, he couldn't bear to wake him. Samuel had stayed up long, worked hard, run off during a walk the brothers had meant to share— and now he was asleep, fiercely so, his brows knit and his eyes ringed with shadows of fatigue.

Colin stepped back, slowly so the floorboards didn't creak, and let the door shut again. All right. He'd read it himself.

Mr. Goddard, it said on the outside. He knew that. And on the inside—

He cracked the seal, only to be faced with lines of what looked like gibberish. A wall of it, all loops and lines linking and interlocking and unlacing again. He'd been eager to set off for Theale Hall, and his concentration was all in pieces.

Squeezing his eyes shut, then opening them wide, he tried again.

Druu Qloom—all right, that had to say *Dear Colin*. But what came next? He couldn't think. He didn't want to know. What if she suspected he'd come up with the *Periodical* questions about her brother? What if she was done with him?

Or what if she merely wanted to ask him to buy a few cakes in the village for the tea she was planning to host in the early afternoon? It could be anything.

If Ada had ever sent him a note before, he'd have a sense of whether this was something he could give Jarvis a coin to read out for him after pleading a splitting head. But she hadn't. So the chance was too great that the note was of a personal nature.

He hoped it was of a personal nature. Surely it would not be bad, if she wanted a reply from him. Yes, that made sense. The best way to find out would be to go to Theale Hall, as he'd intended, and tease out the substance of the note from Ada before making his reply as she'd wished, in person.

Cramming the note into an inner pocket of his coat, he set off, whistling.

* * *

"You didn't even *read* it?" Ada was arranging and rearranging the dishes on a tea service. She was sorely tempted to wing one of them at Colin Goddard's head.

But she couldn't. Everything had to look perfect, for Lord and Lady Wrotham were coming over for tea.

They were staying in the area at some small place of Wrotham's father, and Ada had known since the dinner a week before that she ought to have them over again. If she hadn't once been betrothed to Wrotham, she wouldn't have thought twice about it. New company was thin in the country, and invitations were eagerly granted and seized.

Kisses on the bridle path—and on the lips—had buoyed her throughout the morning. Thoughts of the note she'd scribbled out, of Colin's possible responses, had teased and tantalized her. Would he want...? Did they dare...?

Now she found out he hadn't even *read* the damned thing. Maybe she would throw a dish at him after all.

"I was busy," he said.

"You could have read it as you walked over from the inn."

He looked at her pityingly. "I had other things on my mind. If it's that important, just tell me about it now. Your groom said I might give you my reply in person."

"Yes, but that was assuming you would have read my note and thought it over."

Chalmers appeared in the doorway of the drawing room. "My lady, Lord and Lady Wrotham have arrived."

Good Lord. What had she got herself into? Pasting a smile upon her face, she said, "Thank you, Chalmers. Please show them in."

To Colin, she shot a look of pure venom. He hadn't even *read* the *note*. "There's no time to talk about this right now," she hissed. "We'll speak of it later."

He didn't even bother looking chagrined. He just shrugged, smiled at the entry of the two guests, greeted them in a way that was everything polite and friendly. He had a gift for that, she had to admit—though right now every kind thing she thought about him was grudging, because he *hadn't even read the note.*

Ugh.

With an effort, she set aside that annoyance and guided Lord and Lady Wrotham to a set of comfortable chairs. The four tea-drinkers surrounded a round table on which a tea service and several towers of dainties were set out. Around them, the drawing room's draperies were drawn back to let in early afternoon light and permit a view of the grounds.

"Nice look at the stables from here," Wrotham granted. He put an unbelievable amount of lemon into his tea. "Talbot used to be the horse master here, didn't he? Good old fellow. Really knows his horseflesh."

Ada politely agreed with all of this, then offered biscuits.

"I'd love one," said Lady Wrotham. "I am remarkably fond of shortbread."

Colin took up a plate and passed it over to the viscountess.

"No, those are lemon biscuits," said Ada. "See, there's a little sign." Fussy of her, probably, but when one put out a dozen types of biscuits and cakes, one needed a reminder of what they were. She'd written labels in her neatest script on lavender paper, then folded each into a tiny upside-down vee to rest on the plate.

"My mistake. I overlooked it." Colin grinned. "Too eager to try a biscuit myself, I suppose."

"I will happily have one of those, Mr. Goddard. Don't they look delicious?" Lady Wrotham was all smiles and good cheer. Her neat blond hair and riding habit showed that the couple planned to spend another day at the horse farm.

Ada turned the subject back to that safe direction, asking what the couple thought of the Talbot horses and whether they'd determined which to buy.

"If we only wanted to buy horses," said her ladyship, "we certainly could have chosen them much more quickly! But Wrotham and I are enjoying our stay in the area. So lovely in autumn here, isn't it? And it is nice to get away from London. I've been indulging myself with daily rides on practically every animal in Talbot's stable."

"You must be a fine horsewoman," Ada noted. "I've no doubt the new duchess would love to make your acquaintance if you find yourself in Berkshire after she and my brother return from abroad."

Wrotham cleared his throat. "As to that, I cannot say. Our plans for the future remain unfixed."

Ada blinked. "Well, surely you'll cross paths with Her Grace in—"

"Lady Ada." He struggled to smile. "You will forgive me for broaching an awkward subject, but your family—that is, since your eldest brother's death, it has been known to me that—that is—"

"Spit it out, man," grumbled Colin.

Wrotham sighed. "The Ellis family draws more than its share of scurrilous notice. An acquaintance cannot be too careful."

Colin blinked. "You don't want to meet with the new Duchess of Lavelle because there was a whisper of scandal tied to her marriage with the duke."

"Surely not!" Ada said. "Harriet Talbot is a gentlewoman by birth and behavior, and…"

She trailed off, staring at the three faces arrayed before her. Lord Wrotham looked stony, but superior. His wife looked chagrined. Colin was all grimness.

Ada struggled to understand. "That's it? A few impertinent questions in *The Gentleman's Periodical*, and you won't even meet with a *duchess*?"

She'd not thought Wrotham could sit up straighter, but he managed it. "It's not a respectable journal, but it does a great service by asking the questions others are afraid to."

"Not *respectable*?" Now Colin was piqued. Ada shot him a look of pure *this is neither the time nor the place*. He shut his mouth, but continued to fire darts of loathing at Lord Wrotham's elegant self.

"I am sure Lord Wrotham doesn't mean any insult," murmured his wife. "He only thinks of reputation."

"I know he does." Ada wanted to put her hands to her temples and squeeze this conversation out of her head. Or lace her tea with brandy and drink it down as if it were lemonade. "I know that."

"Lady Ada is constantly thinking of that too," Colin said solemnly—a shift in mood so quick that Ada looked at him warily. "She has done me the honor of permitting my attentions to her, but always with the reservation that I am not worthy of her." He paused. "That was *my* reservation, I should explain. Not hers. For Lady Ada would never for a moment betray any ungraciousness due to her birth, which is, as you are both aware, higher than any of ours."

What the devil…? Ada knew she ought to say something, but she had no idea what. Her mouth was open, waiting for words to issue forth. But all she could think was, *What the devil?* Was he chastising them all? Complimenting them? Chastising the Wrothams and complimenting Ada?

From the expressions on Lord and Lady Wrotham's faces, they were wondering something similar.

"I—" Ada began.

Colin put a hand to his heart, and she snapped her mouth shut. "Lady Ada is the best woman I could ever have imagined," he sighed. "I know I am not good enough for her. I know I have nothing to offer that she needs. Nevertheless, I hoped for her heart, and in the time that I had her hand, I was the happiest man in England."

"Lady Ada and you...you two were betrothed?" Lord Wrotham was squinting, as if this would slow the flow of unexpected information.

"No, we weren't," Ada said. "Mr. Goddard never asked for my hand." She looked murder at Colin.

But he was oblivious. Whatever part he was playing, he was well into it now. "I would have if I had any prayer of success. I should not have implied otherwise. You would never be so dishonorable, Lady Ada, as to jilt someone to whom you'd made a promise."

Lady Wrotham drank her tea, the cup hiding her features. Ada would have given ten guineas to read the other woman's expression.

"You are embarrassing me," she whispered to Colin behind the shield of her own cup. Impossible that the Wrothams would not hear, but she didn't altogether mind that. "Stop. Talking."

"I'll see myself out," Colin cried. "If Lady Ada will but come with me, so I might have a few more minutes in the light of her presence."

Wrotham had gone pale, but he had self-possession enough to reply, "That's not seeing yourself out, then."

Colin sprang to his feet. "What are you playing at, sir? What do you—"

"Oh, for heaven's sake—let's be on with it." Ada stood, cutting him off. "If you'll excuse me for a moment, my lord, my lady, I will see Mr. Goddard to the door."

Fuming, she marched him out of the drawing room and into the entry hall of the stately home. "What are you *doing*?" she whispered furiously.

"Did you like that?" he murmured, an eye toward the open door of the drawing room a few yards away. "Rather good, wasn't it? I've been wanting to get in a few licks at Wrotham since I first met him. He deserves it, you know."

"It's ungracious to try to embarrass a guest. Especially in front of his wife, who is a fine woman who did nothing wrong." And it was ungracious, Ada did not add, to toy with her finer feelings by implying that his were fully engaged.

"I did it for you, so you could get a bit of your own back. Triumph over him."

"By triumphing over you?" She shook her head. "It wasn't necessary. I don't care about Lord Wrotham anymore."

He folded his arms, leaning against the wall. "Right. Which is why you arranged for me to be your devoted slave for two weeks."

Was he bitter? Maybe he was just annoyed. She certainly was. "If you'd read the note, you'd know I don't want that from you anymore." She drew in a deep breath, clenching her hands into fists for courage. "I want more."

"You want more." He bumped his head against the wall a few times. When he spoke, he sounded tired. "And what do you think I can give you, Lady Ada Ellis? I work for every penny. I've nothing to my name but nerve and a glib tongue."

"You can't think so. You've much more to offer than that."

"Compared to your fortune? It's nothing."

She tried for lightness. "Well, if I already have a fortune, I don't need another one, do I?"

He raised a brow. "Strange logic. What do you need, then?"

"I was beginning to think"—she swallowed—"that I needed you. But you didn't read my note. Did it—couldn't you tell that it mattered to me?"

He didn't meet her eyes. "I guessed that it did. In my hurry to reach you, I'm afraid I left it behind at the inn. Won't you tell me about it now?"

Oh, he was good. So calm and sincere, he almost had her placated. "I wanted to cancel our bargain. I wanted you to stay as a guest. A friend. And… so, I said in the note, I wanted to know what you thought of that. If you were interested in anything more than a series of pieces on how someone might wed for wealth."

He pushed upright again, folded arms unlocking. He drummed his fingers on a glossy console table that showed every finger mark. "You put me in a difficult position. If I say that I am interested, am I not making myself the beneficiary of my own articles? But if I am not interested, do you not have the right to throw me out of your house?"

"I do," she said. "But I won't. You've won, you see. I can't make it through the two weeks. I never imagined that would be the case, but so it is."

"Why?" He looked mystified.

"I'm tired of pretense. I want something real. And if you want the same, let's be on with it. And if you don't, better that I know now than that I let myself fall too far." Her voice quavered on the final words. Damnation.

"How far is too far? I ask only because I think I've done it already."

"Do you really?" She searched his face. She'd thought, once, that she was skilled at catching out lies. Now she was desperate for signs of truth in his lineaments.

What she saw there was pain. Did it come from him, or was she seeing her own heart?

"What do you want from me, Colin Goddard?"

He looked away, made a slashing motion with his hand. "Nothing at all. You're right, we should cancel the bargain. I won't even state that I won, because then you'd have to write the articles for me."

She narrowed her eyes. "You are hot and cold at once. What are you hiding from me?"

"Nothing at all," he said again.

"Impossible."

He smiled, though it wasn't the confident grin she was accustomed to seeing. This one rang false. "I promised to lie to you. You promised to catch me out. That was the deal from the beginning."

For the first time since he'd sat across from her in the study a week ago, she had the creeping feeling that they could easily become adversaries.

"Didn't we move beyond that? All our time together, and the kisses, and…" She pressed her lips together. She would not beg. A heart could not be moved unless it wanted to be.

"What am I hiding from you?" He sighed. "Let me reveal all, then. I am hiding my envy. Not at your position, but at the fact that you live near a village where you can buy caramel candies from a confectioner who's known you your whole life. At the fact that you have the confidence to seat a man on a horse and trust that you'll be able to talk him—and the horse—safely through. Or even at your resourcefulness, to turn one who could have been a foe into an ally with a single proposed bargain."

The words were admiring, but the tone was not. He sounded angry, the laughter that so often edged his voice turned jagged and raw.

"Well." He made a fist, bumped it against the wall. "I guess I'm not hiding any of that anymore."

"I'm glad you were honest with me." Sort of. She still felt unsettled. A figurative sword hung overhead; she could feel it swinging, the movement of air making her skin prickle.

"No. No, I'm not. I'm many things, Lady Ada, but honest isn't one of them. I'm not the sort of man you want. It would be dishonorable of me to pretend I am."

In these words, there was the ring of truth. Honest though he claimed he was not, there was everything genuine in these parting words.

So there was nothing more to say. And she let him go.

When the great front door closed behind him, she braced herself against the wall with a flat palm. The bones of Theale Hall held her up. They always would. She was no worse off now than before she had met Colin Goddard, with his glib tongue and his frank eyes and his Londonish energy. She was no worse off than she'd been before she talked with him, laughed with him, kissed him. Told him truths she had hardly dared admit to herself.

All of this was over, and she had been fine before, and she would be fine again.

She would paste the bits of her heart together, a heart she'd never meant to lend. Somehow, she'd said the word *besotted* enough that it had sunk in, and she'd thought it was to apply to her.

She really ought to have confined herself to numbers rather than words.

Slowly, trailing her fingers along the wall, she walked back to the drawing room. Outside of the doorway, she took a deep breath. Let her hands fall to her sides. Raised her chin.

"My apologies for the interruption," she told Lord and Lady Wrotham. Her guests sat still and tentative. Uncertain. She smiled her reassurance. "All is well. Shall I ring for a fresh pot of tea?"

CHAPTER SIX

Sometimes the best advice fails. In that event, be bold, be ingenious.
However, sometimes that fails too.
Vir Virilem, *Ways to Wed for Wealth*

Just a few hours by mail coach, Colin had once told Ada. From
Berkshire to London was an easy journey.

But he'd been wrong. The journey from Rushworth Green to the
London printing house of Botolphus Bright included some of the most
difficult hours Colin had ever passed.

He'd left the White Hare as soon as he could pack his things. A groggy
Samuel, confused and startled, had taken in Colin's explanation and said
he'd follow in a day or two.

So. Ada had won their bargain, and Colin had left. Not because he
couldn't play the part she asked of him anymore, but because he had to
return to writing whatever would pay, even if it skated through lies.

Damn the woman. She'd made him care about her, and she'd made
him care what he'd made of himself. She had defeated him soundly, not
by asking him to be someone else, but by being herself. He couldn't face
her anymore. It was hard enough to look in the mirror.

By evening, Colin was in their rented rooms in London, his belongings
stowed and his brain in a muddle. What would he do next? He wished he
could turn time back a fortnight, so he'd never gone to Rushworth Green,
or met Ada, or had a half-baked idea about making his own fortune, and
Samuel's, through a skill he did not possess.

Well... no, he didn't wish that. Not entirely. He didn't want to forget

Ada, magnificent in her suspicion and throwing caramel candies about. Ada, soft and moonlit and yearning to be kissed.

Ada, asking for more, not knowing how much she did not know about Colin.

He'd returned to London before Bright expected him, so he didn't go into the printing house the following morning. Instead, Colin spent the day at home. First, he took Ada's letter out of his coat pocket and made his winding way through the lines she'd written.

Sweet lines. Hopeful lines. Ignorant lines, unknowing of the truth.

When he'd read it, he wished he hadn't. The very sight of words written in her hand was a shameful reminder, a precious remembrance.

He tossed it into the fire.

Then he raided Samuel's desk for paper, ink, quills, a bit of pencil. Enough of this ridiculousness about wavering letters and switching positions. Letters didn't move once they were down on the page. They were written, and they stayed, and he would make them stay and read them and understand them and then be able to write the sort of piece Ada deserved. Or a letter of apology to her.

Or, as the hours went on and the words he scrawled refused to remain still and obedient, maybe a note.

Or a line or two.

As afternoon faded dim and gray, he looked around him at all the ruined papers, and he put his head into his hands and wished the world away.

In the morning, he was determined anew. He was in London again, he was himself, and his life would go on as it always had. Samuel would be back in London sometime today, he'd promised, and they'd continue on.

So Colin turned his steps toward Botolphus Bright's printing house, which was located near St. John's Gate. Bright copied the prestigious, established *Gentleman's Magazine* in as many ways as possible, including locating his headquarters near that of the magazine's. The magazine's editors operated from a large office and maintained a fast newfangled press for their popular journal. The rents being costly, Bright squeezed his combined business and printing offices for *The Gentleman's Periodical* into less space than one might imagine.

Colin pushed open the door to the cramped space, greeted as always by the sharp scents of ink and machine oil and the sulfurous smell of heated rag paper. It wasn't printing week, fortunately, or he'd also have encountered a clatter from the press that was fit to burst his eardrums, and he'd have wound his way between papers hanging to dry on lines like squared-off laundry across the room.

As it was, Bright was laying type, his fingers stubby but nimble as they whipped between type cases and page forme. About the age Colin's father would have been had the elder Goddard lived, he was a garrulous man of average weight, but with a double chin that softened his look. One could tell nothing of his rapacious ambition from his appearance.

"Goddard!" Bright hurried around the table where he'd been working, hand outstretched to shake. Eyeing the ink all over his fingers, he thought better of it, then motioned Colin into the space and retook his place by the type case. "Good to see you, good to see you. I'm working on the questions for the next issue. You don't mind if I continue, do you? You're back earlier than I expected. Must be good news, hmm?"

In the time that he talked, he'd already pulled a few dozen sorts from the type case and fit them into place. "This is going to be the best issue yet. I think we'll split your pieces, tease them out as long as possible. The page of questions can connect, anything to do with society gossip. We'll make it fit. We always do, hmm? Brought your pieces in person, did you?"

He finally looked up, Colin's silence sinking in. Which meant that now Colin had to determine what to say.

"Samuel has all our notes," he began. "I expect him here within the next day."

"Fine, fine. What've you got for me before then? What can you add to the questions page?" He tapped an inky finger on his chin, leaving a blackish smudge behind. "Something to do with Lavelle, I think, to tie into your new series. What have we run before on Their Graces? It'll have to be something new. 'Did the Duchess of Lavelle seduce the duke into marriage?' No, not enough punch. 'Was the duchess with child when they wed?' Better, better. We'll get there, hmm?"

"I don't have any questions," Colin said slowly.

"Ah, you already know everything." Bright winked broadly. "Confidence of the young! What a gift. But of course you can think up questions. The questions page is your baby, much as this press is mine. Hmm?"

"I don't want to give you any questions for the new issue," Colin said, his voice firmer this time. "I don't—it doesn't seem right."

Birdlike and quick, Bright darted back around to Colin. Looked him over, prodded his face until Colin swatted away the inky fingers and wiped at his cheek.

"It's you, right enough," Bright said. "But it doesn't sound like you. What the devil happened to you in Berkshire? Lost your nerve?"

Colin set his jaw. The less said around Bright, the better.

But silence was clue enough. Bright whistled. "Lost your heart, hmm? Well, well. Well, well, well. Who's the lady?"

Colin gritted his teeth.

Bright burst into laughter, easing back around his worktable. "The duke's sister? Oh, this is rich. Too rich, hmm?"

"I didn't say it was the duke's sister. Or anyone at all. Maybe I came to this conclusion all on my own."

"You don't have to say a word. Your expression says it all. Want to flay me alive, hmm? Oh, Goddard, you've got it bad for her. I can get a dozen questions out of this. 'Did Lady Ada Ellis fall in love with a writer of scandal?' Or maybe more salacious. 'Was the duke's sister seduced by a rogue traveling under false pretenses?'"

"The duke's sister," Colin ground out, "was not. You won't put her in the questions, will you?"

"'Course I will. There's no harm in a question or two, and they do bring in the coin most marvelously." Bright stabbed the page forme with a forefinger. "There's good work here, Goddard, and it'll get better yet once you give me your pieces. Vir Virilem, wasn't that the name you decided on?"

He'd thought it so comical when he came up with the name. Now it seemed foolish. Presumptuous. An apt enough description of the whole trip to Rushworth Green.

"I don't plan to write that series after all," he told Bright. "Sorry. It just doesn't interest me."

"I don't give a damn whether it interests you or not. It'll interest the *Periodical*'s readers right enough." Bright looked at him shrewdly with eyes like shiny black currants. "You don't want the lady's name in it, do you? You needn't mention any name. Or you could make up ridiculous ones, like in that novel *Glenarvon*. We'll have all of London guessing who Lady Ella Adis is, hmm? Maybe that's too close to the real name. You can come up with something better."

The smell of ink and the closeness of the office were making Colin's head pound. "I can't keep you from writing it yourself, but put it under your own name. I want no association with it."

"Are you saying you don't want to be paid?"

Colin pressed at his temples. "I have to be paid, sir. I can't live on air and hope. But I don't want to be connected with lies."

Bright eyed him closely, then softened. "She really did get to you, didn't she?"

He let his hands fall to his sides again. "I don't want to talk about it."

"Do you want to write about it?" Colin must have looked murderous, for Bright lifted his hands. "All right, all right. But consider this a firm offer. If you'll write for the *Periodical* about your love affair with Lady Ada Ellis, I won't have to put in the page of questions."

"A bribe?"

"A business proposition." Bright winked. "If you do it right, you'll have that editorship. Just one piece, Colin, and you and your brother won't ever have to worry about money again."

* * *

Chalmers, who knew everything, as good butlers always did, told Ada that Colin Goddard had departed the White Hare the afternoon before.

She had suspected as much, but thanked him for the information. Then she went to the study. Put on her spectacles. Prepared to work.

After writing a brief letter of inquiry and having it posted.

There, that was done. She didn't need Colin Goddard to be a part of her life. She'd miss him, but so what? She missed her parents, she missed her brother Jonas. Colin was one more person to miss. She would set that feeling aside, along with the Lavelle ledgers—once she'd finished her day's work with them.

For the work needn't consume her. She realized she'd let it; she'd tied herself to it too closely. But a day's work on the estate's accounts could be finished, and finished well, and then set aside. And if that wasn't enough for Philippe once he and Harriet returned from their wedding trip—well, then, it wouldn't be enough, and they would sort that out between themselves. Maybe he'd hire a steward.

She paused, quill in hand, before she'd made a single entry in the current ledger. A steward. Now, that was an idea. Maybe Philippe should have hired a steward years ago. Maybe she should have demanded that for herself, instead of clinging to every scrap of the familiar.

But she'd done what she thought was right. What she'd needed. And Philippe, being a good brother, had gone along with it.

For now, she had work to fill her time. And she was in her study, surrounded by books. The little volume of German poetry that always sat on the desk bore the remembrance of Colin's touch on its binding. She bore the same on her hands, her lips, her throat, her face, and the promise of more on her breasts and thighs, spoken in secret words by moonlight.

She shut her eyes, remembering.

And then she opened them, found a fresh ledger intended for the next quarter, and dipped her quill again.

Bother the accounts—just for now. She was of a mood to write, and she would write as she hadn't allowed herself to for some time. Oh, there was a great deal to write about now. A heart split and confused, a fortune in emotion gambled and lost. All the truths and worries she'd carried within.

The lines she wrote were dark and clear. She was angry. She hadn't even known how angry until the feeling spilled forth in harsh, sharp words.

Not at *The Gentleman's Periodical*, for all its tactless feasting on grief and scandal. Not at Wrotham, for dropping her hand as soon as it lost its marble perfection.

Only one person had kept her from London for the four years since. Only one person had trapped her with ledgers in this study, resigning her to a solitary life.

She, Lady Ada Constantia Ellis, had done all of that to herself. And the wound she'd inflicted was deep. Even now, she did not know how deep. But she would get to the bottom of it.

She had covered two pages, front and back, in a neat and regimented hand, by the time Chalmers announced a Mr. Goddard to see her.

Her head snapped up.

"Mr. Samuel Goddard," added the butler. She thought she heard pity in his voice.

She squared her shoulders. "Show him in, Chalmers."

As she waited, she removed her spectacles and wiped the quill she'd been using.

When Samuel appeared in the doorway, a young man of slight build and dark coloring, she stood up on impulse. "Mr. Goddard. Let's go somewhere brighter to speak, shall we? Let's go to the blue parlor. Or the pink one. Ah—do you have a preference?"

He nodded several times. "I'm partial to stripes, myself."

"The blue one, then." She smiled, then led him from the study—God, she had almost been *living* in there, hadn't she?—to a smallish parlor, sunny and pleasant with its striped blue paper and velvety chaise longue.

"Tea for you?" she asked Samuel as she seated herself. He swayed, then dropped into a chair opposite hers.

"No, thank you. I came to give you something, that's all." Samuel held out a thick packet of papers. "He hasn't been sending them to London."

Ada took the papers from Samuel. "Who hasn't...what...*oh.*" She flipped through them, page after page written in a clear hand, and realized. Colin. The articles he'd described to her, the ones that would win him the coveted editorship. This was everything he'd drafted since arriving in Rushworth Green, left behind, handed over to her.

When she looked up at Samuel, wondering, he ducked his head. "Surprised me too. Seems he wants something more than money or that editorship."

Ada looked at the sheaf of papers in her hands. "Which is?"

"Honor. You." He chuckled. "He lost, according to the terms of the bargain you made. He didn't convince you he was in love with you."

Ada let the papers fall to her lap, caught Samuel's eye. "He didn't have to convince *me.* Our bargain was for the sake of others."

"Who better to convince than you?"

She shook her head. "I lost the bargain. I called it off, forfeited it. I'd promised your brother if I lost, I'd write all the pieces myself. In fact, I've written a letter to the editors of *The Gentleman's Magazine*, promising them just such a series."

"No, it's *The Gentleman's Periodical.*"

"Mr. Goddard, I couldn't bear to enrich a publication that profited off my brother's death. I promised your brother I'd write the pieces myself, and so I will. I didn't promise where I'd send them."

A grin spread over Samuel's angular face. "You are sly, my lady."

"I think I will like writing them. I can make certain there isn't anything in them I don't want there to be."

"The power of the written word." He smiled. It was a sweet smile, making him look very young. "I ought to have thanked you before for giving my brother the sack of candies. He shared them with me. They were excellent."

The caramel candies. She had almost forgotten about them. "I don't deserve much credit. I did it on impulse."

"A generous impulse. Would that the world were full of them."

"I can't argue with that." She smiled back, then collected the papers in her lap. "Here, you must have these. You and your brother can sell them where you see fit."

Samuel took the papers from Ada with a hand that clenched and unclenched, almost scattering them. He seemed hardly to notice. "Lady Ada. I wonder if it's occurred to you that everything Colin said in front of the other guests was true. About hoping for your heart and all that."

She gaped.

Samuel hunched his shoulders. "He told me about it. He said you didn't receive it well."

"I didn't, because he sounded as if he were mocking me. He made a fool of me before..." She trailed off.

"Did anyone else think he was mocking you?"

"No, I don't suppose they did." Lord and Lady Wrotham hadn't looked amused. They'd looked uncomfortable at the unexpected display of emotion.

Ada had to think about this for a while. If Colin had not been mocking her—if he had been perfectly sincere in everything he'd said—

Dear God.

"But he didn't read my note," she said. "He couldn't have cared that much for what I felt about him. He didn't even bother to read it."

Samuel's eyes, as blue as his brother's, had clouded.

And she realized, all at once. The book of poetry—*it's not in English, is it?* The little cards on the tea treats, dismissed. The reading he was asked to do night after night, which he'd refused time and again.

The note he had left untouched.

"He cannot read," she realized.

Slowly, Samuel shook his head. "He can, but not well. It takes him a long time. He says the letters wiggle and change when he looks at them."

Ada had never heard of such a thing. But she had never heard of a man having Samuel's condition of twitches either, and here he sat, large as life and friendly as anything.

"How can he be a writer," she asked, "if he can't read?"

"He remembers everything," Samuel said. "He tells me who he talks to and what he learns, and I write it down. It's been a good partnership for years."

"Has it? It allows neither of you to have all the credit you deserve."

"What's credit worth? You can't spend it." Again, that sweet smile. "We've got by, and that's all we could have asked."

No, she thought. They could have asked for more. They could have asked for admiration or love or an editorship or…why, anything.

But that was her upbringing talking. Dukes' daughters and sisters weren't shy about asking for what they wanted. Unless it was the heart of a stubborn, wily, kind, exasperating man.

"He told me he wasn't real. That he was dishonorable. Did he mean that too?"

"How would I know? I'm only his brother. He doesn't confide everything in me. Especially not when he's heartsore and discouraged and trying to convince himself he did the right thing by leaving Berkshire."

"He thought up the questions, didn't he? About my brother's death, for the *on-demandes*?"

Samuel swayed, nodded. "He always thought up the questions."

She looked at him, perched uneasily in her chair, and smiled. "I thought so. I think I've known it since the first time he apologized."

He'd looked so troubled, so sincere as they sat in her study. His were lies of omission, but he'd never lied in how he felt. She thought he regretted what he'd done, truly.

At this distance in time, she didn't. Colin's questions, tossed off for coin and scandal, had pushed her life onto a road entirely new. It had brought her home from London, led her to constrain herself. But she'd kept traveling, and after all this time, the road had brought her to a place she quite liked.

"He didn't know you then," Samuel excused. "When he wrote the questions."

"It's all right," Ada reassured him. "I am beginning to think I didn't know myself." She searched the face of the young man across from her, looking for further hints. "Did you encourage him to leave Rushworth Green?"

Samuel looked insulted. "Of course I didn't. He was wrong to leave. But I didn't say that. All I said was that I was tired and would take a mail coach and return by night. I'm usually awake at night."

"Not today."

"No. Not today. And maybe not more days from now on. I want to venture out more."

Ada regarded him. Yes, he twitched. He had also carried his brother for years, just as Colin carried him. "I think it a good plan. How can you get the credit you deserve otherwise?"

He laughed.

"What will you do, Mr. Goddard? You didn't want to go with him?"

"Samuel, please. No, he and I disagreed on the timing. I thought he had unfinished business here."

Ada waved this off. "I had forced his hand enough. If he wanted to go, I'm glad he left."

Samuel looked skeptical at this. "Maybe so. Anyway, I'll be leaving too, by the next stage. Colin and I have rented rooms. I have a few friends. It's not a bad life at all." He shook the papers in his fist. "I'll be Vir Virilem yet. And I'll make sure there isn't anything in here you don't want there to be. Though I don't think there is." He leaned forward, confiding, "Colin was yours at once. He probably wouldn't like me telling you his secrets like that, but he's not here, is he?"

Now she had to laugh, even as she flushed. "Right you are. And you'll like that, you think? Going about in London?"

"Taking up a bit more of the life Colin and I've shared? I think so. I've been hiding."

"Yes," she said faintly. "I have too. But writing is one way around that, isn't it?"

"If it feels like it, then it is."

"You're a wise man, Samuel. And what will he do?"

There was only one possible *he*. Samuel did not misunderstand. "That depends on you."

She squinted. "I can't see up close," she murmured. "I don't have my spectacles with me. Samuel, will you wait for a few minutes while I return to the study? And when you return to London, will you take a parcel along?"

CHAPTER SEVEN

If this advice brings you success in marriage, why—
One half of her is yours, the other half yours,
Her own, she would say; but if hers, then yours,
And so all yours.
Vir Virilem (with apologies to William Shakespeare), *Ways to Wed for*
Wealth

You are real.

That was all the note said. It was easy for Colin to read; Ada had printed the letters square and big. She had also wrapped the note around a packet of caramel candies, though only two had made it all the way to London. Samuel refused to say how many had originally been in the package.

"The note is what matters," he said, pacing the sitting room of their lodging.

"She knows, then," Colin said. "About the wiggling letters. And the questions I wrote?"

Samuel nodded. "She sorted it all out. And she sent you this note. I think she would say much more if she saw you in person."

Relief lifted boulders he'd not even realized he'd been carrying. Relief, and the queasy awareness that he'd been granted unwarranted forgiveness. *You are real,* she had told him on the duke's bridle path, seeing him as no one ever had before. Seeing his well-meaning ways, his careless selfishness, his ambition, his worry, his joviality, his heart. Was it any wonder he had fallen for her? Who could resist being seen and known and accepted all the same?

You are real, said the note, after she knew it all. He'd not rung false in his feeling for her. Thank God, she knew that part of it too.

Colin held the paper. Stared at it. Stared some more at this missive from Ada, until Samuel grew tired of waiting and said he was going to order a meal from the charwoman.

"I'll do it in a minute," Colin said. He always ordered the meals, or spoke to the charwoman about whatever cleaning they needed done.

"No need." Samuel bobbed his head. "Mrs. Cobb was married to a surgeon. She's seen much worse than a man with twitches."

This finally tugged Colin's attention away from the note in his hand. "Samuel. Really? You don't mind it?"

Samuel shrugged. "Traveled by myself from Rushworth Green, you know. It wasn't so bad. If anyone backed away from me, I got more room in the carriage." He put a good face on it, though Colin could tell he wasn't unbothered. Still, he'd done it. A first for him.

"Well done. I didn't feel right about leaving you, but I see you're fine on your own."

"I'm not the one you should feel wrong about leaving. But that's up to you. I'm getting some food, then I'm for Bright's."

Colin rubbed his fingers against the soft paper of Ada's note. "Why?"

"The Vir Virilem articles. I offered them to Lady Ada. She gave them back."

"I told Bright I wouldn't sell them to him. Nor would I write a special piece about Lady Ada Ellis, though he offered me a spot as co-editor on the strength of that piece alone." The refusal had been instant, unthinking. There was no way he'd sell Ada's name. Not now that she'd made him understand the harm words could cause.

Now that he knew her, cared about her, he would hurt himself before he'd allow her to be injured again.

"I think Bright and I are done with each other," Colin added.

"All right for you. I didn't tell Bright anything of the sort." Samuel looked devilish, telling Colin of Ada's plan. Her offer to the editors of *The Gentleman's Magazine* to write a series of rival pieces. "She said she'd promised you she'd write the pieces herself, but didn't say where she'd send them."

Colin laughed. "Heart of a reporter, she has. What a woman."

"So you see, she's going to profit from our time in Berkshire, and she gave us her blessing to do so too."

"She doesn't need to profit," Colin replied, but he thought he understood. She was taking control of her story; she would tell it herself, in the way she chose.

"If she writes about marrying for wealth, will it seem too much like copying?" Samuel drummed his fingers on the well-used desk at which he'd written many a piece.

Colin scoffed. "Given the same topic to write on, no two people would ever think up the same result. Besides, if Bright can get Vir Virilem's work into the next issue, the *Magazine* will seem to be copying the *Periodical* for once."

Samuel gathered up the sheaf of papers they'd written together, then hesitated. "You don't mind? If I sell all of this to Bright?"

"Don't sell it." At Samuel's crestfallen face, Colin explained, "Trade it to him for the position of co-editor and a regular salary, just as he promised me. You can do the work as well as I, Samuel."

"But you've always been our eyes and ears."

True, and how good it had felt to make use of his abilities. But there would be other ways. "You have excellent eyes and ears too. You can do this." Colin grinned. "Maybe you can even think up something better than the questions page. Drag the *Periodical* toward respectability a bit."

"You might ask too much there." Samuel paused. "You're sure you don't want it yourself?"

"Very sure that I don't. I couldn't take the post, or even go to Bright's printing house again. I have a journey to take."

Samuel beamed. "To Berkshire?"

"Where else is there?"

* * *

I have decided that I am not the sort to avoid scenes or topics that might give rise to awkwardness. Therefore, let me be frank.

My name in Latin is Nobilem.

I was jilted after my eldest brother died.

I have returned to London first in my words, soon, in my person.

I have a talent with numbers, but I prefer words.

I have fallen deeply in love with a man who won't have me.

And I have never been happier.

One of those statements, but only one, is false. Which one?

Ada laid down her quill, stretched her fingers, then arose to walk around the blue parlor. It was sunny and bright, drawing her mood upward. She was pleased with the tone of the piece she'd begun.

The Gentleman's Magazine had sent a reply at once: They would take whatever pieces she chose to write at five pounds each, provided that she allowed her name to leak out at some point in future.

The money was rather nice; it was the first she'd earned herself. It was nothing to the interest on her dowry, but it would still buy a great many caramel candies. Or cover a portion of the cost of a special license to wed, should there be an opportunity.

That was for Colin to decide. She'd said all she dared in that note of three words. She thought he would remember how much more had passed between them, or guess how much more those two words represented. *You are real.* A sentence not often bandied about by the *ton*.

They were the only words that mattered to her now—other than, perhaps, *I love you madly*, or *I can't live without you another day*, or—

"Mr. Goddard is here to see you, my lady."

Or those.

Ada blinked at Chalmers through her spectacles, hardly daring to believe what he'd just said. "Ah—would that be Mr. Colin Goddard?"

"Indeed, my lady. Shall I show him in here, or will you meet him in the study?"

The study was more usual for her. But she felt like being a bit unusual. "Here will do. Thank you, Chalmers."

When the butler disappeared to fetch the visitor, Ada went into a frenzy of motion. Removing spectacles, rubbing at ink stains on fingers, wiping them on a handkerchief, then shaking out her skirts and smoothing her hair.

"You look lovely."

He'd caught her unawares as she picked at her appearance. From the doorway, he smiled at her: golden and tall and travel-rumpled and, by God, real.

"Colin," she said, standing at a safe distance. "Come in, then, and tell me why you've come back."

"Simple enough." He loped into the room, all easy grace and charm. "Once I knew you knew everything—that you didn't hate me—it was impossible for me to be anywhere else."

"Hate you? No, I never could. I'm not saying I'm fond of *The Gentleman's Periodical*, and yet"—she closed the distance between them—

"it brought us to this point, didn't it? So maybe I'm a little fond of it."

"A little?"

"A very little." She caught his coat lapels in her fingers, tugged. "But that's not how I feel about you."

"It would be ungentlemanly for me to ask for further details, wouldn't it?"

"Not as ungentlemanly as what you're doing with your hands—oh! Not that I am complaining."

Scoundrel that he was, he stilled his wandering hands and took hers in them. "Ada. My dear. I admire you and adore you. You make me want to do better, to be better, and to make more of myself."

"I have to sit down," she said. "My knees aren't quite working right."

"Ha! I knew you liked what I was doing with my hands." He guided her to a settee, then said, "I know it's fast, and it's sudden, so if you like, I'll take a room at the White Hare and moon after you for months until you trust in my feelings for you. But I think—I think I've been yours ever since we first struck that bargain."

She shut her eyes, collecting his every word within her. It was everything she'd hoped, everything she wanted. It was real.

When she opened her eyes, his face filled her sight. He was so handsome and roguish and familiar and…and just now, his heart was in his eyes and she had him at her feet.

"None of us have been happy without you," she said demurely. "When I saw him in the village earlier, Squire Martin said no one understands the troubles he has with elegant dress so well as you. The vicar says no one recites as well as you. Equinox looks past me each time I enter the stable, as if hoping to see you entering after me."

He pulled a face. "You could go on listing, and I would be impressed. But what of you?"

"You could be a gentleman if you wished," she said. "I've told you so before. And a gentleman would reveal his true feelings before asking a lady about hers."

A smile spread over his features, slow and mischievous. "Is that so? I'll reveal my feelings for you, all right."

And he did.

Ada loved words, and she had a talent for numbers. But at this moment, she found she needed none of those things, and all that mattered was a kiss from the man to whom she'd given her heart.

* * *

By the turn of the year a few months later, Vir Virilem's satirical articles in *The Gentleman's Periodical* had become the talk of London. The dreadful rag, as Ada always referred to it, had garnered a steady level of sales as a result, even without the *on-demandes* that had first drawn notice to it. As the founding editor had never achieved such success, Ada and Colin gave credit to the new co-editor. Not that credit was worth anything to that gentleman, but they gave it all the same.

Meanwhile, Ada and Colin worked on pieces of their own. Her love of observation, his glib tongue and wry humor—there was no one with whom they wouldn't speak and nothing about which they wouldn't write. They could have lived simply on the sales of their work—but since Ada had a fortune, they didn't have to. Colin had needed a little persuading to adopt his bride's style of living, but she reminded him how easy he'd once thought it to get used to fine clothes and plentiful food.

He wore his own clothing, though. On that, he would not negotiate. And he much preferred to visit Equinox in the stable and then leave without ever climbing on horseback again.

From her new home in the long-abandoned dower house, Ada was able to walk over to Theale Hall as needed to assist the duke's new steward with his duties. The young man was capable, and before long, she wouldn't have to do even that much.

Philippe had been surprised when he returned, suntanned and several horses the richer, from his travels with Harriet to be faced with Ada's reluctance to continue keeping the accounts. "I thought you enjoyed it."

"More that I thought it necessary to hold our family together. I'd always done it since our father's day. I thought if I kept doing it, maybe we wouldn't have lost every bit of the way things used to be."

"When our parents lived and Jonas too." He understood at once.

"But our family is different now," she said. "And I'm ready for a change. It'll be good, not sad."

And he understood that too and agreed.

He and Harriet would never have booted Ada from her rooms in Theale Hall. But newly wed couples liked their own space, and so did couples about to marry. The dower house on the grounds had been unoccupied for years, and Philippe was happy to grant its lifetime use to Ada and Colin as a wedding gift. A charming cottage of a mere twenty rooms or so, it was at an easy distance for the couples to visit.

And it was easy too for them to walk the bridle path to their favorite places, whether home or to neighbors' or to the village for a treat or a visit with friends. Daylight or twilight, Ada and Colin had developed a tradition of flirting as they walked.

"We're ending the year by walking on the bridle path," Ada said, taking her new husband's hand.

"I noticed where we were walking, yes. Can't think of a better way to bid farewell to December."

"Do you want to kiss me?"

"Always." Colin wore a wicked grin.

"Must we wait for the full moon?"

"Indeed not." He swept her into his arms, heedless of anyone on the Talbot lands who might see them through winter-bare hedges. "Lady Ada Goddard, I shall kiss you on the lips, and on the bridle path, and anywhere else you might permit—are you laughing at me?"

"Not at all," she choked out. "Go on. This sounds nice."

"It will be. Just wait." He suited his actions to his previous words.

When they both paused for air, flushed and gasping, he added, "I will bring you here by the next full moon and kiss you again, if you like. But legend or no, I've no doubt in my mind, my darling wife, that you are my true love."

She beamed up at him. "And you're mine. Now, won't you kiss me again?"

THE END

ABOUT THERESA ROMAIN

Theresa Romain is the bestselling author of historical romances, including the Matchmaker trilogy, the Holiday Pleasures series, the Royal Rewards series, and the Romance of the Turf trilogy. Praised as "one of the rising stars of Regency historical romance" (*Booklist*), she has received starred reviews from Booklist and was a 2016 RITA® finalist. A member of Romance Writers of America and its Regency specialty chapter The Beau Monde, Theresa is hard at work on her next novel from her home in the Midwest.

To keep up with all the news about Theresa's upcoming books, sign up for her newsletter here: http://theresaromain.com/contact/ or follow her on BookBub.

Visit Theresa on the web at http://theresaromain.com * Facebook. com/authortheresaromain * Twitter @theresaromain * Pinterest.com/theresaromain

Read on for an excerpt from Theresa's upcoming historical romance, LADY ROGUE—out in spring 2018! *How to Steal a Million* meets the Regency *ton* in this passionate tale of forgery, a daring heist, and an unexpected love to last a lifetime.

BOOKS BY THERESA ROMAIN

Stand-Alone Works
Those Autumn Nights (novella) in A Gentleman for All Seasons
My Scandalous Duke (novella)
The Prodigal Duke (novella) in The Dukes of Vauxhall

Romance of the Turf
The Sport of Baronets (novella)
A Gentleman's Game
Scandalous Ever After

Royal Rewards
Fortune Favors the Wicked
Passion Favors the Bold
Lady Rogue

The Matchmaker Trilogy
It Takes Two to Tangle
To Charm a Naughty Countess
Secrets of a Scandalous Heiress

Holiday Pleasures
Season for Temptation
Season for Surrender
Season for Scandal
Season for Desire

LADY ROGUE

©2018 by Theresa Romain

HER SECRET SCANDAL

As far as London's high society knows, Lady Isabel Morrow is above reproach. But the truth is rarely so simple. Though the young widow's passionate fling with dashing Bow Street Runner Callum Jenks ended amicably months ago, she now needs his expertise. It seems Isabel's late husband, a respected art dealer, was peddling forgeries. If those misdeeds are revealed, the marriage prospects of his younger cousin— now Isabel's ward—will be ruined.

For the second time, Isabel has upended Callum's well-ordered world. He's resolved to help her secretly replace the forgeries with the real masterpieces, as a . . . friend. A proper sort of friend doesn't burn with desire, of course, or steal kisses on twilight errands. Or draw a willing lady into one passionate encounter after another. Isabel's scheme is testing Callum's heart as well as his loyalties. But with pleasure so intoxicating, the real crime would be to resist . . .

* * *

She raised herself up onto her elbows, watching as he turned the key in the lock. "I am so sorry you were hurt in helping me. I should never have involved you."

"Probably not." His footsteps crossed the carpeted floor to the window, where he tugged open the draperies. In the faint light of the moon, he became a broad, strong shape silhouetted against the window.

"There is a lamp on the writing desk," Isabel said. "And though I meant what I said, now I am even sorrier that you agree with me."

"I'm being honest." He laid hands on the tinderbox, struck a spark, then lit the lamp on her desk. It flung warm light on his features, showing their wry expression. "I wasn't telling you how I feel about the matter. I'm glad you involved me."

He carried the lamp to the table at her bedside, then set it down. There he hesitated.

She shook the decanter at him. "Sit with me. Have a drink."

Gingerly, he sank onto the bed. His feet remained on the floor as he tested the ropes of the mattress, bouncing his weight. "Good bed," he commented. "But how are you? Besides your ankle, did you come through all right?" He hiked up one knee onto the mattress, twisting to study her. "Are you afraid? Shaken?"

She tugged out the crystal stopper, then handed it to him to set on the table. "Why are you asking about me?"

"I want to know everything. Hazard of the profession." His mouth crimped. That trying-not-to-smile look.

She tipped the decanter to her lips, imbibing courage as well as sticky-sweet port—then traced a fingertip over the line of his lips. "I want to know everything too, and I'm no Officer of the Police."

His eyes lowered, lashes shadowing his cheekbones. "Ah, you got the name right this time. And tonight, you were as much one as I was."

"Which is to say, not at all?" She took another sip. The decanter was heavy in her hand, expensive lead crystal. "Don't use your profession as an excuse, you wily man. You'd have been just as blunt and prying if you were a grocer."

"You make me sound like a crowbar." He tugged at his boot, wincing.

"Look at—at your leg! Oh, I'm so sorry." She sat up, all but flinging the decanter at him. "Let me take that ridiculous shawl off of your wound."

He set the decanter on the table beside the lamp. "It hurts like the devil, but I'll be fine if I bind it. It's not the first time I've been shot."

"Don't say that. Don't tell me that. Now I'll just worry about you more."

"I'm honored." His tone was so dry that he made it sound like a jest—but when she looked him in the eye, his gaze was serious and stark.

Unknotting the shawl from about his calf, she quickly made a cushion of it to cradle the injured leg and protect the coverlet. "It's ruined your boot," she chided. "That's just annoying."

Callum frowned at the hole in the thick leather. "Shame the duke's servant wasn't an even worse shot. But I've faith that Brinley will still adore my footwear."

"You and that dog." Isabel shook her head. "He did take to you uncommonly quickly. Will it hurt you if I pull off the boot?"

"Maybe. But I can't live forever with it on."

That was fair enough. She seized the heel and tugged hard. When the boot hit the carpeted floor of the bedchamber with a *thump*, she ventured a glance at Callum. He wore a tight expression, but said nothing; he only took the roll of bandage they'd brought upstairs. Tugging off his ruined stocking, he wrapped a band of gauze around the raw scoop the bullet had taken from his calf. Once around, and the bandage turned red; around again, and it stayed white. A third time around, then he tore it and tied it off. The shawl that had served as a bandage, he shoved to the floor.

"All better." He dropped the remaining bandage onto the table beside the lamp.

"I wish you were." Isabel swallowed. "I would have been so scared without you. I was scared all the same, but without you..."

"It wouldn't have been wise to go alone," he said gravely. "Investigators often have partners. Or informants, or consultants. It's more than twice as easy to work with the help of another."

"Is it? Well, I'm trying to thank you. So, thank you." She rubbed her lips together. "The port isn't strong enough to dull pain, but it's quite good. You ought to have some too."

"I will, then. We ought to celebrate our success." He took up the decanter, waving it before his nose. His brows lifted. "Why, Lady Isabel, you lay in a fine port."

As he tipped it back, sipping, she hissed, "It's not a celebration! We can't celebrate your bullet wound!"

"It's only a scratch." He darted a sideways glance at her. "I mean—you are right. It is very severe. I am in incredible pain. You should minister to me with your kindest attentions."

She snatched the port from him, suppressing a smile, then sipped from where his lips had touched. The port was sweet on her tongue, warm in her throat and belly. Yes, her ankle still ached, but she didn't care as much as she had. Callum Jenks was ample distraction.

"You"—she reached over him to return the heavy crystal to the table—"are a rogue. But I won't protest at all. Any sort of bullet wound is worthy of kindest attentions."

He arched a brow. "And how do you define those?"

"Much the same way you would, I imagine." When she again traced the line of his lips, he nipped at her finger. Startled, she laughed—and then leaned forward, brushing a kiss against his jaw. The muscle jumped beneath her caress, so she had to kiss it again, then back around to his lips to sip the sweet, heady taste of port, the headier heat of his mouth on hers. Tenderly, he brushed the tip of her tongue with his—then he pulled back.

"You are intoxicating," he said. "But you're also injured. You need kind attentions too." Without waiting for agreement or protest, he nudged her back so she lay flat on the bed. For a moment, he merely looked upon her. She would have given a great deal of money to know what he was thinking.

Then he turned away to remove his other boot and stocking, letting them fall to the floor beside their mates. He slid to the foot of the bed then, crossing his legs atop the coverlet with a hiss of discomfort. She raised herself up on her elbows. "Callum, please don't hurt—"

"Please don't hurt my feelings," he said dryly. "I've never taken the boots off a lady with a sprained ankle, and I don't want to muck it up."

At that, she had to smile. She sank back again and let him minister to her. What would his kind attentions be?

At first, they didn't feel particularly kind, though they were necessary: as she'd done for him, he removed her boots. The left one was not a problem but the injured right ankle protested his slow, tender movements. She moaned as the tight kid slid free from her swollen ankle. A pulse beat in her ankle. How was that possible?

"May I go on?"

"I'm still waiting for the kindness," she grumbled. "But yes, whatever you think best."

She sucked in a sharp breath, prepared for another pain, as he slid his hands within her trouser-cuffs to find the tops of her stockings. They were tied just below the knees. Gently, he untied them. The left one first, he rolled down and off, leaving her foot bare. Then the right, slowly and carefully.

She exhaled, wondering. His fingertips on her skin were a tiny pleasure; even over her ankle, he did not hurt her. With the stocking off, her foot up on a pillow, he pressed at the sides of the joint, then up, down, around again.

"It is not broken," he said. "But you will not dance a cotillion for some weeks."

"It was not in my plans."

He asked for the bandage; when she handed it to him, he wrapped the remainder of the roll about her ankle. Around the arch of her foot. Back, looping, again, then tucked the end under. "I confess," he said as he worked, "I am eager to know your plans."

"At the moment," she said, "they involve you."

* * *